"Didn't you ever see **Attack of the Killer Cucumbers?"** *Angie asked.*

"Yeah," Mike said. "You were in the shower, and they attacked you. So?"

"So I survived the attack—because I knew the secret."

God help him, but he wanted to know the secret. He wanted to be pulled in by the sparkle in her eyes, by the laughter in her voice. "And what is that?"

"You can only beat them if you have help."

"That's it?" He felt ridiculously disappointed. He'd wanted magic, a miracle. He wanted all their problems to disappear. He'd become easygoing and noninterfering. She'd become less independent, more willing to be sheltered by his love. "So you're my help?"

"Maybe." She sat back on her heels, smiling like a cat that had eaten a canary. "And you know something else?"

"What?"

"Love's the real killer cucumber—and there's no escaping from it."

Dear Reader,

Welcome to Silhouette **Special Edition** . . . welcome to romance. Each month, Silhouette **Special Edition** publishes six novels with you in mind—stories of love and life, tales that you can identify with—as well as dream about.

April has some wonderful stories for you. Nora Roberts presents her contribution to THAT SPECIAL WOMAN!—our new promotion that salutes women, and the wonderful men that win them. *Falling for Rachel*, the third installment of THOSE WILD UKRAINIANS, is the tale of lady lawyer Rachel Stanislaski's romance with Zackary Muldoon. Yes, he's a trial, but boy is he worth it!

This month also brings *Hardworking Man*, by Gina Ferris. This is the tender story of Jared Walker and Cassie Browning—and continues the series FAMILY FOUND. And not to be missed is Curtiss Ann Matlock's wonderful third book in THE BREEN MEN series. Remember Matt and Jesse? Well, we now have Rory's story in *True Blue Hearts*.

Rounding out this month are books from other favorite authors: Andrea Edwards, Ada Steward and Jennifer Mikels. It's a month full of Springtime joy!

I hope you enjoy this book, and all of the stories to come! Have a wonderful April!

Sincerely,

Tara Gavin
Senior Editor

ANDREA EDWARDS

MAN OF THE FAMILY

Silhouette®

SPECIAL EDITION®

Published by Silhouette Books New York

America's Publisher of Contemporary Romance

To all the survivors of sexual abuse, may you continue to grow strong and may your spouses and friends provide you with the support you need to be healthy and whole again.

Special thanks to Ann Volk of the Sex Offense Services of the Madison Center, South Bend, Indiana, for her help and advice.

SILHOUETTE BOOKS
300 East 42nd St., New York, N.Y. 10017

MAN OF THE FAMILY

Copyright © 1993 by EAN Associates

ISBN: 0-373-09809-X

First Silhouette Books printing April 1993

Printed in the U.S.A.

Books by Andrea Edwards

Silhouette Special Edition

Rose in Bloom #363
Say It with Flowers #428
Ghost of a Chance #490
Violets Are Blue #550
Places in the Heart #591
Make Room for Daddy #618
Home Court Advantage #706
Sweet Knight Times #740
Father: Unknown #770
Man of the Family #809

Silhouette Intimate Moments

Above Suspicion #291

Silhouette Desire

Starting Over #645

ANDREA EDWARDS

is the pseudonym of Anne and Ed Kolaczyk, a husband-and-wife writing team that concentrates on women's fiction. "Andrea" is a former elementary schoolteacher, while "Edwards" is a refugee from corporate America, having spent almost twenty-five years selling computers before becoming a full-time writer. They have four children, two dogs and four cats, and live in Indiana.

Classics from your favorite scary show!

It's a real
Night of Horrors
this Saturday on FunTime

9:00 PM *Rabbits' Revenge*
When a bunny dies in Angel's garden, she is targeted for revenge by the local rabbit population.

11:00 PM *The Monster Merry-Go-Round*
Angel goes to the local carnival and is held hostage by a merry-go-round gone bad.

1:00 AM *Jealousy of the Giant Ants*
After Angel's sugar cookies win first prize at the county fair, giant ants kidnap her to cook for them.

3:00 AM *Deadly Dust Bunnies*
Radioactive spray gets mixed up with furniture polish and Angel gets attacked by mutant dust bunnies while housecleaning.

5:00 AM *Attack of the Killer Cucumbers*
It hasn't rained for weeks and the cucumber plants in Angel's garden are angry. They come up through the shower to get their revenge.

Starring Angel Heart
Check cable listings for local channel.

Chapter One

Mike Minelli listened to the endless ringing at the other end of the phone line as he tapped an impatient tune on his kitchen counter. Someone finally answered.

"Hey, that was five rings," he griped. "What are you running there, a police station or a dentist's office?"

"Stuff it, Minelli," the dispatcher snapped. "You know 911 calls get priority."

Mike rolled his eyes toward the ceiling. What was it about police dispatching that turned little white-haired grandmothers into full-fledged dragon ladies?

"You're absolutely right," Mike replied. "Now could you just put me through to Sergeant Glaswell?"

"I'd be happy to."

Ignoring the smirk in the dispatcher's voice, Mike just waited for his call to go through. He was getting antsy, ready to roll. Moving into his new apartment hadn't been nearly distracting enough. Glaswell came on after only half of a ring.

"Hey, Len. What's happening?" Mike asked.

"Everything's shipshape, Lieutenant."

"You talk with the county and state police?"

"We're all set up. They're each gonna send a car and two officers, so there'll be ten of us."

Mike could feel the fire building. "That should be enough to take the drug-pushing scum down and put them in a hole for the rest of their lives."

Glaswell sighed. "And the higher-ups will get another house, another set of runners. They'll be putting more junk out on the streets in less than a week."

"And we'll close them down again," Mike said. Glaswell was a good cop, but sometimes he got discouraged too easily. "My dad always said, 'Keep hacking off the top and eventually the roots will die.'"

"Yeah, right."

If Len was any indication, the boys were going to need another pep talk, a reminder that every rat caught meant one less on the streets. "I'm going to take a shower and grab a sandwich. Be there in fifty minutes. We'll go over things one more time—then put on our dancing shoes."

Mike hung up, whistling tunelessly to himself as he set the alarm on his watch. They were going to come out winners tonight. Good, solid police work broke open a lot of cases, but when Lady Luck was on their side, there was no way they could lose.

And luck was definitely with them on this case, from spotting the crack house during a routine traffic stop to that tip from an informer. But the topper was today's date—April first. Hell, if that wasn't a sign from the gods, he didn't know what was. They could shout "April Fools'" as they broke down the door.

Mike pulled off his T-shirt and tossed it into a far corner of the master bedroom. Right now the room was sparsely furnished with an inflated air mattress, a sleeping bag and one large suitcase of clothes. Those, and the selection of boxes stacked in the living room, were the sum total of his belongings in the place. He'd spent most of the day in his old apartment, packing up stuff for the big move over the weekend. For now he had the basics—a place to sleep, a refrigerator for fruit and wine, and a shower.

He slapped his bare stomach once, satisfied that it was still flat and hard even if he had passed thirty-five, and dropped to the floor. Thirty one-handed push-ups with the right hand, then thirty with the left. Thirty sit-ups were topped off with fifteen bent-knee chin-ups on the bar he'd put in the bedroom doorway that afternoon. He worked out in the gym three times a week; these little exercises were more of a pregame ritual—sharpening the body and tuning the mind before the opening whistle sounded.

Puffing just enough, he marched into the bathroom and hung his towel on the hook before stepping into the tub. He set the lever to shower, turned the water to cold, then straightened up, leaving his eyes closed to protect them from the stinging bombardment of the water.

Except it never came. After a half second, he opened his eyes. A weak spray was slobbering all over the tub.

"Damn."

It was one of those telephone showers. The head was at the end of a flexible hose that someone must have used for a teething ring. Water was spitting out, pretty much missing him, but wetting the walls, the ceiling and the floor.

"Of all the—" No, no need to worry. It wasn't bad luck, just a little mishap. Annoying as hell, but not a sign that the gods were no longer smiling on him.

He climbed out of the tub and went down the hall to the kitchen, leaving a damp trail on the rug.

"Where's that number?" he growled as he picked up the receiver. "It's gotta be here someplace."

Fortunately, he found the business card stuck in the space between the wall and the telephone before he had to wreck the kitchen. He jabbed at the buttons on the phone.

"Hello." The voice was businesslike but quite young, and definitely feminine. His cop's ear picked up a tentative undertone. Great, the perfect time to meet the manager's kid.

"Let me speak to your father, please," Mike said.

The reply was silence.

"You father?" Mike ground his teeth. "Where is he?"

"I really wouldn't know."

Ouch. Mike held the phone away from his ear for a moment. With all the ice the kid put into her words, his ear was turning blue.

"Listen, kid—"

"I'm afraid you must have the wrong number."

The dial tone reverberated in his ear. Mike took a deep breath and dialed the number again.

"Yes." This time her voice was sharp, the defenses were up.

Maybe he'd miscalculated. He knew how touchy his little sisters had been about their age when they were young. Better to err on the side of maturity. "This is Mike Minelli. May I speak to your husband, please?"

More silence. Now what?

"Do you have trouble speaking to women, Mr. Minelli?"

"Huh? Look, I—"

"Have you considered counseling?"

"Counseling?" What the hell was going on? Mike could feel the throbbing in his temples. This couldn't be happening. Not on an evening when all his luck had to be of the good variety. "Why are you trying to aggravate me?" he asked.

"Me? Aggravate you? Look, if you don't quit bothering me, I'll have to report you to the police."

It was the final straw. "Damn it, lady, I am the police!"

Silence again. A stunned kind of silence.

"Look, let's start over." He took one deep breath and let it out. "I'm the new tenant in apartment 3-B, and I have a little plumbing problem."

"Well, why didn't you say so?" she said. "I'll be right up."

Mike slumped against the wall as the phone went dead. *She'll* be right up. Great—a female apartment manager with an attitude. There'd be no shower tonight. He just knew it.

Breathing deeply and slowly for control, Mike padded over to the door, ready to snatch it open as soon as she knocked.

All right, so maybe this qualified as a little bad luck, but it didn't mean a thing. He only had to worry when the tally got up to three. He was just at one.

The skirmish over the phone with Miss Manager didn't count as anything but a simple misunderstanding. Convinced that he was in control, he reached down to hitch up his pants and found nothing but skin.

"Damn it."

Another mishap. No, just plain forgetfulness, he told himself as he raced back to the bedroom. His pants lay in the corner, and he snatched them up.

It was time to enter stress management. This was not his normal pregame ritual. Had to ease up on the throttle. One leg in. A deep breath. The other leg in. Slow breath out. Everything was mellow. He adjusted his pants around his waist and pulled on his zipper. It went part of the way up.

That's okay, he told himself. The thing was just a bit stuck. No problem. Just work it slow and easy, and it'll slip right up.

The front doorbell rang, jolting the silence as if with a sudden charge. his right arm jerked and gave a mighty yank on the zipper.

"Ahhh!!!!" It slid up, all right. Bringing a few million hairs along with it. Oh, the joys of being Italian.

He managed to swallow his pain before he got to the door. He pulled it open and found a young woman in baggy jeans and a sweatshirt standing there. She was small, almost fragile-looking, and in her mid-twenties. Not as young as she sounded over the phone. And she had the biggest, brightest green eyes this side of the ocean.

"Mr. Minelli? I'm Angie Hartman. I'm here—"

"Yeah, right." He didn't have time for distractions. Mike looked away from those eyes, pulled her into the apartment, then started to push the door shut. "Come on, I don't—"

Suddenly there was a roar, and the door came flying back in his face.

"Jeez!" Mike jumped back, his hand automatically reaching for the gun he wasn't wearing. "What the hell is that?"

Standing in the doorway was a huge monster the color of mud, ugly as sin, and with the meanest set of fangs Mike had ever seen. The monster's eyes fixed on him and Mike suddenly seemed to find air a little hard to come by. He wasn't sure his heart was still beating.

"This is Fudge. He's my partner and all-round good buddy." Angie led the beast into the apartment. "He doesn't like doors slammed in his face. He takes it as a form of rejection."

"I wouldn't reject him," Mike said, moving back so they wouldn't all be crowded together in a small space. He might shoot the thing if he had a cannon, but he certainly wouldn't reject the beast.

"He doesn't handle rejection very well," Angie said. "You see, I got him as he was about to be put to sleep, and that's really an ultimate form of rejection."

"I guess. Just what kind of beast is it?"

"He's a dog, silly." Her laugh tinkled like a tiny silver bell as she leaned over to kiss the monster. "But mostly he's a baby."

That thing was about as close to a baby as Godzilla was. Mike just pointed toward the back of the apartment.

"Right," Angie said briskly. "Your plumbing problem."

She walked toward the bathroom, the puppy from hell following close at her heels. It wore a pack on its back filled with tools. That was fitting. The damn thing was the size of a donkey.

Mike forced his eyes away from the beast and let them wander over Angie. She was much easier on the eye. On the small side and with the most delectable curves, she reminded him of a French pastry that had to be eaten in small portions because it was so rich.

Her baggy jeans and sweatshirt fit like a tent but couldn't hide what a doll she was. She looked gorgeous enough to be an actress or a model. What the heck was she doing managing an apartment building in South Bend, Indiana?

"Okay," she said, pausing at the doorway to the bathroom. "What's the problem?"

"The shower," Mike said as he squeezed by her. "The hose has a crack in it."

"Whoops."

"You just have to replace the—" Mike stopped dead as his mind caught up with his ears. "Whoops?" This was bad—he knew it.

"I don't do showers."

"What?" He wasn't hearing this. "You don't have the tools? You don't have the supplies? What are you talking about?"

"Oh, I have everything," she replied. "I just don't do showers. Sinks and drains are okay, but not showers."

Mike stared at her a long moment. She stood there looking small and delicate, like the kind of woman you would hold gently and protect. Except that the streak of stubbornness in her face could make you want to wring her neck.

His watch beeped. Damn. Time to leave.

Then, suddenly, he smiled. "Okay. I get it. April Fools'! Right?" He was still a little annoyed, but he could take a joke.

"Wrong. I'll get a plumber," she said.

His smile dried up. "I need a shower now. I have to be out of here in a few minutes."

"Take a bath instead," she said.

"I never take baths."

"I can put a sprinkler outside if you want to run through that a couple of times."

"I want a shower."

Her grin disappeared, replaced by a look that bordered on panic. "Look, it's just a quirk of mine, okay? I have a thing about showers."

Mike could feel the seconds ticking away. "You have 'a thing about showers'?" he repeated. "Who ever heard of an apartment manager having 'a thing about showers'? Who ever heard of anybody having 'a thing about showers' unless it was that woman in *Psycho* who got murdered in one?''

Her look turned grim. ''I'll call a plumber and get this fixed tomorrow.''

''What's the big deal?'' he said, reaching out to take her arm. ''You just take that hose and—''

The roar of the dragon filled the apartment again, and Mike leapt away from Angie. ''I'm not doing anything!'' he shouted. ''I didn't touch her!''

''Oh, Fudge.'' Angie moved over to scratch the dog's ears, eliciting disgusting groans of ecstasy from the monster. ''Chill down, baby.''

Mike glared at the dog, but bowed to the inevitable. Whoever held the leash, held the power.

Damn, he hated baths.

''Hey, Mike,'' the woman behind the convenience-store counter called out.

''Hey, Rose,'' Mike grumbled as he trudged in. The smell of stale nachos was making him gag.

''Boy, aren't we in a good mood?''

''Good left long ago.''

''Poor baby.''

Mike went around some kids trying to see through the bubble-gum wrappers to the cards inside and stood by the magazine rack.

''Ham and turkey on rye with one slice of Swiss and the hottest mustard I got?'' Rose called.

''Hey,'' Mike said, turning toward the counter. ''Do I need a big sign on my chest? I order the same thing all the time.''

''So maybe one of these days you're gonna surprise me.''

''I don't want to think about what kind of sandwich to eat,'' he said. ''I got other things on my mind.''

''Lighten up,'' Rose said. ''It's not good to eat food on a grumpy stomach.''

He turned his attention back to the magazine rack. People just didn't understand. The reason you cultivated habits, good ones at least, was so that you didn't have to think things through all the time. Like how to brush your teeth or what kind of sandwich to have for dinner. It left your mind free for the important things in life.

Suddenly, his eyes were drawn to the cover of a magazine, one of those gossip ones about show-biz personalities. The head shot of a girl in the upper right-hand corner looked darned familiar. He picked up the magazine.

A little pixie with green eyes and light-brown hair stared up at him. A soft, little smile was on her lips, making her whole face look as vulnerable as a little girl's.

Nah, it couldn't be. They didn't put apartment-house managers on the cover of magazines like this. He opened to the table of contents.

"All right, everybody freeze."

Mike's head jerked up. A tall, skinny teenage boy stood at the counter. His right hand was in the pocket of his nylon jacket, sticking out like he had something more dangerous than just his finger in there.

"You, put all the money in a bag," the kid said to Rose, then looked at the handful of customers in the store. "The rest of you just relax."

Mike's left hand slid the magazine into his pocket, while his right hand pushed back his sport coat and closed on the butt of his pistol. "You'd better relax, son," Mike said softly but firmly. "I'm a police officer."

The kid blinked once; then his foot shot out to kick over a display of plastic soda bottles. He was out the door and running across the parking lot as the bottles rolled around Mike's feet.

"Call 911!" Mike shouted as he took off after the perp. He sped out the door and turned the corner. He saw the boy ahead, loping through the long shadows of oncoming dusk. Damn kid was built like a greyhound and could move like one. Speed had never been Mike's forte, but persistence was.

He kept after the kid, down the street and around a corner. Mike was losing ground slightly, but he didn't pull his gun. The kid hadn't hurt anyone, nor had he shown a weapon. The track star turned into an alley, and Mike followed.

"Stop!" he shouted. "Police!"

The kid kept on pumping those skinny legs of his. Mike was hoping a patrol unit would come by when a tall, chain-link fence came up. The boy grabbed the top and pulled himself over, dropping down on the other side and continuing his run without missing a beat.

Mike pulled himself up to the top of the fence but, as he struggled to keep from catching his pants, he slipped and fell. Sharp pain shot from his knee and spread through his whole body.

"Oh, Lord," Mike gasped.

He couldn't move without hurting and just lay there in shock. He was through chasing anything, even rainbows, for now. He'd be lucky if he could crawl out of there.

"Are you hurt?" An old woman had come out of a house nearby, cautiously advancing only a few steps from her door.

"I'm a police officer," Mike shouted. "Call 911."

The woman went inside, and Mike dropped his head back on the ground. Would she call the police or would she just let him lie there and rot?

A short while later the old woman came back out on the porch. "They're coming," she said. "I told them you was hurt bad."

In too much pain to talk, Mike just waved his hand. Boy, what a day. No matter how he counted it, his bad-luck tally was beyond three.

The magazine in his pocket made an uncomfortable dent in his back as he listened to the sound of sirens converging on the spot.

Oh, great. Little Granny Dispatcher probably put out an officer-down code on all the channels. That meant all the on-duty officers in the city would be there in five minutes or less. And in half an hour all the off-duty officers would know he couldn't scale a fence anymore and would be busting a gut over it.

Damn. He'd always hated April Fools' Day.

* * *

Angie stared at the cold pizza for a long moment, searching for the one piece that would be too delectable not to eat, but not finding it. She finally just put the cover back on the box and stood up.

"Come on, Fudge. Let's go get the paper."

The big dog raced her to the door, then slid out ahead of her as if his sole joy in life was to scout out hallways. With a wag of his tail, he looked an "All Clear" at her.

What a great friend he was, Angie thought as they walked out to the front lobby of the building. She couldn't believe that she'd only had him for the eight months since she'd moved here. He was so huge—a rottweiler-mastiff mixture—that she'd had to argue long and hard with the humane society to get him. They'd wanted him to go to a farm. Someplace where he would have a lot of room to roam.

But, as no farmer or anyone else had come forward to adopt the giant dog, Angie had gotten him after promising to fence in an area behind the apartment house. And she had, paying for it with her own money. Angie pulled her newspaper from the box in the lobby as Fudge raced to the outer door.

"Okay, but just for a few minutes," she warned him. "I've got a lot of business-math homework."

Fudge's look promised he'd be quick as he trotted over to investigate the bushes near the parking lot. She walked out onto the step. It was getting dark, but she unfolded the newspaper in the glow of the entrance lights. A picture of two little boys in T-shirts enjoying the warm spring day graced the front page. Angie smiled. That was the nice thing about a small-town newspaper; they could show happiness. In Los Angeles, the front page was full of accidents and evils. She wondered why her mother had ever left the Midwest.

"Hey, lady."

Angie looked up. A gray-haired, heavyset man had come up the walk while she was daydreaming and now stood a few feet from her. His eyes were hidden beneath the brim of an old baseball cap, but his mouth was curved in a frown.

Her stomach plummeted, leaving a hollow void in her midsection. She was really starting to get careless in this small-town atmosphere.

But even as she took a step backward, she heard Fudge's reassuring, low growl from her side. The man came to an immediate stop, his eyes widening as he stared at the dog.

"Ah, you got a Mr. Minelli living here?" the man asked, pointing over his shoulder with his thumb as he kept his wide eyes on Fudge. "I got this fare."

Angie looked around the man and saw his taxicab in the street. A young girl had climbed out of the backseat. Her short, dark hair bounced around her face as she pulled a lightweight jacket on over her sweatshirt.

"She said she was supposed to be delivered here," the cabdriver said.

"I'm not sure Mr. Minelli is in," Angie said. Actually, she was pretty sure he wasn't. He had been awfully definite about having to leave without his shower. "Was he—"

The child, who looked about ten, was skipping up the walk toward them, her eyes locked on Fudge.

"Fudge," Angie called, even as the dog bounded off the step. "Honey, look out—" But Fudge was dancing around the girl, his tail wagging nearly hard enough to come off.

"He's really neat," the girl said, patting the dog's head.

"I hate to interrupt this love-in," the cabdriver said. "But I gotta earn a living."

The girl looked up. "My bags are in the trunk."

"And somebody owes me four dollars," the cabdriver said.

Angie sighed. Apartment-house managers accepted deliveries for residents when they weren't home, but this seemed a bit much. "Is Mr. Minelli expecting you?" she asked the girl.

"I don't think so. This is kind of a surprise for him."

"A surprise?"

"My name's Emily Minelli." The child stuck her hand out toward Angie. "Mike's my father. He's a cop."

Angie shook the girl's hand. With her thick, black hair and bold, brown eyes, she certainly resembled Mike. "But you said your father wasn't expecting you?"

"Nope." Emily shook her head. "Mom put me on a plane, and here I am. Sort of like an April Fools' joke."

"That's awful," Angie cried.

"We really should give the guy his money," Emily said, nodding toward the cabdriver. "It ain't fair to make him wait around."

"But your father isn't home right now."

"I figured that," Emily replied. "He's always working. But he'll pay you back when he gets home. Mike's no deadbeat."

Angie stared at the child. Fudge's smile and wagging tail said he thought the kid was good for the money, but then that wasn't really the issue. It was the involvement that made Angie hesitate. Yet what could she do?

"I'll open Mr. Minelli's apartment," she said and turned to the cabdriver. "Could you bring the child's bags?"

"Sure," the man replied, giving Fudge one last wary look.

The cabdriver took two big bags from the trunk, and Emily grabbed a smaller one; then they followed Angie and Fudge up to Mike's apartment. Angie unlocked the door, and Emily rushed into the apartment without any qualms. Her lack of restraint chilled Angie. How had this child been raised? Hadn't anyone explained the need for caution to her?

"Hey," Emily shouted, then grinned at Angie. "Neato! This place sounds like a cave."

"That's because your father has no furniture." Angie watched as the cabdriver put the bags down in the living room, then came back to the door. "Emily, we have to go downstairs. I don't have any money with me."

"Okay." But the little dark head disappeared down the hallway with Fudge following close behind.

"You can't stay up here by yourself," Angie said. "Come on."

"All right." The voice wasn't happy, but Emily emerged from the bedroom and trudged out of the apartment. Angie could have sworn that Fudge gave her a dirty look, too, but she chose to ignore it.

By the time she'd paid off the cabby, Emily and Fudge were lying on the floor of Angie's living room watching a cartoon show. The child had kicked off her shoes and was totally at home. Angie couldn't believe it. The kid didn't know her at all.

"Why didn't your father meet you?" Angie asked. She couldn't believe that parents would just let a kid drift from city to city.

"He probably doesn't know I'm here," Emily replied, her eyes still glued to the TV set. "Mom said she'd call him once I was on the plane, but she hardly ever does stuff she says she's gonna do. Especially when it means talking to Dad."

"Are your parents divorced?"

"Yeah, they've been that way a long time. Mom's pretty laid-back. She says Dad's sort of hyper."

Angie remembered the man, his piercing brown eyes and the way he dashed around his apartment. "Sort of hyper" was putting it mildly.

"Mom says I'm a lot like him," Emily went on. "She says I got too much of his blood in me to relax like a regular person. She says California just ain't my thing."

California hadn't been her thing, either, Angie thought. Did that mean she wasn't a "regular person?"

A commercial came on the screen, and Emily rolled over to look at Angie. "I can go back upstairs if you have stuff to do."

"No," Angie said. "I don't think it's right for you to be up there alone."

"Fudge can come with me."

And leave Angie alone? "Fudge is my dog," she said. "He stays with me."

A sly smile turned the kid's lips. "We can ask him what he wants to do."

"Let's not," Angie said, rather surprised at the firmness in her voice. At least Marshmallow hadn't abandoned her, not that her cat showed a preference for anything but solitude.

The cartoon came back on, and Emily rolled over onto her stomach again. She and Fudge stared at the picture while Angie frowned beyond them, out the sliding glass doors at the hedge along the property line now disappearing in the dusk.

That selfishness was unlike her; she didn't really begrudge Emily Fudge's friendship. She had never had to share him before—that was all. It made her feel vulnerable to think he might not be all hers.

She walked over to the doors and closed the drapes, as if she could keep the darkness at bay. What was she supposed to do with this kid? Her past experience had not included dealing with kids, not even when she was one herself.

"Did you eat on the plane?" Angie asked.

"Yuck, no," Emily replied. "They give you cardboard with barf poured all over it."

The child's colorful language resembled her father's also. "Would you like something now?"

"Yeah." Emily popped up from the floor and raced into the kitchen, followed by a happy, giant puppy. "Whatcha got? Wow, pizza."

By the time Angie got to the kitchen, Emily was halfway through her first piece. Angie handed the girl a plate.

"Want some milk to go with that?"

Emily shrugged. "How come there's only one piece gone? Don't you like pizza?"

"I wasn't hungry."

As Angie poured the milk, Emily filled her plate with pizza. They went back into the living room, her big canine companion following Emily. Angie gave Fudge a glare, but he totally ignored her. Once the girl was settled down in front of the TV again, Angie went into the kitchen to call the police station.

Emily was certainly welcome here, but Mike should know that his daughter had arrived. From the little Angie had seen of the man, she really hated to interrupt him, but what else could she do?

"I need to speak to a Michael Minelli," Angie told the woman who'd answered the phone.

"I'm sorry, he's not here. May I take a message?"

Angie felt a tickling in her stomach and wiped her sweating palms, one at a time, on her jeans. She really hated these little decisions. Maybe she should just leave him a note on his door and let Emily sleep here tonight. No, a note at the station was more responsible than a note on his door.

"His daughter is here from California."

"His daughter?"

"And I don't think he was expecting her," Angie said.

There was a long silence before the woman spoke again. "Minelli's had an accident. He's in the emergency ward at St. Joseph's Hospital."

Oh, no! Was Emily about to lose her father? "What happened?" Angie asked. "Is he badly hurt?"

"I'm sorry," the woman said. "We can't give out that information."

"But—" Angie stopped, remembering her own sense of loss when her mother was dying. She got off the phone. It was more important to get the girl to the hospital than to be denied more information by the woman.

"Emily, get your shoes back on," Angie called into the living room as she found her purse. "We're going to see about your dad."

"Now?" Emily was quickly at the kitchen door, her face mirroring her surprise. "But isn't he at work?"

"Sort of." Angie pulled the car keys out of the bowl by the phone. Fudge was already waiting at the door.

"Is Fudge coming?" Emily asked.

Angie let them all out into the hall, then closed the door, checking to make sure it was locked. "Fudge always comes with me."

Chapter Two

"Nice outfit."

Mike glared at the emergency-room nurse, hoping to dim her wide smile, but it didn't do any good. He slumped back on the gurney.

The ambulance crew had split the right leg of his pants so they could immobilize his leg with an inflatable cast. Then the cast had been removed so he could be duly poked and prodded by various medical personnel. Now his ripped pants framed his swollen knee for all to see.

"What's going on, Janelle?" Mike asked. "I gotta be out of here. The city doesn't pay me to lie around on my butt."

"We're waiting for the doctor," the nurse replied. "She's going to put a soft cast on that knee."

Mike shot back up to a sitting position. "A cast? I won't be able to bend my knee. I can't work with my leg immobilized."

"Lieutenants have desk jobs," Janelle pointed out. "You don't have to do anything but sit on your can."

"Not me," Mike said. "I'm out where the action is."

A smirk danced on the nurse's lips as she stole a quick glance at his swollen knee. "Maybe you're getting to the age where you need to redefine action."

Right, fold up his tent and slink away. Give up his police work and he'd have nothing. He'd be nothing. Suddenly, a ruckus could be heard out in the hallway. Mike groaned and let himself fall back. He really didn't need this.

"Hey, Mike." The curtain around his cubicle was ripped back, and four husky men pushed their way in.

"Hi, guys." His voice was short and curt, heavily loaded with dignity as befitted an officer of the city's finest. "How'd everything go?"

"Great."

"Got the whole gang."

"Loads of evidence."

"No casualties."

With most of his people here, it might be a good time to hold a meeting. Anything to keep them from eyeing his knee and smirking.

"Where's Polanski?" Mike asked.

"Calling to have your car picked up from the convenience store."

Mike's stomach sank. If they were doing that...

"Don't bother calling my mother," he said quickly. "I'll take care of that myself later."

"Sorry, Mike."

The expressions on their faces belied their words, though.

"You know your family has to be notified. Standard departmental procedure."

Mike stared at their grins. For two cents, he'd wipe those smiles right off their faces.

"Hey, Lieutenant." Another hulk stepped into the room. "Looking good."

"Thanks, Polanski," Mike replied.

"I hear your takeoff was real good, but your landing stunk." His men snickered.

"You got a 6.85 overall," Glaswell said.

"Sorry, Mike," Polanski said. "You don't make the Olympic fence-jumping team this year."

"There's always next time."

His men and Janelle roared with laughter and were still laughing when the doctor stepped through the curtains. *About time,* Mike thought. He'd had more than enough of this damn place. Janelle herded the men out of the cubicle, leaving the doctor alone with Mike.

"Just put a small Ace bandage on it, Doc. I don't want to be too much of a gimp."

"We're going to immobilize it, Lieutenant."

"Doc, I said—"

"Would you prefer an operation, Mr. Minelli? As in reconstructive surgery?"

Boy, give some people a little authority and right away they play hardball. "All right. Do your thing. I have to get to work."

"I can't see you going to work for a week at least."

"For crying out loud, all I did was—"

"Mikey, Mikey, what happened?" His mother rushed in, sweeping up his head and crushing it to her bosom.

"I just fell, Mom," he stammered into her ample chest. "I'm okay."

His mother turned to a higher authority, letting Mike fall back on the gurney. "How is he, Doctor?"

"He's severely strained his knee ligaments," the doctor said. "I want to immobilize the knee, then check it when the swelling goes down. I don't think we'll have to operate, but you never know."

His mother turned to look at him, shaking her head. "Mikey, Mikey. You're too old for these kind of games."

"Mom," he protested. "I'm only thirty-eight."

She continued shaking her head, when suddenly she saw his ripped trousers. Storm clouds filled her dark eyes. "And your new pants."

"I didn't cut them, Mom. It was the ambulance guys."

The doctor moved in to wrap his leg, and his mother glanced around the cubicle, aggravation still filling her face. "Where's Margaret? I told her to meet me here. We're supposed to work at the Lenten supper tonight."

"Just go ahead," Mike said. "Catch her at the door. Save yourself some time."

In spite of the fuss everyone was making, this was not a big deal. He didn't need his whole family here to watch him get his leg bandaged. They should save their energy for more important things.

"We have to get you home first."

"You go on to your dinner. I'll catch a cab."

"What cab? Then who's going to help you into the house? You'll be on the first floor, but you still have to climb the porch stairs."

Porch stairs? First floor? "Mom, my new place is on the third floor, and there's an elevator."

"That is not your home," his mother pointed out. "That's just where you live. Home is where you grew up."

"Mom."

"You need to be where we can take care of you."

"Mom, I've only got a bum knee."

What was all the fuss? He didn't need a nursing home or a nursemaid. He was the man of the family, for Pete's sake, and had been since he was fifteen and his father had died.

"Look, Mom. I'm fine. I don't need any help."

"Mike, what happened?" Emily cried as she came rushing around the curtain. "Are you okay?"

Emily? And behind her was Angie with her ever-so-green eyes. What the hell was going on here? Did his men place an ad on the TV stations across the country? *If you want to see Mike Minelli flat on his back, come to the emergency room at St. Joseph's Hospital.*

"Emily," his mother exclaimed. "What are you doing here?"

"I'm staying with Mike," Emily replied.

"He is your father. To you, he is not Mike."

Mike closed his eyes, feeling his blood pressure on the rise. His only hope of avoiding an explosion was finding out that this was all a dream. All he had to do was be patient and this impending nightmare would disappear.

He took several deep breaths and opened his eyes. Nothing seemed to have disappeared. He turned to Emily.

"Why are you here?" he asked.

"Mom sent me," his daughter replied. "She says I'm supposed to stay with you."

How was he supposed to do that? "But she never called to—"

His mother turned to Angie. "I am Mrs. Minelli. Mikey's mother."

"I'm Angie Hartman."

Angie stepped forward, thrusting out her hand. His mother smiled; she liked take-charge women.

"I'm the apartment-house manager where Mike lives. Emily was waiting with me."

"You have beautiful eyes. Kind, with a touch of mischief." His mother reached down to take her left hand, holding it in both of hers. "Doesn't she have beautiful eyes, Mikey?"

"Absolutely. Look, Mom, why don't you go on to your supper? I'm fine." He knew exactly where his mother had been headed, just as he had known why she'd chosen to check Angie's left hand. Poor Mom—she never stopped trying.

"Ah, Margaret," his mother exclaimed as his sister stepped into the cubicle and greet everyone.

Mike nodded gratefully in her direction. Good, she'd take their mother away, and the place would start to clear out.

"We can't go to the Lenten supper," Mike's mother was saying. "Call Louie and Bobby and tell them they should get the recliner and the roll-away bed from the basement. And the trundle bed from upstairs. They should get a card table and chairs from Clara's; then they should take everything to Mikey's new place. He moved in with no furniture."

"I thought he was hurt," Margaret said. "Is he staying alone?"

"I'll be okay," he snapped.

"He has me to help him," Emily chimed in.

"Right, kiddo," Margaret said. "That must be why you dropped in for a visit."

His mother patted Angie's arm. "And I bet this nice Angie will help, too."

Angie looked startled at that. "Uh, I'm not really a nurse," she stammered.

His mother patted Angie's hand, and Mike felt a stab of evil glee at seeing her confusion.

"And Fudge, too," Emily added. "Angie's got the greatest dog."

His pleasure fled as quickly as it had come, stomped flat by reminders of the puppy from hell.

"Well, Mr. Minelli." The doctor smiled and patted his bandaged leg, before helping him sit up. "Looks like you're going to be well taken care of."

Mike just gritted his teeth. Why wasn't anybody listening? He didn't need to be taken care of. Soft laughter rumbled in the far distance, and he knew it was all the gods on Mount Olympus laughing. April Fools'.

"This is so dumb," Angie told Fudge. "Why am I such a weenie?"

His only response was to fog up the back windows even more with his breath. Angie pulled her Escort to a stop at the emergency entrance and wiped the windshield with her hand. Inside the doorway, she could see Mike in his wheelchair and Emily hovering over him. They were in the spotlight, while Angie was in the darkness of the audience. Just the way she liked it.

"I should have told his mother that I couldn't take him home," Angie muttered. "Lord knows, he seems to have family coming out of the woodwork. There's got to be somebody else who could drive him home."

Fudge just leaned forward over the seat back and laid his head on Angie's shoulder, snorting wetly into her ear. She patted his head and opened the car door. "I don't even particularly like him," she confided in a half whisper as if Mike could hear. "He's too pushy and much too hyper for my tastes."

Fudge agreed. Angie gave him a last scratch behind his ear and got out of the car. "Might as well get this over with."

She took a deep breath and walked back into the hospital. Enter stage right. "Your chariot awaits," she called out.

Emily jumped up and attempted to wheel her father's chair over to the door, a feat that was made more difficult by the fact that he was trying to wheel himself over at the same time.

"Jeez, Em, I'm not a cripple," Mike grumbled.

"Then how come you're in a wheelchair?"

"Because of some stupid hospital regulations. Let me—"

"I can get it."

Angie just laughed and moved upstage. Out of harm's way, she hoped. Somehow Mike made it out the door and over to the car.

"Hope you don't mind togetherness," Angie said.

"I could take a cab," Mike said as he started raising himself from the chair. "Why are the windows all fogged up?"

"Fudge," Emily said and opened the car door for her father.

The dog looked out at him and growled. It was a small, pleasant victory that Angie did not allow herself to dwell on.

"Fudge!" she scolded lightly. "Come out here. Emily, I thought you and Fudge could sit in the front. Your dad can stretch out on the backseat."

"Okay."

Angie turned to Mike. He looked like he was steeling himself to face a firing squad.

"He won't hurt you," she said.

"Who? The dog?" Mike made a show of propping himself up. "I never thought he would. I was just planning how best to get into the car."

"I see."

She enjoyed his discomfort. It made him seem less intimidating. She waited as he climbed awkwardly into the backseat of the car, easing backward onto the seat and pulling himself along with his hands and one good leg. Once he was settled, she closed the back door and helped Emily and Fudge into the front seat.

"You look like a pretzel," Angie said to Emily with a laugh. Fudge was sitting on the floor, with his front legs in the girl's lap.

"More like a sardine," Mike grumbled. "We should have taken a cab."

"It would take too long to pry Emily out now," Angie said. "We might as well just go on home."

She went around to the driver's side, took a deep breath and congratulated herself. It had been a long time since her "we" had included anybody but herself, Fudge and Marshmallow. She was doing pretty well.

Some butterflies reappeared, though, when she shut her own door. The air was so close in the car, so confined. She could feel Mike behind her in the backseat, looming, lurking. She wished she had put him in the front seat where she could see him. Fudge grunted reassuringly, as if he could read her mind, and she started the motor.

"Well, here goes nothing," she said, revealing her vast repertoire of repartee. She was going to have to hire a scriptwriter if she joined any more of these outings.

Even though he was out of sight, Mike seemed to fill up the car. His good knee was partially between the seats, which made it all too close to the gearshift. His left arm, as he leaned against her seat back to brace himself, was all too close to her shoulder. All in all, there was just too much of him in the crowded car. She tried to ignore her stomach, which was rapidly tying itself up in knots, and concentrated on driving out of the parking lot.

"Now, tell me again what you're doing here," Mike said to Emily.

He moved forward slightly to look at his daughter, which brought him even closer to Angie, but she was able to relax a bit. His attention was on the girl, while Fudge's gaze was on Mike. Angie was forgotten, invisible, just a chauffeur.

"Mom said I should live with you for a while," Emily said.

"Just like that?"

Emily shrugged. "She said she'd call."

Mike grunted and moved back again. Angie cast a quick glance over her shoulder at him. He seemed huge. Tall certainly, but it was more his bulkiness. His shoulders were broad and muscular; his legs were thick. He was a man of power, of strength. Someone who wasn't afraid of violence. It was very obvious he was a police officer. Her hands tightened on the steering wheel.

"What if I was on vacation?" Mike said suddenly. "You could have gotten here to find nobody home."

Angie squirmed slightly at the passion in his voice, though she knew he was talking to Emily. Fudge flicked his eyes in her direction, and she patted his head reassuringly.

"I would have gone to Grandma's," Emily said. "Besides, I got your letter. I knew you were moving. You don't go on vacation when you're moving."

Another grunt was his answer, and they rode the last few blocks to the apartment building in silence. Unless, of course, Angie counted Fudge's heavy breathing or Emily's murmurs to the dog.

Mike cleared his throat as they pulled into the parking lot. "Thank you for your help. You really didn't have to," he told Angie. His voice was more reluctant than his words. It was very obvious that Mr. Macho Man didn't like depending on anyone else.

Well, that was just fine. She wasn't one to be depended on; that wasn't a role she was auditioning for. She concentrated on navigating around a parked car before speaking. "That's okay. I was there anyway."

No one spoke for a moment. "You always bring your dog with you?" he asked. His tone was joking.

"Yes." Hers was not. "Well, here we are. Safe and sound."

She pulled up to the walk, noticing in the glow from the streetlight that a pickup truck was sitting off to the side of the parking lot.

"Jeez, just what I need," Mike muttered. "My little brothers."

"You have a big family?" Angie asked.

"Big doesn't begin to describe it," Mike said.

She turned off the motor, ready to go around to his side to let him out, but he didn't wait. He had the door open and was struggling out on his own. Angie got Fudge out, then Emily.

"Hey, Uncle Louie, Uncle Bobby," Emily cried, dashing off.

Angie put a light hand on Fudge's head as Mike limped past them to the sidewalk. Her touch was enough to keep the dog at her side, watching the others from the shadows. This was fine. Mike's family would get him upstairs and settled in. She could go back to her own place and get to her studying.

"Let's park the car, Fudge," she said. The dog hopped back into the front seat, and she pulled it into her reserved spot. After they got out, she checked that all the doors were locked.

"Angie can help." Emily's voice pierced the darkness, and Angie felt that all eyes suddenly seemed to be on her.

"I can what?" Angie asked, walking slowly back across the lot and back onto the stage. Fudge tensed, feeling her apprehension.

Emily skipped over to Angie's side. "Show Uncle Louie where the elevator is. Or I can do that and you can help Mike."

Angie's gaze went from Emily to her two burly uncles, waiting next to the truck, to Mike, a powder keg of irritation waiting to explode.

"I'll take the uncles," she said on a sigh. It would be faster.

But that was debatable a while later as she waited at the elevator door for them to maneuver the trundle bed in. Fudge was semi-well-behaved. Angie was just plain tired of trying to be cheerful.

"Bet Mike makes you crazy," Louie said once they finally got the bed into the elevator.

"He just moved in today."

"Give him another day or two," Bobby said with a laugh. "He'll be telling you how to breathe and everything else."

"Fudge gives him the willies," Angie said.

"Can we borrow him?" Louie asked. "Be nice to have someone like him around when Mike gets on our case about something."

Both men were laughing when they reached the third floor. She held the Open button while they maneuvered the bed out again. As they carried it down the hall, she went ahead and unlocked Mike's apartment. Mike and Emily reached it as the uncles were going back down for their second load.

Good, Angie thought. Her evening was finally over.

"I'll help them this time," Emily offered and ran off with her uncles.

Angie was left alone with a visibly exhausted Mike. Her goodbyes died in her throat—she couldn't just leave the guy standing there alone. Not with him on crutches. But standing there in silence made her uneasy.

She glanced around her. Fudge was settling down on the floor, yawning and sighing as he found just the right position.

"This whole thing was so stupid," Mike said with unexpected vehemence. "And that punk got away."

Angie edged away from the anger in Mike's voice, not knowing how to respond. "We should have brought the recliner up first," she said. "I didn't think."

He looked startled at the change in subject, then shrugged. "No big deal."

"I hope it was all right that I brought Emily to the hospital," Angie said, then wished she could retract the words. She sounded so unsure of herself, like she was seeking his approval. "I called the police station, just to let you know she was here, and they told me you'd been hurt."

"Probably made it sound like I was on death's door instead of the nothing it really is."

If it was nothing, why couldn't he stand on his own? But she didn't say anything. Reading people wasn't her specialty, but even she could see his pride had taken a beating tonight. Emily's voice reached them from down the hall, and Angie felt relief surge through her.

"She's a nice kid," Angie said.

"I don't know what her mother was thinking of, sending her like she did." He glanced at his watch. "She ought to be home from work by now."

He limped into the kitchen, and Angie wandered back into the hallway. Mike's brothers brought the recliner into the living room, while Emily pushed a roll-away bed on wheels.

"This'll be my bed," she told Angie.

"Always good to have a place to sleep."

The sound of the phone being slammed down killed any stray smiles hanging in the air.

"No one answers," Mike announced as he limped out into the living room. He turned to Emily. "Do you know who your mother's friends are? Who she might go to visit?"

Emily's face darkened. "Don't you want me to live with you?"

Mike hobbled over to his daughter. Using only one of his crutches, he pulled his daughter close to him with his free hand.

"I can't think of anything else in the world that I'd like more." His voice had turned slightly husky.

Angie felt a lump in her own throat. For all his gruffness, Mike was just an old softy. Like Fudge in a number of ways.

"But I still have to talk to your mother," Mike went on. "I have to check out stuff. There's medical records. Dental records. School records. I don't even know what size shoes you wear. There's a whole bunch of stuff."

"I wear size five shoes," Emily said. "And I'm on spring break, so I'm not in school."

He looked down at her, his smile so unexpectedly filled with love and caring that Angie had to look away. "I think I still need to talk to your mother," he said.

What would it be like to have someone so concerned about you, so filled with love that you were all that mattered?

Angie wasn't sure she wanted to explore those questions, so she turned her attention to pushing Emily's bed down the hall. Besides, how did she know what Mike was feeling? She was about the world's worst judge of people's motives.

She opened up the bed in the smaller bedroom, finding sheets folded up inside and shaking out the fitted one over the mattress. Fudge came in, looking around the bare room, and found it nonthreatening enough to settle down on the floor by the closet.

And if Mike cared so much about Emily, why was she living halfway across the country?

Everybody was an actor, playing a preassigned role, Angie decided. Some were just better at it than others. Emily came dragging in, pulling a suitcase.

"He doesn't want me here," she said, sinking onto the edge of the bed. Her voice was quivery, on the verge of tears. "He's gonna send me back as soon as he talks to Mom."

Angie's heart melted. "Hey, you don't know that." She sat down next to Emily, putting her arm around her shoulders. "It was just a surprise. He didn't expect you."

Fudge shuffled over to put his head on Emily's lap. His big brown eyes watched the girl, telling her not to cry.

"A girl's got to have a dad," Emily said, scratching behind Fudge's ears and blinking back the tears. She was afraid, just a kid who was lost in a grown-up world. "You can't grow up without one."

"Well, I'm not sure about that," Angie said. "It might be harder, but not impossible."

Emily looked up at her. "Didn't you have a dad?"

"Technically, everybody has one," Angie said carefully, not certain she should have started the conversation. "But mine wasn't around much."

"How come?"

Angie shrugged. "I don't know. I guess he wasn't into this fatherhood thing. He left when I was three, so it wasn't like we had discussed it."

"Didn't you miss him?"

"Not that I remember. My mom and I took care of ourselves all right." And now that her mother was gone, Angie was taking care of herself and doing just fine. Emily was silent, too pensive, and Angie squeezed her shoulders. "Hey, that was me and my dad. Yours is different. Even if he sends you back, he's not going to duck out of your life. He was part of it before, wasn't he?"

"Yeah."

"Then he will be again."

"I guess." Emily slid off the bed with a sigh and knelt on the floor to open her suitcase. She took out a pair of pajamas. "I'm supposed to get ready for bed."

Angie glanced at her watch. It was after ten. "It's late." She stood up. "I'll see you tomorrow."

Emily nodded and Angie, after mussing the girl's hair fondly, led Fudge out into the hallway. The uncles seemed to have left. Mike was limping into the kitchen.

"Want something to drink?" he asked, pulling open the refrigerator.

"Thanks, but I don't drink." She tried to keep the stiffness from her voice, but didn't quite make it.

He gave her a strange look as he pulled a soda out of the refrigerator. "How come you haven't dehydrated then?"

She felt silly, like he was laughing at her and that she deserved it. "I thought you meant beer or something."

"And that you don't drink."

"No." She felt obligated to explain. "All alcohol does is make you lose control."

"And you don't like to be out of control."

"I don't like anyone out of control." She wanted to leave, to get back to her own apartment where she didn't have to play a role. Where she could be alone and safe. But her feet wouldn't leave just yet, not until she said what needed to be said.

"Emily thinks you don't want her here."

He took a drink of his soda and looked straight at her. "I don't."

So that loving-father bit really was just an act. "She's your daughter," Angie said. "And a great kid. She really loves you."

"I know that," Mike snapped.

Fudge growled softly, deep in his throat. Angie put her hand on his head to silence him.

Mike gave the dog a sour look. "I love her, too," he said, but more softly this time. "But cops make a lot of enemies."

"Your daughter isn't one of them."

He shook his head, staring at the can of soda in his hand. "She was about four years old." His voice was still soft, as if dredging up the memories could awaken some demon. "A perp I'd arrested met up with a judge who felt sorry for him. Gave him a bail he could make. Wasn't more than a couple of hours after he was released that the crud was pitching a Molotov cocktail at my house. I was on duty at the time."

"Was anybody hurt?" Angie asked.

"Not physically, but it made me see the light. Sometimes you can't have the things you love best. Em and Susan were on a flight to San Diego before the week was out."

"Susan's your wife?"

"*Was* my wife. We'd been having problems and were heading for divorce anyway." Mike bit off a sigh. "I never thought I'd be sending Emily away from me, though."

Silence filled the kitchen. The sound of Emily's singing from down the hall seemed a painful reminder of her presence.

"Do you get to see her much?" Angie asked.

"A couple times a year," he replied with a shrug. "I go out to California, and we go to Disneyland and stuff like that."

"Don't you miss her?"

"I'm awfully busy with my work, but we talk on the phone a lot. We stay in touch."

Angie could see pain in his eyes that she was sure had nothing to do with his knee. He crushed the empty can in his hand and flung it at the back of the counter. Fudge jumped to his feet, but Angie settled him with her touch.

He'd seemed like an awfully gung-ho cop, and now Angie could see why. He had nothing else in his life except his job.

"I can't watch Emily all the time," Mike said. "But I can take care of her. I can send her far away from here to somewhere she'll be safe. Somewhere she can grow up like a normal, happy kid."

"No place is safe."

"Some are safer than others."

How could she argue with that? It was what she had been counting on herself. There seemed to be nothing more to say, so Angie nudged Fudge toward the door. "I'll get that shower taken care of tomorrow."

He nodded, lost in his own thoughts, as she opened the door.

"Hey," he said, as if just realizing she was leaving. "I've been meaning to ask you." He moved awkwardly after her, then reached around to his back pocket and pulled out a magazine.

"Is this you?" he asked, pointing to a head shot on the cover.

Her stomach twisted as the past came back to laugh at her. So much for trying to hide.

"Angel Heart," she said and opened a whole flood of locked-away memories. The perfect sixteen-year-old, virginal victim. The silly, innocent, naive fool who had played too many parts, mixing up the roles with reality. Believing evil couldn't really be disguised and that heroes came with a lifetime guarantee.

"Yep," she said. "That was me when I was a superstar, but it was such a bore, I quit." She followed Fudge out into the hall and shut the door firmly.

"Whatcha doing?" Emily asked.

Mike's head snapped up from the magazine article he'd been reading. "I thought you were asleep."

"I can't sleep. My body's still on California time."

Emily crawled into the chair with him. Her foot knocked the desk lamp he'd balanced on a moving crate, and he reached out to steady it.

"Hey, that's Angie," she said, pointing to the magazine. "Yup."

"Is she a movie star?" Emily's voice was filled with excitement.

"She used to be."

"What do you mean 'used to be'?"

"She used to be in movies and on TV," Mike said. "She isn't anymore."

"How come?"

"I don't know. I guess she doesn't want to be."

Emily turned back to the previous page to look at the pictures, from an ad for a candy bar Angie had been in at age five to the recurring role she'd had as a victim in "Night of Horrors." He could remember the made-for-TV series of movies, though it must have been five years since the last one had been on. She was always walking into the wrong place at the wrong time and having to be rescued. You wanted to shake some sense into her, scream out a warning before it was too late, but you also always wanted to rescue her, keep her safe. There was something she did with her eyes that made her look so vulnerable.

"What else does it say?" Emily asked.

He forced his attention back to the article. "That there was talk of reviving her show for a movie sequel, but it fell through."

"Really? That would've been so rad. I mean, I could've told everybody she was my friend."

Emily took the magazine from his hands and studied the pictures more carefully. Emily pointed to one picture. "This is Angie and her mom. Does her mom live with her downstairs?"

"No, it says her mother died of cancer last summer."

His daughter looked thoughtful for a moment. "Then it's a good thing you moved in here," she said.

Mike just looked at her.

"That way you can take care of her."

He just glanced away, seeing Angie's deep-green eyes staring up at him. The last thing that lady needed was somebody to take care of her. Those eyes definitely flashed an I Can Take Care of Myself signal, which was good. He didn't have time to take care of anybody else, not with Emily, the family and the city counting on him.

Chapter Three

"Damn," Mike muttered as he slammed the phone down in its cradle.

"Grandma said you're supposed to rest."

Mike spun to find Emily frowning at him. "I was just using the phone."

Judging from her expression, that wasn't a reasonable excuse, so he hopped over to a folding chair and dropped down into it. "Where is your mother anyway?"

"Mom said something about going to Hawaii with Ron," Emily said. "I think she wants me to live with you."

"You can't," he snapped.

"Why not?" Her dark eyes challenged him.

What could he tell her that wouldn't scare her? "I have a full-time job."

"So does Mom. After school, I'm in day-care and during the summer, I go to a day camp."

So that's what childhood was these days. He saw his own youth, rushing home from school to a home that had been warm and welcoming with his mother's presence. They hadn't had much to spare on his father's cop salary, but they were always together. Even after his father was shot and killed, they'd had each other. He'd denied that to Emily, and that denial spread the shadow of guilt over him.

Yet what was worse—keeping her from her family or exposing her to danger? She could live without him. But could he live without her if he let her back into his life again? He got to his feet and hobbled back over to the phone.

"Are you calling Mom again?" Emily asked.

"No, I'm calling your Aunt Margaret. You have to stay with someone while I'm at work." There he could continue to try to reach Susan by phone without Emily's accusing stare.

"It's Saturday."

Mike turned away from his daughter's eyes and faced the wall while he punched in his sister's number. "Hey, Margaret," he said jovially. "How are you?"

"What do you want, brother dear?"

Boy, was he the only friendly one in the family? "I need somebody to look after Emily this morning while I'm at the station."

"I thought Louie and Bobby were supposed to help you move today."

"This afternoon. That doesn't mean I can't put in a few hours at the station this morning."

"Well, I can't help. I've go to do an estimate for a decorating job."

"You're five months pregnant."

"I'm just bringing some of the lighter fabrics and colors."

"Fine," Mike snapped. He was sure that there was some interior-decorator's joke in there someplace, but he wasn't in any mood to go searching.

"Just chill down, Mikey. The rest will do you good. Besides, you and Emily ought to spend some time together. I mean, visiting the kid a couple times a year is hardly being a father."

How was he supposed to spend more time with her? He only had so much vacation.

"And if you need any help, you can always call that nice little landlady of yours."

"She's not my landlady," Mike pointed out. "She's the manager. Just does odds and ends around the place."

"Well, there you go. She can run to the store, play with Emily, rub your back. Just odds and ends."

He wanted to give a real snappy retort, one that would lay his sister flat, but the dial tone was already buzzing in his ear.

"What happened?" Emily asked.

"She has to work today."

"Women have to do a lot of that," his daughter replied.

"I work, too," Mike protested.

"You're not supposed to today. Grandma said you're supposed to stay home and rest."

"What Grandma doesn't know won't hurt her."

"She could find out." A sly look came in his daughter's eyes. "Somebody could tell her."

"Nobody likes a snitch," Mike said.

"I thought cops used them all the time."

"They may use them, but that doesn't mean they like them." He took a deep breath. "Let me splash some water on my face, and you put your shoes on. We'll go out for breakfast."

The closest restaurant was a greasy spoon over on Mishawaka Avenue that was four blocks away, but the distance didn't matter. They didn't have any food in the house.

"Emily?"

"Yeah. Okay. Swell."

She picked up her shoes from where she'd left them by the recliner and sat on the floor to put them on. He hopped down the hall toward the bathroom. Damn. Now his other leg was hurting.

He shut the bathroom door, hopped to the sink and leaned forward on his hands. Alone, he allowed himself the luxury of a long groan.

Great father he was. No one to take care of his daughter, no food in the house and practically no furniture. He didn't even know if she had the right clothes for this climate or if she brought a toothbrush with her. What if she needed girl stuff? No, he shook his head. She was too young to need any of that, wasn't she?

Angie's face floated through his thoughts. Angie could ask her. Angie would have an idea what a girl Emily's age would need. But he didn't want to ask Angie. He didn't need to ask Angie. Emily was only going to be here a short time.

"Come on, Minelli. Take charge," he told the face in the mirror, then brushed his teeth. He hopped into his bedroom to put on a clean shirt and a fresh smile before going back to the kitchen.

"Hey, Emily," he called out. "I'm ready. Are you dressed?"

Woof.

The big mud-colored beast stood in the hallway, blocking his way. There was an evil glint in its eyes and foamy slobber dribbling from his mouth.

"Assaulting a police officer is a felony, fella."

The creature wagged its tail and its grin grew even larger. Why was he always without his weapon when the puppy from hell was visiting?

"Fudge."

A slight chill ran up Mike's spine as Angie walked into the hall. She had on the same baggy jeans, but today the sweatshirt advertised Indiana University. She looked as fresh and alive as the forsythia bushes that were starting to bloom. He felt a tightness in his belly, a longing that came on hard and strong.

"Fudge." Her voice had a scolding tone to it, but it did nothing to dim the dancing light in her eyes as she hugged the beast around the neck. "Are you being a pest?"

Monster beast made the sound of death deep within its throat and wagged its tail vigorously.

Angie looked up at Mike. "He's never seen anyone hopping around on one leg. He thinks you want to play."

Mike could imagine what kind of game the beast wanted to play. Probably something like Grab-the-Man-by-the-Neck-and-Shake-Him. Or Listen-to-the-Man-Scream-Before-His-Neck-Breaks.

"What are you doing here?" Mike asked, liking the sensation of seeing her in his home and disliking himself for that.

"Making breakfast." Angie pulled Fudge to the side of the hallway. "Come on, get to the table before it gets cold."

"Ladies first," Mike said as he tried to avoid looking at the devil dog.

Angie made a face, but she went off, floating in the company of her bodyguard. Mike hopped along behind her, watching the gentle sway of her body.

At least he thought there was a gentle sway. That baggy outfit of hers was sexier than any bikini. It left everything to his imagination, which seemed to be working in overdrive at the moment.

Emily looked up as he came into the kitchen. She was sitting at the card table, shoveling syrupy pieces of pancake into her mouth. "Guess what, Dad? Angie really was a movie star. She said that was her in the magazine."

"I told you that last night."

"I was just checking," Emily said.

The dog ambled over to a corner and dropped his three-thousand-ton frame to the floor, all the while keeping an eye on Mike.

Mike hesitated in the doorway. Things looked a little too settled here, a little too comfortable. Definitely too domestic.

"Did you call Angie?" Mike asked.

"I had to," Emily said. "I was starving to death, and there's no food around here."

"I thought we were going out for breakfast."

"Grandma said not to let you do too much."

Like fending for himself? He knew how to manage his life and those who belonged to him. He didn't need everyone in the world trying to take over. Angie came over with a frying pan and flipped three pancakes onto a plate set in front of the empty chair.

"Sit down," she said. "They taste best when they're warm."

"And even bester with syrup," Emily added.

Mike thought about arguing, thought about insisting that they go out for breakfast as he'd planned. Hell, they could even invite Angie to come along, providing she was willing to leave the beast from hell at home. He glanced at the two females in his kitchen, then stared for a long moment at the monster dog.

The dog turned so that its tongue hung out the side of its mouth. Its tail was wagging slightly as its eyes followed Angie around the kitchen.

Mike's dad had often said that a few key decisions shape a man's life, and Mike knew he was at one of those junctures right now. He could be firm, take charge and clearly demonstrate who was in control here.

Mike could see that the choice was clear. On the one hand, he had principle, on the other, he had death.

He slipped down into his chair at the card table and reached for the syrup bottle.

By the time he was halfway through the stack, Angie was ready with more. He just shook his head and tried to swallow. "It's your turn," he said. "You eat those; then I'll make the next batch."

"I ate long ago," she said and gave Emily one of the fresh pancakes, then dumped the others onto his plate.

So she just came up here to wait on them? The idea gnawed at him. Damn it. He didn't need taking care of. "Then pour yourself some coffee and sit with us," he said.

She frowned at him and bit at the edge of her lip for a moment, as if it were some huge decision. Was she believing the hound from hell's opinion of him?

"I've just got a sprained knee, not leprosy," he said.

A smile peeked out from behind the clouds. Though it hid itself pretty quickly. She poured herself a cup of coffee and sat down. The ordinary old kitchen seemed warm suddenly, but then freshly brewed coffee always did that.

"What's leprosy?" Emily asked.

"A disease people used to think was *real* contagious," Mike said as he watched Emily polish off the rest of her snack. He turned back to Angie. "This was really nice of you. We were just going out to eat, but this was even better."

"It was nothing." She held her cup with both hands, flashing those big green eyes at him over the edge. "I wasn't doing much, just waiting for the plumber to call back about your shower."

"No big rush. I can't shower for the time being anyway," he said, nodding at his leg. "I never was good at the one-legged jump-in-the-tub event."

Those eyes were such a mystery. Sometimes they seemed to laugh at the world. And other times they seemed to be filled with dark, forbidding clouds. He wondered what the key was to keeping them dancing.

"Lucky you feel that way. I suspect it'll be Monday before it's fixed."

"I guess I can wait. If not," he added with a grin, "there's always that sprinkler in the yard."

"Can I use it, too?" Emily asked.

Angie chuckled, a soft, teasing sound that belied the shadow in her eyes. He leaned back, sipping at the last of his coffee. Why was he assuming something was wrong? The woman was an actress, a professional victim no less. She was probably hired for that job because she could turn on that worried look in her eyes.

His stomach tightened with annoyance because he'd been taken in. He saw con artists every day of his life—not that she was deliberately trying to con somebody. Still, he shouldn't have been so gullible.

"Say, can I ask you for one more favor?" he asked. "Can Emily stay with you this morning? I want to go into the station for a while, and I need to stop at the grocery store—"

"We were going to do that," Emily said. "Me and Angie already got a list made up."

"A list?" he snapped.

The beast from hell raised its head, and a low rumble filled the room.

"Fudge." Angie sprang out of her chair and was quickly at the dog's side, patting it with one hand while holding on to its choke collar with the other. Emily was also at the beast's side.

"Everything's cool," his daughter told the dog. "Mike's not mad. He's just Italian."

"Fudge isn't used to shouting," Angie explained.

Shouting? Who was shouting? All Mike wanted to do was take back some control of his own life. He stared into the dog's brown eyes, seeing the flames of hell glitter within them. They hadn't heard shouting yet. He took one last look into the beast's eyes.

And they wouldn't.

"He equates shouting with hostility," Angie said. "And hostility is just another form of rejection."

"I see." Mike's voice was grim but quiet as he got to his feet. "Have you thought of counseling for him?"

Angie laughed. "No." She nuzzled the slobbering beast on the neck. "I just give him tons and tons of love."

Mike stared at them for a moment, astounded at the sudden wave of hunger in his own heart. He wanted to hold her, to have her nuzzle him on the neck and give him "tons and tons of love."

What was happening to him? Had he damaged more than his knee when he fell yesterday?

"I'll clean up," Mike said and, balancing himself on one crutch, he piled the plates together. "Angie, thanks again for your help."

"Sit down," Emily ordered. "We can do this."

Mike glared at his daughter. "I will clean up," he hissed in a near whisper. No need to upset the neurotic dog and delay his own escape. "Then I am going to the station for a few hours."

"I'll tell Grandma," Emily threatened.

Enough was enough. He didn't need some half-pint shrimp to come in and manage his life. It was time to assert himself. It was time to bring some control to the situation at hand.

He looked into the dog's red-rimmed eyes. It was time for him to go sit in his recliner in the living room. The sooner Emily and Angie cleaned up, the sooner they could take the dog downstairs and go shopping. Then he could do whatever he wanted.

"Come on, Fran. I can't believe she didn't tell you what was going on." Mike would have slammed the phone down, except that wouldn't have gotten him the straight answers he needed. "You're Sue's big sister. You practically raised her. She always confides in you."

"Hey, what's there to tell? We're all adults. She doesn't need my permission for anything," Fran said.

"Look, I called her office, and they said she quit last week. There's no answer at her apartment. Emily said she was going away with somebody named Ron. I have the right to know if something's wrong." He paused for a moment. He and Sue had been divorced almost six years. He didn't have any rights. "Emily has the right to know."

Fran sighed. "Look, nothing's wrong. Ron's her latest, and she just wanted to get away with him. And she thought that Em needed you. No big mystery."

"Yeah, but how long is she going to be gone? Should I enroll Emily in school?"

"Not unless you want her to be as ignorant as you are."

The urge to hang up was growing even stronger, but he fought it. He and Fran had never gotten along. She was so opinionated, always trying to influence Sue.

"You know, it would have been nice if she'd talked to me about this," he said.

"And give you the chance to say no? She knows you too well."

"Thanks a lot."

For all practical purposes, Emily had been abandoned by her mother and dumped into a life that he couldn't let her stay in. He was still a cop, and now there wasn't even a mother to help care for her. So now what?

"Ask Sue to call me, will you?" he asked.

"If I hear from her."

Mike hung up then, not with the force that he wanted to earlier but with a slow resignation. How was he supposed to take care of a ten-year-old girl? School, day-care, Girl Scouts, dollhouses. Not to mention keeping her safe.

Mike limped slowly into the living room, the silence making him edgy. Since Emily and Angie had been determined to go to the grocery store, there seemed little reason for him to flee the apartment to use the phone.

Now he wished he had gone to the station. He felt useless hanging around here. He limped over to the recliner and sank into it, picking up the movie magazine from the box beside the chair.

Angie's photo smiled up at him, her eyes wide and innocent with just a touch of imp to them. There was something so appealing about her, something so intriguing in her smile. Maybe he should get to know the lady better.

Not that he wanted a real steady. He shook his head and tossed the magazine aside. He didn't want any kind of attachments; he didn't have time for any. He just wanted someone to go out with once in a while, when it was convenient for both of them.

And someone like Angie might be ideal. Growing up in a fast-paced society like L.A. had probably made her a no-permanent-attachments kind of person herself. The entrance buzzer rang, forcing him to get up.

It took him a moment to reach the intercom, enough time for two more buzzes, and by then he'd lost his patience. "Yeah," he barked.

"Mike, it's Louie. Open up."

Mike pressed the door-release button, but wondered what he was doing here already. He'd thought the move was set for this afternoon. Louie came off the elevator, wheeling a dresser on a dolly and followed by Aunt Lucille.

"Michael," she called out. "Thought it was about time you gave that child of yours some decent furniture."

"She's not staying."

But neither slowed in their descent on him. Louie went past, wheeling the dresser down the hall toward the second bedroom. Aunt Lucille came in, too, to prowl the rest of the apartment and scowl her disapproval.

"You need some furniture, Michael. This is no way to raise a child." She stopped in the living room, her hands on her hips.

"I'm not moved in yet," he pointed out.

Her gaze took in everything, from the lack of drapes to the packing box pretending to be an end table. She frowned and pounced on the movie magazine.

"What is this?" she cried. "This isn't the type of reading material that should be around. You have a child in the house now."

He took the magazine back, not an easy feat while trying to balance on a crutch, but the magazine was his. Or would be, once he went by and paid Rosie for it.

"Right. From now on, only Shakespeare."

"Is this for me?" Emily squealed from the doorway, trailing Louie and a bunk bed. She had a grocery bag in her arms. "Does this mean I'm staying?"

The excitement in Emily's voice hurt as much as the joy in her voice warmed him. Mike kept his eyes on his feet as he hobbled over to her. "Need help with those groceries?"

Lucille snorted. "What are you going to do, carry the bag in your teeth?" She turned to Emily. "I brought you the set, honey. All my kids are grown up now, and I needed to find a new home for it."

"Wow. Bunk beds!" Emily looked over her shoulder at Angie who was standing in the doorway, a bag in each arm. The ever-present Fudge was at her side. "I always wanted bunk beds." Emily thrust the grocery bag at Mike and went over to give Lucille a hug. "Thanks, Aunt Lucille."

"You're very welcome, honey. You have a friend stay over real soon and have a great time."

A frown settled on Emily's face. "I don't have any friends here yet," she said, then brightened. "'Cept for Angie. Can you stay over, Angie?"

Lucille laughed hard and long. "I'm sure that Michael wouldn't mind," she said.

Angie blinked momentarily, but she quickly put a smile on her lips. "I really can't," she said as she looked down at her giant devil dog. "I already have one male in my life, and he tends to be the jealous type."

"Fudge can stay, too," Emily assured her.

Enough was enough. It was time to take over. "Em, why don't you help Louie bring up the rest of the stuff? You know, like hold the door open for him."

"Okay." She was gone in a flash.

"Slick," Lucille murmured as she walked toward the door herself. She stopped just short of the hallway, though. "You should let her stay, Michael. You need her more than she needs you."

She went out into the hallway, leaving Mike to wonder whether she had meant he should let Angie or Emily stay. Angie and Fudge slipped past him. He could have sworn the dog glared at him as it followed Angie into the kitchen.

"Here, let me take that." She was back and taking the grocery bag from his hand.

"I can manage," he said.

"Right." She took the bag anyway and carried it to the kitchen, setting it down on the counter next to the other bags. He followed her.

"So where do you keep your cereal?" she asked.

"Nowhere yet." He frowned as she kept on unpacking the bags. "But you don't have to worry about it," he said. "I can put the stuff away. I'm not exactly helpless, you know."

"I never thought you were." She started putting things away in the empty cabinets as she unpacked the grocery bags. "So what's Emily's mom like?"

He shrugged. "Quiet. Sort of indecisive. Very protective."

"Yet she sent Emily here unannounced."

Mike frowned. He hadn't described a woman who would do that kind of thing. "I can't figure that one out myself."

Angie took a package of margarine out of the bag and put it into the refrigerator. "Have you talked to her yet?"

"No. Her sister claims nothing's wrong, though. Just that she thought Emily needed a father's influence for a while."

"Sounds logical."

He frowned at Angie. Had she forgotten what he'd told her last night about the attack on his family? "She's too precious to me to put at risk."

"I think you'd be risking a lot more by sending her back."

What was that supposed to mean? "You don't—"

"Mike, look who we found outside in the parking lot. Uncle Bobby and Timmy." Emily produced her uncle and cousin like a magician making a tiger appear. "They've got stuff from your old apartment."

"Great." He moved out of the kitchen. Angie didn't understand. The risk to Emily was being here with him. "Hey, Bobby. Tim. That stuff can go in my bedroom. Em, want to show them where that is?"

"Sure."

He watched wistfully as she led them down the hallway. She brought so much sunshine into his life. He was sure going to miss her when she left.

Mike suddenly started, noticing that Angie was slipping past him and heading for the door. "Hey, where you going?"

"Back to my apartment."

He didn't want her to go, either. The apartment would be a cold and empty place, but that wasn't the only reason he wanted Angie to stay. After all, Emily needed a woman around her.

"How about having dinner with us?" he asked. "I owe you."

"You don't owe me anything."

"You made breakfast and did my grocery shopping."

"And paid the cabdriver yesterday," Emily chimed in as she skipped down the hall toward them.

Angie just shrugged. "No big deal."

"It is to me," he said. "Minellis always pay their debts."

It seemed like shadows were back in her eyes. Those eyes changed moods more often than Indiana changed weather. He didn't dislike that brooding look; it made him feel like protecting her and that wasn't all bad. But he liked her laughing eyes better, bringing no burdens along with them. He wanted the sunshine back and thought he knew how to get it.

"There's this great restaurant out in Lydick where a lot of the local Hell's Angels types eat," he said. "What d'ya say we take a nice drive out there, stuff ourselves with food and liquor, get obnoxious, get thrown out and end up with a chains-and-knife brawl in the parking lot?

"Then we'll drive home, stop along the way to throw up a couple of times, drop in at the emergency room to get any loose parts sewn back on, then come back here and make some popcorn, watch TV and relax."

Both Emily and Angie stared at him, neither even cracking a smile.

"How's that for a great evening?" he asked. "Planned out to the last detail."

Still no one said a word. If anything, the shadows in Angie's eyes looked deeper. So much for his great sense of humor.

"I was joking," he said slowly. "You know, like in making ridiculous statements. Statements so far out that they couldn't have a shred of reality connected with them."

"Thanks for the invitation," Angie said. "But I have a lot of studying to do."

"Okay," Mike said. "We'll go someplace closer and save Lydick for when you guys are more in a fun kind of mood."

"I really can't," Angie said and without another word, she left. Fudge trailed along behind her, the heavy tread of his paws on the rug lingering in the air.

Mike felt ridiculously disappointed. She didn't want to spend time with them.

"I think it was the throwing up," Emily said.

"Huh?" Mike looked down at his daughter.

"It wasn't cool," she said patiently. "Nobody wants to go out on a date and throw up."

"It was a joke. Besides, it wasn't a date," he said and turned to hobble back into the kitchen. It hadn't been. It'd just been an effort to repay his debts. There was no reason to be disappointed.

Angie was asleep; she knew it and yet she didn't know it. She was at the beach house, searching. Sounds from the past floated onto the sun deck. Her mother was watching an ancient episode of "Night of Horrors" on the VCR, keeping the volume loud as if noise could accomplish what the painkillers couldn't.

Angie cringed as the sound of her own youthful voice surrounded her.

"Please, let me help you."

"Why, thank you, little Angel. I'd never find my way in this old castle alone."

She was cold, so cold. It had never been this cold in Los Angeles before. She longed for a sweater, for gloves, for a thick blanket to wrap around her, yet she couldn't find anything. Every drawer she looked into was empty, every closet bare.

"Please don't."

"You don't mean that. You like this. You want this, I can tell."

"No, please. I have to go."

"Angel."

"Stop."

The voices were the same but reading from a different script, one she wanted to forget. She tried to cover her ears, but the screams in her heart and his laughter echoed around her. The terror clawed at her, holding her prisoner. She had to escape it, had to get away, yet she was frozen. His hands were on her again. Breath came from somewhere, filling her lungs and giving her one moment of strength.

"No!"

She sat up as she awoke, the pounding of her heart deafening her. It was over. It was just a dream. She was here in her bedroom, safe with Fudge and Marshmallow, safe, with her lights blazing as they did every night.

Fudge licked her hand, whining with worry.

"I'm okay, honey," she said, patting the dog. Angie fell back against her pillow in exhaustion, her heart was racing, and she was covered with sweat.

Somehow Fudge believed her. He padded back to the big old love seat in the corner. She lay quietly, staring up at the ceiling. It was silent in the room, too silent. Edges of the dream started to creep back into her subconscious.

She got up and joined Fudge in the love seat. It was a tight fit, but his warm, furry body brought her comfort. She was safe there.

"I am all right," she told him. Told herself.

Her voice was a shallow whisper, a mere breath on the night air. She forced her shivering to stop. She was not afraid anymore. It was time she put that night behind her, really behind her.

She leaned against the chair back, closing her eyes and letting Fudge's even breathing set the pace for her. She had come to South Bend to start living again and that's what she needed to do. She had to stop being afraid to meet people. She needed to open up and let others meet her.

Her dreams had grown far distant that night. He'd taken more than her body. He'd taken her ability to believe in the future.

She wanted such normal things—a home, a family to love and take care of, and someone to love and cherish her. Yet the search seemed a terrifying process now. Who could she trust? How could she ever judge what lay behind a man's eyes?

Opening her eyes, she took a deep breath. She'd been hiding too long, believing the time would come when the memories would stop holding her back. But the memories weren't fading with time. The nightmares were still there; her appetite was still spotty at best. Maybe it was time to stop waiting for a bus to come along and take her back to life. She needed to flag down a cab, and the sooner the better.

She got to her feet carefully, trying to let Fudge sleep, and pulled a clean nightgown from her drawer. She would start dating, start leading the life of a normal twenty-seven-year-old, even if the idea sent icy shivers through her.

The next time Mike Minelli asked her out, she would accept. No, she wouldn't wait for him to make the first move. She would. She would heal herself.

Chapter Four

The phone was ringing as Mike unlocked the door. Emily jumped over his crutch and was in the apartment before he could say a word.

"I got it," she cried as she picked the receiver up.

Mike just frowned and hobbled after her. The pan of lasagna, leftovers from Sunday dinner at his mother's, was balancing precariously on the edge of the counter where Emily had shoved it. Emily may have answered the phone all the time when she lived with Sue, but he didn't like her doing it here. He didn't want to advertise to the whole world that his daughter was here now. And likely to be here for a while, since he still hadn't reached Sue.

"Great. Sure," Emily was saying. "Okay."

Mike put the lasagna into the refrigerator as she hung the phone up. "Listen, young lady," he said. "We need to get some things straight if you're going to be living here."

Instead of frowning in worry or looking apologetic, Emily's face split with a wide grin as she flung herself at him. He almost lost his balance under the assault of her hug.

"You mean, I'm staying?" she cried, hugging him fiercely. "You want me to stay?"

The relief in her voice could only be mirroring the pain and fear she'd suffered over the last couple of days. Mike extricated himself carefully and limped over to one of the folding chairs that was still serving as his dinette set. He pulled Emily over, holding her hands in his.

"It wasn't that I didn't want you here," he told her. "I just worry when you're here."

She nodded. "Because of the fire."

"You remember that?" He had hoped that she would have forgotten the attack and the fire that followed.

"Sure. And you're afraid some nut'll hurt me. Mom told me all about that. But I can be careful. And we're safe way up here on the third floor. If anyone tried to break in downstairs, Fudge and Angie would get them."

Fudge maybe, but Angie was a tad on the small side. She looked more like she needed protection rather than being able to provide it. Not that she wanted any. Certainly not from him. Her attitude made that point quite clearly.

"There's just a lot of things we need to get worked out and number one is that I want you to be careful."

"Sure."

The doorbell rang then, and Emily took off.

"Em!" he cried, but she was already opening the door.

Mike got to his feet and followed her. What had he just been telling her? Couldn't she remember even basic caution?

He turned the corner into the foyer and found Angie at the door, a wide smile on her face and a pie in her hands. Her appearance so stunned him that he forgot about being annoyed with Emily.

"Hi," she said and held out the pie. "Hope you like chocolate."

"Huh?" Her words didn't seem to make sense. Not that his did any better.

All he saw at the moment were her eyes. Bright, sparkling but with a touch of clouds. He didn't know whether they were signaling sunshine or storms.

Of course, either would be fine with him. He could always use a little sunshine in his life, but storms were good, too. They shook things up and washed the dirt out of the air, left things smelling clean and fresh.

"Angie called," Emily told him. "That's who was on the phone. She asked if we wanted to have dessert with her."

"Oh."

He moved aside, feeling awkward and ungainly even though he was better with his crutches today than yesterday. Angie and the ever-present puppy from hell came in.

"Hiya, Fudgey," Emily said, dashing over to cuddle the devil's disciple. The damn dog was so big that Emily barely had to bend over to hug it.

"Why do I have the feeling he'd eat me alive if I tried that?" Mike asked Angie.

"Because he would," she said. Her eyes were suddenly alight with her smile, inviting him to laugh with her. "He'd sense your insincerity."

"So it would be my fault?"

"Isn't it always?"

Her laugh was so light and cheerful. It was like one of those car ads on TV with no car and birds singing in a meadow at sunrise.

She looked good. He wanted to take her into his arms, but he reached for the pie instead. "Want me to take that?"

"I think I'd better."

She carried it around him into the kitchen. He turned, trying for a semi-graceful movement, but by the time he executed it, he found himself following behind Fudge and Emily. Angie was wearing a sweatshirt again but, instead of baggy blue jeans, she had on a pair of shorts. Not too short—they were almost down to her knees—but the right length to show him that his imagination had been right on target. The lady had very nice legs.

"Guess what, Angie?" Emily cried as she got plates from the cabinet. "I'm staying."

"Are you? That's great!" She hugged Emily with one arm even as she put the pie down, but her eyes caught Mike's. *Right move,* her gaze seemed to say.

Her approval seemed wholehearted, not the least bit grudging, and Mike's heart felt lighter in some strange way. This was crazy, he told himself. He wasn't looking for approval from some stranger, even one as attractive as Angie.

"I think I'll find a seat if you don't need my help," he said.

His voice was gruffer than he had intended, but no one seemed to notice. Emily and Angie were busy cutting up the pie.

"Let's eat in the living room," Emily said. "Fudge and I want to watch the circus on TV."

By the time Mike made his way to the sofa, Angie was there with their pieces of pie. She held his while he sat down; then she sat next to him, close enough to touch. He just took his plate from her. Emily and Fudge were settling down in front of the television. If Emily's pie tried anything funny, the dog looked ready to take it out in a New York minute.

Mike took a forkful of pie. It was sinfully delicious. "This is great," he said. "It's okay if you forget to take the rest home."

"I'll think about it," she said with a laugh and started in on her own piece. "I love your decor."

He gazed around the room. It was slightly more furnished since the family had carted stuff over from his old place, but most of the furnishings consisted of unpacked boxes. The actual pieces of furniture had looked better in the cramped confines of his old apartment.

"At least I can seat more than myself now," he pointed out.

"Your end tables are lovely."

"Rare and valuable antiques," he agreed. They were the TV trays that together used to form his kitchen table. His old place had been a lot smaller and hadn't had any room at either end of the sofa. One hanging lamp had provided light, and the part of the sofa he wasn't sitting on had provided space to dump the newspaper.

He eyed the little elf sitting next to him and wondered if he dared to test their newfound friendliness. "Still willing to play the Good Samaritan? I could use some help picking out new furniture. My mother says it's time I lived like a regular person instead of like some cliched version of a private eye.''

''Now that you've got a new place to live?''

''Now that I've got family living with me.''

''I probably could,'' Angie said, jumping back to answer his request.

The words weren't exactly enthusiastic, but what about the eyes? They seemed to be sparkling, but sparkling with what?

He turned to watch Emily as he ate his pie. She and Fudge were shoulder to shoulder, watching a trapeze artist as if they were both planning it for a career.

''I'm glad you're keeping her,'' Angie said softly. ''She really, really wants to stay.''

He just shrugged, then felt he was being less than honest. ''It's only because I can't reach Sue. I still don't feel this is the right place for Emily. I put in a lot of hours in my job, and I can't be here all the time to take care of her. Apparently, Sue's gone off with her boyfriend after deciding Emily needed time with me.''

''She does,'' Angie said. ''She's at a critical age.''

''The age when she needs a woman,'' Mike said.

Angie shook her head. ''She's on the verge of so much. Physical changes are just a part. She needs to learn about the world. She needs to learn things that only a strong man, a father, can teach her. Things a mother can't.''

Emily had said that Angie had never known her own father. Yet it didn't seem to have done her any harm. She seemed a straight-up kind of person. What did she feel that she had missed? He supposed he could ask, but he didn't want to pry.

''You know what the worst part of parenting is?'' he asked Angie, surprised that he was going to open up so much. ''Watching your kid enter a world of chaos, a world that, no matter how strong you are, you can't set right for her. It scares the hell out of me.''

''You can't change the world,'' Angie agreed. ''But you can make Emily strong enough to take it on.''

Her voice made him almost believe he could, that even if life was a roll of the dice, he could make sure that Emily was in a position to make good use of whatever the gods had handed her.

He looked at Angie. Her green eyes were soft, unguarded for a moment. There were shadows lurking in the background. What uncertainties and fears lay hidden there?

"Maybe you're right," he said, and reached over to lay his hand on hers. "But it doesn't matter in any case. I've got to do my best for Emily. I've been dealt my hand—now I have to play it."

Her eyes opened wide and her hand stiffened in his, like a bird freezing when captured. Then, just as suddenly, she relaxed and smiled.

He'd surprised her, he decided. With his usual hollering and stomping around, she hadn't known he had a gentle side to him. Mike returned her smile. He'd have to make sure that Angie saw more of that side of him. She was nice, and they might hit it off for a while.

"Want me to take your plates?" Emily asked.

"Sure," Angie replied.

Startled, Mike's hand jumped off Angie's. She passed her plate and fork to Emily.

"Need some help?" Angie asked.

"Uh, I think I've got it," Emily said. She took Mike's plate and carried them all out to the kitchen.

"She's such a nice kid," Angie said. Her voice quavered slightly. She wiped her hands on her shorts in a quick, nervous motion and glance around the room.

Mike looked away, pretending not to notice Angie's sudden uneasiness. Most of the time she seemed like a pretty up-front type of lady, but there were other times that she seemed on the verge of running away. Maybe it was because she didn't really know him yet.

"Hey," Emily exclaimed as she popped back into the room. "The light over the sink doesn't work."

"Probably just the bulb," Mike said and started to struggle to his feet. "I'll fix it."

Angie jumped up. "I'll do it."

"Don't worry about it," Mike said.

There was a growling rumble as the mountain of evil stood up. Damn, he was going to have to whisper all the time or buy that fool dog some earplugs.

Mike cleared his throat. "We got by without that light last night and we can do the same tonight. The room's bright enough without it."

"No. It's my job to maintain things like that."

"Angie—"

"It'll only take a few minutes. I may not do showers, but I'm quite capable of changing a light bulb."

Mike just stared at her. Her earlier unease was gone and she was back to being her regular pushy self.

Angie and Fudge left and returned a few minutes later, all brisk business. The dog was playing packhorse again, carrying her bag of tools. Angie was dragging a small stepladder behind her.

Mike glared at it, visible proof of how useless he was. "I'm not going to be crippled all my life," he grumbled. "I could fix the light in another couple of days."

"This is my job."

Why? But the question stayed locked in Mike's mind. He watched her quick, light movements as she opened the ladder and climbed up to take off the light cover.

As he looked up at Angie, it dawned on Mike why men put women up on pedestals. It brought out all their better points. Being three feet up off the floor certainly put Angie's trim legs in focus. And the bottom of her sweatshirt flopped out enough to show Mike that the package also contained a slender waist.

He shook his head slightly to himself. Were his tastes changing as he got older? Usually he preferred a woman with a little more heft to her, somebody sturdy enough that she wouldn't fall apart with the first decent hug.

On the other hand, although Angie was on the small side, she did seem to be wound tight. She was filled with a vigor and a sense of boldness that awoke a fascination in him.

"Okay, Emily," Angie said. "Flick the switch."

They all watched the fluorescent light flicker, then beam its rays out over the sink and counter area. Mike hobbled closer to the sink as Angie put the light cover back on. He felt useless and wasn't enjoying it.

"You want to take the screwdriver, please?" Angie asked, handing the tool to Emily.

"Sure." Emily put the screwdriver in Fudge's pack as Angie started down the ladder.

Well, he could at least be a gentleman. Mike reached up to help Angie down, putting a hand on her back to help her balance.

"No!" Angie's cry was loud and sharp even as she pulled away from his touch.

"What the—"

It was as if a bomb had dropped. No one moved. The dog didn't growl or make any kind of noise, but filled the room with a strong sense of menace. Its eyes grabbed Mike and held him tighter than a three-hundred-pound wrestler.

Angie forced a laugh up out of her throat. "Sorry. You startled me."

Mike let his hands fall slowly. "I was just going to help you down."

"I've been up and down this ladder a thousand times," Angie replied, embarrassed, and scrambled down as if to prove it.

"I was raised to be a gentleman."

She smiled at him. Or at least in his general direction, as her gaze was on the ladder she was closing up. "You only have one good leg," she explained. "I don't want anything to happen. I don't want either of us to get hurt."

So that was it. She was afraid that the cripple would knock both of them down. Mike could feel his spirits sag even further. "This cripple thing sure is getting a little old."

"You'll be healed soon," Angie replied.

She folded up her ladder, bid them a cheerful adieu, and left with her beast. If she'd meant to leave some joy behind with the remaining slices of her chocolate pie, Mike had trouble finding it.

* * *

"You almost ready?" Mike called toward Emily's bedroom. He had the breakfast dishes in the dishwasher, the milk put away and the answering machine turned on.

Emily shuffled into the kitchen. "I guess." She was dressed in jeans and a clean blouse. Shoes were on her feet, and her hair was still damp from her shower. "This isn't fair, you know. I'm on spring break."

"If you were here on vacation, you'd be on spring break. If you're here to live, you've got to get started in school."

"Can't we pretend it's vacation for a week?"

"We're just registering you for school." He gave her a hug. "You don't have to start today if you don't want to. You can decide once you see the place."

"Okay." She headed toward the door. "I'll go get Angie."

Mike had been hobbling along after her, but stopped at the mention of Angie. "What for?"

"So she can drive us."

"I can drive."

"But—"

"But nothing. I'm fine."

Emily wore her doubting expression as they left the apartment and went down the hall. They didn't need Angie, not to drive, not for anything. A man needed to be in control, to be able to take care of his own.

"You're going to love St. Joseph's," he told Emily. "They have all kinds of sports. Soccer, basketball, softball, volleyball."

She stopped, her hand keeping the elevator door from closing, even though he didn't need that much time to get in.

"Will I have to wear a uniform?" she asked.

"I don't know." He frowned, trying to remember what Louie's kids looked like coming home from school, but couldn't picture them. Had he ever been there when they got home? "We did when I went there, but that doesn't mean they do now."

"Gross."

Mike didn't say anything more as they rode down and walked out to the parking lot. By that time, his leg twinged more than a little, but he told himself it was fine.

"Look," Emily said. "There's Angie and Fudge."

He looked over to where Angie, shadowed by the puppy from hell, was heaving garbage bags into a dumpster. Her regular costume of baggy jeans had replaced the shorts she'd worn yesterday, her sweatshirt was bright yellow. In the fresh-morning sunshine, she looked like spring.

"Hey, Angie," Emily shouted. "We're going to register me for school!"

Angie smiled and Mike forced a pleasant but distant smile on his face. He was just another father driving his daughter to school. The crutches were a very temporary addition to his attire, and one to be discounted, if not ignored, when taking his measure as a man.

"I'm gonna go to St. Joesph's," Emily went on. "It's the school Mike went to when he was a kid. Can you drive us?"

"Sure," Angie replied and tossed the last bag in. "I'd be glad to."

Mike's jaw dropped to the ground while his irritation level soared. He glared at Emily.

"Then you can take him to the doctor's. He's got an appointment this morning."

"Okay." Angie had come over. "I'll get my license and be right back."

"Maybe we'd better take Mike's car. It's bigger."

Angie's lips twisted as she thought. "I'd better leave Fudge at home then. Come on, boy. Inside with you." She and the dog left.

Mike ignored the scent of lilacs that seemed to linger in the air after her and turned to his daughter. "Why did you do that?"

Emily's jaw was set in the same stubborn line that he recognized in his mother. "Grandma told me not to let you do anything stupid."

"This is my home, not Grandma's."

"You can't drive," Emily said.

"I'm the adult here, young lady. So I'm in charge."

They stood there glaring at each other.

"Is something wrong?"

Angie's soft voice defused a truckload of Mike's anger while, in some perverse way, it generated another new spate of it. "I thought Emily was being very rude," he said. "She had no business imposing on you."

"You mean asking me to drive? I don't mind. I'm done with my morning chores, and I don't have a class until eleven-thirty. I have lots of time."

That wasn't the point. He was a man, and a man didn't need help. "It's not right."

"Nonsense," Angie assured him. "What are neighbors for, if not to help? Let me have your keys, please."

Grimacing, he reached down in his pocket and pulled out his keys.

"Thank you." Angie took the keys and walked toward his car. The gentle sway of her body added fuel to his annoyance.

"Mike can sit in the backseat," Emily announced.

"Isn't that too close?" Mike asked. "Wouldn't you prefer I sat in the trunk?"

"Now, now." Angie smiled at them both over the roof of his car. "Emily just wants you to be comfortable. The backseat will give you room to stretch your leg."

The morning sun seemed to lighten her eyes with laughter. He searched for something, anything, to focus on besides her. "You sure you won't have any trouble with the stick shift?"

"My car has a manual transmission," she reminded him.

"Oh, yeah."

They all got into the car, and Angie pulled out of the parking lot onto the street. He stared silently out the window.

Spring was really bursting out all over. The trees by the river were faintly green along their branches. The grass on the banks had been kissed into life by the recent rains. Even the old stone bridge arching over the river ahead of them seemed newer, stronger.

"Was it fun to be in the movies?" Emily asked, and Mike turned his gaze away from the street.

"Most of the time," Angie said.

The curve of her cheek begged to be touched. Her hair was short enough to curl around her ear, tickling it in a way he suddenly longed to. He turned to stare back out the window.

"Were you a star?" Emily asked Angie.

"No, not at all. Just one of the cast. The one always getting attacked by monsters, bugs, killer plants and all kinds of villains."

"And always had to be rescued by that same old guy," Mike added dryly. So much for staring out the window and ignoring her. "What was his name? Randall Somebody."

"Sheridan."

Her voice was suddenly clipped. Mike didn't know if it was his imagination or if he'd done something dumb again, but the temperature seemed to have dropped about fifty degrees.

"Jeez, couldn't you beat the bad guy yourself?" Emily asked.

"Not then," Angie said, then seemed to force a smile. "Hey, some of those bad guys were pretty bad. I was once attacked by killer cucumbers."

"Killer cucumbers?"

Mike could see Emily swearing off salads for the rest of her life. "I don't think they were the kind we eat," he said.

Angie laughed, and this time it sounded natural. They were turning away from the river now. The street was lined with old houses, towering as high as the treetops and covered with old Victorian trim. It felt warm and safe, and he could sense Angie relax.

"It was just a stunt for the show," she said. "The plants attacked me in a shower."

He had a sudden longing to share in her memories. "And turned you against showers for the rest of your life?"

"Yep." Angie's sunshine had come back. "They put me in the shower and then shot some film with the plants around my ankles. Then they'd move the vines up and shot some more film. They did this for days until they had the vines covering my whole body."

"That doesn't sound very scary," Emily said.

"It doesn't seem like it should have been," Angie admitted. "But it was. Maybe because it was one of my first shows and I was only twelve. I had nightmares for years about being choked by those vines. And the worst thing was that every time I had a nightmare, I got the rash back that I got from the plants. I'll never get into a shower again the rest of my life."

Angie laughed, minimizing for Emily the horror that Mike had heard in her voice. What kind of mother would put a child through such an ordeal? He had his own ideas, but he wasn't about to voice them. Maybe that was one of the reasons Angie came out here, to be her own person.

They pulled into the lot behind the yellow-brick school building. Diamond-shaped kites hung in a second-floor window, bunny-shaped silhouettes danced in another. The place looked inviting, and Mike was glad. Emily would feel at home here.

"Are you ever going back to Hollywood?" Emily asked as Angie parked the car.

"No way," Angie said. "I've had enough of waiting around while people poke, pull and primp you until they think you look good enough to take a picture of. I'm going to college."

"Whatcha gonna be? A ranger or an astronaut?"

Angie laughed again. "I'm going to be a financial planner. They help other people take care of their money and get paid real well for it."

"Oh," Emily said, obviously not impressed.

"But right now, I'm struggling with my first finance course. I have trouble with math."

Mike frowned a bit. A financial planner who had trouble with the mathematics of finance?

Angie was smiling at Emily. "This looks like a nice school. I bet you'll make lots of friends here."

"I guess I might as well stay the day." Emily got out of the car. "Give Fudgey a hug for me."

Mike worked his way over to his door and stopped, one hand on the door handle, the other on the seat back.

"You don't have to take me to the doctor's," he told Angie. "I can get a cab."

A big smile lit up Angie's face as she reached over to pat his hand lightly. "I'm not driving your car without you. You'd probably report it as stolen."

Her touch was pleasant, but her smile was great, lighting up her face and his heart like fireworks on the Fourth of July. So what if she was on the small side? His father used to say that the only thing that needed to be big in people was their hearts.

"I'd never do that," he insisted.

"Yes, you would," she said with a laugh. "With me locked up, you'd be able to change all the light bulbs in your apartment without any interference."

The unexpectedness of her reply made him laugh. She was fun; they would have to get together one of these days.

His mood suddenly soured. They would get together once his damn knee healed up; there was no way someone like Angie would go out with him now. Hell, she'd have to help him around, open doors for him and cut up his meat. It would be like taking her great-grandfather on an outing from his nursing home.

Emily was waiting by the school entrance, no doubt wondering what was taking him so long. He took another moment to adjust his crutches and get his impending grumpies under control.

There were some interesting feelings coming into play here, ones he'd like to explore a bit more, but would Angie? Would she be attracted to him once he was healthy, or would she think of him as the cripple she had to drive around?

"You okay?" Emily asked.

"Just peachy keen," Mike snapped and swung his crutches into action. "We go in that door."

She was doing great, Angie told herself as she leaned against the car. She'd been a little jumpy yesterday around

Mike, but today she was fine. Those first steps toward normalcy had been taken, and Mike had proven trustworthy. Today she would take a couple more. Before she knew it, those nightmares would be a thing of the past.

A group of little kids, kindergartners maybe, walked across the parking lot to another building in some semblance of a line. She smiled at them. They were so full of life and energy, so ready to trust. If only they could all remain that way.

"You didn't have to stay."

Angie turned to find that Mike had come out. "She all registered?"

"And in her classroom."

His voice was sour, as if he were trying to swallow anger. Had something happened inside to upset him or was it her? Stop blaming yourself, she scolded. His knee must be bothering him, that's all.

She debated about opening the door for him, but then remembered how sensitive he was about his injury. She just slipped into the driver's side and stared straight ahead while Mike struggled into the backseat.

"Where's your doctor's office?"

"On Cedar, just across from St. Joseph's Hospital."

"Just about everything around here seems to be named after St. Joseph," she said as she started the car.

"Yeah, he spent a lot of time here as a kid," Mike said. "Then when his mother died, he went to live with relatives in Nazareth."

His words were fun, but Angie wasn't too sure about his tone. A look into the rearview mirror confirmed her fears. Her heart sank and her smile zipped away as if pursued by a pack of dogs.

Mike was staring out the side window, his jaw tight and his eyes mere slits. She sighed and clutched the steering wheel a little tighter. The man was such a bundle of contradictions; there was no way on earth she'd ever get a handle on him.

She shouldn't have driven him. She shouldn't have interfered. Most of all, she shouldn't have assumed he could help her win her battles against the past. She needed somebody solid and open, someone gentle and calm. An even-tempered, dependable man. A hero straight from the script of "Night of Horrors?" a little voice asked mockingly.

Oh, who cared? She'd take Mike to the doctor's and home; then she'd stay out of his life. Maybe she wasn't meant for happily-ever-afters. Not that she was looking for that from him. No, just a little bit of healing and a little bit of fun.

They drove past the wide expanse of parking lots around the hospital and up the hill to the offices. There was a parking space close to the door. She pulled into it.

She had barely turned off the engine when Mike had the door open and was squirming out of the car. She had to move quickly to catch up with him as he propelled himself across the parking lot.

"Boy," she said. "You're certainly anxious to see the doctor."

"I don't like taking up your time," he snapped. "You've got better things to do than haul a gimp around."

"It's all right."

"It's not all right," he insisted. "You don't need to baby-sit some fool who forgot he wasn't nineteen anymore."

The building's outer doors opened automatically, and they went inside. Some teenage boys were there, pushing and shoving each other. They pulled back and out of the way as Mike came in.

"Sorry, Pops," one kid said as he jumped aside to avoid bumping into him.

For a moment, it looked as if Mike were going to say something. Angie held her breath and, noting the color in his face, wondered if he'd swallowed his tongue. They continued down the hall, every muscle in his body seeming to vibrate with irritation. When they reached his doctor's office, she tried to open the door for him, but he pushed her hand away.

"I can do it," he snapped.

Angie had had it. She hated confrontations, hated displays of anger, but she had just plain had it with his grumping. This was worse than her battles with Fudge when he would want to go one way on their walks and she another. If she could handle a hundred-plus pounds of animal stubbornness, she should be able to handle Mike. Of course, he didn't wear a choke collar, and she wasn't sure he was obedience-trained, but he was on crutches. She gave his arm a good yank, enough to move him away from the door, but not enough to knock him down.

"This really has gone on long enough," she said. "If you don't want me to help you, fine. In another hour or so we'll be back home, and I promise I won't volunteer to drive you again. But in the meantime, I would appreciate not being treated like everything that ever happened to you was my fault."

Mike had the good sense to look sheepish. "I've been acting like a jerk, huh?"

"Yes."

"It's not that I don't appreciate your help, it's just—"

"That you'd rather you didn't need it," she finished for him.

He nodded. "I didn't mean to be an idiot, though. I'm sorry."

His smile seemed genuine and genuinely sweet. It touched her in ways she didn't expect. She found herself wanting to smile back at him, to laugh and tease him about his male ego, but that seemed to giant a step to take. Besides, she didn't want to give him the idea that a sweet smile was enough to wipe out all his boorish actions.

She glanced down the empty hallway, away from the softness in his eyes. "Apology accepted," she said, and hated herself for sounding so stiff and formal. "Now you'd better get in for your appointment."

He nodded and took a step toward the door, then stopped. "You want to wait in here or down in the lounge?"

"In the lounge," she said. She didn't need to sit here with him, waiting for his turn. Some time alone would help her regain her equilibrium.

She watched Mike hobble into the office; then she walked back down to the lounge off the lobby. There were only a few people there, so it wasn't hard to find a quiet corner. She sank into a chair and stared at the potted plant on the round table in front of her.

It didn't look all that healthy. Maybe they needed a plant doctor to take up residence among all these other physicians. Maybe they needed to let the plant have a little sunlight. She leaned back in her chair and closed her eyes, wishing life were that easy.

Feeling fearful? Worrying all the time? Try a little sunshine and a good dose of fertilizer.

Well, that's what she had thought Mike would be, but she had been wrong. He was too volatile, too unpredictable to relax around. The scene in the emergency room came to her mind—the tough, aggressive police officers out in the waiting room, Mike's loud, boisterous family around his bed. That's where he was most comfortable; that's where he belonged. Mike Minelli was not a loner, seeking subdued acquaintances.

But that scene was quickly replaced by the gentle expression in his eyes. Eyes that showed concern, that were gentle and caring when he spoke of Emily, when he talked of keeping neighborhoods safe for the old people who lived in them.

She frowned. He was too complex, that's what he was. And that still made him wrong. She would take a little time and then look around again. Maybe there'd be someone in one of her classes, though so many of her fellow students were young guys just out of high school and—

"Surprise."

Angie opened her eyes to find Mike standing there, a huge chocolate bar in his outstretched hand. The smile on his face was almost as big.

"Are you done already?" she asked.

He shook his head and sat down next to her. His knee nudged hers, but it was so accidental that there was no way she could be threatened by it.

"They're running a little late. I decided to get you a peace offering." He nodded toward the chocolate bar.

"I see." She took the candy bar slowly. It was so big, it felt like a slab of concrete. "Where in the world did you get it?"

"The gift shop."

"Seems like a strange thing to sell by doctors' offices," she said. "Or is it healthy candy?"

"Maybe it's an attempt to drum up more business. Although I think it would work better in a dentist's office. Big piece of chocolate like that is bound to give you a zillion cavities."

"At least," she agreed. His voice and his manner were so infectious that she had to laugh.

He nodded toward the bar. "So open it. I'm hungry."

"I thought it was for me," she pointed out, but she unwrapped it and offered him a piece. The chunk he broke off was relatively small.

She broke off a piece for herself and munched on it slowly. The urge to open up to him was strong, and she leaned forward, closer to him, as if shortening the distance her words had to travel would make their meaning all the clearer.

"You know," she said. "For just one minute there, I felt like snatching your crutches away and letting you hop around on one leg."

Mike laughed, and she knew he didn't realize how serious she was. It was suddenly important that he understand her feelings and even share them.

"I don't like feeling angry," she explained. "Anger is a form of violence, and I abhor all violence."

"I agree," he said. "I'm all for peace and love myself."

He didn't get it. Why had she thought he would? "Don't patronize me." She leaned back in her chair, away from him and that urge to confide.

Mike frowned. "I'm not. Hell, why do you think I'm a cop?" he asked. "So I can go riding around on a motorcycle and shooting people? I'm out there to help people live peaceably."

They stared at each other for a long moment. Angie knew they were both speaking English, but in so many ways they seemed to come from different solar systems.

Slowly, his smile grew, a sweet, teasing one that wanted to charm her out of her irritation. Angie didn't want to soften. He wasn't the right one to help her fight the past, but she almost forgot that when he smiled at her that way.

"So when are we going to look for my dinette set?" he asked.

Angie just shook her head slowly, fighting the urge to run screaming from the room. This man was going to drive her crazy. She needed to get out now.

"How about tomorrow?" he asked. "I want another chance to prove I'm a nice guy."

Why did she want to give him that chance?

Chapter Five

"How come you didn't ask your sister Margaret to help you find furniture?" Angie asked as they walked across the parking lot to the furniture store. "She is an interior decorator, isn't she?"

"She's too bossy."

"Oh, and I can see how that would really bother you."

Her tone was definitely teasing, and Mike smiled in response. He'd been a little worried after that blowup yesterday. He still wasn't crazy about her having to drive him around, but he'd be on his best behavior. Once he was off these damn crutches, he would show her what a man could do.

Angie slowed down to watch him maneuver between two parked cars. "Will you be okay with just one crutch?"

"Did something happen to my mother?" Mike asked.

Angie blinked in bewilderment. "How would I know?"

"It just sounded like she'd died and left you to be my boss."

"Very funny, and after I got your shower fixed and everything," Angie said. "Let's see how humorous you can be without my help." And she went ahead into the store.

A smile had flashed on Angie's face, but she had turned so quickly that he hadn't been able to tell if it was fueled by a sense of teasing. It must have been; the fluid motion of her body as she walked proved there wasn't a bit of tension in her. Not that he could say the same for himself. He could spend several lifetimes watching her walk, but his nervous system might never recover.

Speaking of recovering, her dashing off let him prove that he was on the road to being healthy, that he wasn't a ball and chain. He followed her across the lot without any trouble at all, and opened the double doors easily. Unfortunately, a good, stiff breeze was blowing and the doors swung closed on him before he was all the way through. He was stuck between them. He swore under his breath; this crutches gig was sure getting old.

A store employee started to come forward, but Angie stopped her. "Please don't help him," Angie said. "He likes to do things himself. He gets very upset when well-meaning people try to help."

The woman stopped, which was lucky for her. Mike would show both the saleswoman and Angie just how a real man could cope with inconveniences. He got an elbow against the door and gave a good push so that it stayed open long enough for him to slip through. He paused just inside the threshold and gave the two ladies a look of satisfaction, totally unmarred by arrogance.

"He did that very well," the saleswoman said.

"Oh, yes," Angie agreed. "He's very talented."

You ain't seen nothing yet, Mike thought. Those green eyes were going to really sparkle with appreciation when she got to know him. He hobbled over to where the women were waiting.

"Well, what can I help you folks with?" the saleswoman asked.

"He'd like a dinette set," Angie replied. "And maybe some end tables and lamps."

"Okay."

The saleswoman seemed to be addressing herself to Angie, but Mike didn't really care. He welcomed Angie's input, just as he welcomed her smiles. Besides, if she was concentrating on the furniture, he could concentrate on watching her. Altogether a most enviable way to spend a few hours.

"Let's start at this end and then work our way around."

Mike followed them, catching up when the saleswoman paused at the top of a small flight of stairs.

"Should we wait for him?" she asked Angie.

"No," Angie spoke in a stage whisper. "He's very sensitive about his injury. We have to act like there's nothing wrong."

The woman nodded sagely, and the two of them continued walking toward the back of the first room. Mike slowly climbed the three steps. It was a trade-off, actually. If he followed Angie from a distance, he could enjoy the magical sway of her body, but if he was up close, then her faint scent of lilacs would tease him.

"This is a nice dinette set," the woman was saying as he hobbled up. "Solid oak, but very reasonably priced."

"Too big," Angie said.

The saleswoman looked at Mike. It was his chance to get a little teasing payback.

"Yeah, I agree," he said. "It needs to be smaller."

"I see," the woman said as she turned to look at Angie, "so the dinette area is fairly small."

"Not that small," Mike said. "But a smaller table is better. I gotta be close to my sweetie."

The saleswoman didn't lose an iota of composure. "I see," she said.

"It's best not to encourage him," Angie said and wandered off toward another display of dinette sets.

Mike wasn't really sure, since her back was to him, but he'd thought her face had gone rather tight. He was sure her voice had been strained. He frowned and followed along after them. Why was it okay for her to joke around but not for him?

For the next hour or so, they walked up stairs and down stairs. Went into dining-room settings and fake kitchens. Saw tables under bright lights and dim lights. He got up and he sat down, but mostly he walked as Angie and the saleswoman had deep conversations about wood, color and finish. Every time he was about call it quits, Angie would smile at him and he'd forget all his impatience. If was a relief, though, when he had a dinette set, two end tables and two lamps picked out.

"When do you want your furniture delivered?" Angie asked him.

"I don't care. Whenever you like. You're the one home most of the day."

The saleswoman smiled at Angie, waiting.

Angie looked startled. Her green eyes turned murky. "We're not married." Her voice held a thread of tension.

"That's okay," the saleswoman said. "You don't need a marriage license to buy furniture in Indiana."

Angie shook her head vigorously. "We're not even living together."

"It'll be our secret," the woman replied with a quick wink as she finished up her paperwork.

Angie just sat, staring off into space. Her eyes were giving off little flashes, like lightning in dark thunderclouds. Mike felt a twinge of guilt for letting his words be misunderstood, but she'd been teasing him all afternoon. Turnabout was fair play.

When the papers were all signed, Angie stood up, and Mike reluctantly dragged his carcass up the stairs one more time. The saleswoman followed them to the door.

"We don't live together." Angie tried once more. "I have my apartment, and he has his."

"Whatever suits you," the saleswoman said with a slight shrug. "There are times when I wish my husband and I had places of our own to go to."

Why was it so important to make their relationship perfectly clear? Mike wondered. What did it matter?

"We're really not at all alike," Angie said.

"I know," the woman said. "But you complement each other so beautifully. I mean, like black and white. Rough and smooth. Reserved and joking. You couldn't get it better if you tried."

Angie smiled, though it appeared to require effort. "Thank you for your help."

She hurried out of the store with Mike hobbling along after her. He hoped she wasn't mad. She had teased him, and he was just teasing her back.

It was so hard to know how far to go with Angie. She'd laugh at his joking; then she'd come to a screeching halt and pull back. He wished they could reach some peaceful water. He sensed life could be fun if they'd get in tune with each other.

"I really owe you," he said as he settled himself in the car.

Angie simply shrugged. "It's nothing."

"It means a great deal to me."

"Well, I don't want to make a big deal out of it," she replied. "You needed a little help, and I was available. No big deal."

"That's what you said when you drove us home from the hospital, took Emily to school and me to the doctor's, not to mention breakfast, grocery shopping and a great chocolate pie. That sounds like a whole lot to me."

"I didn't mind," she insisted.

"That doesn't matter. It's out of our hands."

She glanced his way. "What's out of our hands?" Her green eyes were cloudy with suspicion, like a snow-filled glass paperweight someone had shaken.

"It's become a matter of honor," he said.

"Whose?" she asked.

"If you don't let me repay my debt to you, I'll be thrown out of the Minelli clan."

Her smile was twisted with equal doses of humor and cynicism.

"Hey, believe me," he went on. "I'll be stripped of my Italian heritage. I can see the headlines now. Mike Minelli Barred From Eating Lasagna, Talking With His Hands and Bringing Joy to All Women."

"Oh, dear," she exclaimed. "What I can do to avert thi tragedy?"

It wasn't just her eyes that could put magic in the air; was her voice, too. Her laughter was like a song, unheard b the ears as it raced straight to the soul. "Go out with me to night."

Angie looked away, concentrating on starting the engine He couldn't see her straight on, but he sensed that the jo had slipped from her eyes again. Now what?

All right, so he didn't know her all that well, but he hadn' seen any guys hanging around. If she had no emotiona commitments, then why the hesitation?

"What about Emily?" she asked.

"Louie's oldest girl can stay with her."

She stayed silent as she pulled into traffic. "Okay," sh said slowly. "It's a date."

Great. She wouldn't regret it.

The curtain came down for the final time and the ap plause tapered off. Mike looked over at Angie.

"Up to your standards?"

"My standards?"

"Sure, you're the expert, aren't you?"

He'd realized just a few minutes into the revival of *Th Music Man* by a local theater group that he might have beer rather foolhardy. After all, Angie had probably seen som of the best professional performances when she lived in Lo Angeles. An amateur production in the Midwest was likel to be about as exciting to her as an after-dinner nap.

"I don't know how you decided my expert status," sh said. "But I enjoyed the play. Nice to see people all starry eyed and enthusiastic about performing."

That raised other questions in his mind, but there wa something in her tone that made him decide not to pusl further. He just glanced around the theater. Once enough o the main crowd had filed out to make it safer for him and hi crutches, they'd leave, too.

He wondered if Angie wanted to go home right away Emily would probably prefer that he stay out longer. If h were home, he'd be shooing her off to bed; Emily would rather sit up late with her cousin and watch horror movies. Besides, he didn't really want to take Angie home yet. He was still trying to probe the mystery behind those eyes.

"This used to be a movie theater, didn't it?" Angie was staring up at the ornate plasterwork above the stage.

"Yes. It used to be called the Palace," he said. "Now it's the Morris Civic Center. I guess it's named after some guy named Morris, but I don't know his last name. Or maybe that is his last name. Hell, I don't know."

"I certainly get my money's worth talking to you." There was a little smile pulling at her lips. "Ask a question, and I get six or seven answers."

Mike glanced at the dwindling crowd. He wondered if it was uncrowded enough for them to move now. Sitting around wasn't a good idea. It made his tongue itch, and then he rambled like an idiot.

"You ever do any live theater?" he asked.

She made a face as if she'd bitten into something sour. "I was in summer stock when I was fifteen," she said. "My mother decided the exposure would be good for me."

"The exposure? Like to the sun, wind and rain?"

Laughter came floating back into her eyes. "Believe me, I would have preferred those. My 'Night of Horrors' contract was up for renewal, and Mom decided that she'd have more bargaining power if I became a star away from the show."

"Why do I suspect it didn't work out that way?"

"Great wisdom?"

"Great exposure to reality?" He took her hand in his, holding on as lightly as if she were a goldfinch that might dart away at any moment.

"Well, I wasn't used to having no retakes, to doing a show straight through from start to finish, to having an audience there."

"Didn't like them watching you?"

"Didn't like them not watching me," she said. "It was a dinner playhouse and, not only did they eat through the performance, they talked and got up to walk around. It wa so disconcerting.''

"So you didn't gain stardom, I take it?"

"Nope. My mother was quite disappointed in me." He tone was so matter-of-fact.

"Was she a typical stage mother?"

Angie shrugged and leaned back to stare up at the ceil ing. "In some ways. She got me into commercials acciden tally. A friend was shooting an ad and decided I was wha the sponsor was looking for, but once I got into 'Night o Horrors,' I was our main source of income. She made sur nothing threatened that."

"Not killer cucumbers or anything?"

"Not even grumpy old cops who can't scale a fence."

He laughed out loud. Her attack had been unexpecte and all the more enjoyable. "It's not nice to tease the bi bear," he said gruffly. "It can be dangerous."

Suddenly, the atmosphere around them changed. His ol cop's nose could almost smell it. He didn't know how o why, but he was sensing fear. Angie was still at his side, bu now she seemed almost distant, emotionally scrunched bac in a far corner.

What had he done? He could have sworn on a stack o Bibles that he hadn't threatened her. He was just making little joke, going along with her razzing him. This sam thing had happened at the furniture store when he'd tease her.

He fussed with his crutches for a moment before turnin back to her. "Want to go somewhere for a drink or some thing?"

"Sure. Got any place in mind?"

Her voice seemed reasonably strong. Maybe he wa imagining things. Maybe what he liked to call his cop's sens was just an overactive sense of the dramatic. He wished h knew her better, but then going out for some spirits and chat should help that.

"I thought we could go to the Heartland," Mike said "You like country music?"

"I like most kinds of music."

She was relaxed; he was sure of it. Her gentle smile was back, as was the sparkle in her eyes.

"It's just down the street," he said. "About a block beyond where we parked the car."

"It's not too far for you to walk?" she asked.

"Nah. I could walk it on my hands if I had to."

They were among the last to leave. A few other stragglers were on the sidewalk in front of the theater, and a broken line of people on the side street hurried toward the parking lot. A light April shower had fallen while they'd been watching the play, leaving a wet sheen on the streets and a clean, fresh scent in the air.

Mike stopped, talking Angie's hand with his free one. He felt as if he'd captured spring. Whatever he thought he had seen inside the theater had been his imagination. Maybe the spirits of past performances were in the air and had captured his senses for a moment.

He and Angie continued walking and crossed the street. He looked out at the barren landscape of parking lots and office buildings. This part of the city was really only alive during regular working hours. Now the street echoed only emptiness and desolation.

"Mom told me that when she and Dad were dating, this street was filled with stores and restaurants. No one would be rushing home. They'd all be strolling to some favorite spot for some good cheer with their friends and neighbors." He looked again at the people rushing toward their cars and thought of a string of ants. "People don't really do things together anymore."

"You should see L.A.," Angie said softly. "I think the only time folks get out of their cars is to go to the bathroom."

They were two souls alone in a desert, held together by the silence. He could feel her next to him, feel the warmth of her skin and the softness of her heart. Words were unnecessary.

A band was playing when they walked into the nightclub. A woman singer was wailing something about men and women and cheating, but the atmosphere was comfortable.

Mike felt himself relax as he and Angie found a table. She ordered an iced tea and, though he would have liked some wine, he followed her lead and had a soda.

"Care for a snack?" Mike asked, nodding toward the complimentary buffet spread out along one wall.

Angie shook her head. "I'm not too hungry, thank you."

She was never hungry. Had her mother made her feel she had to stay extra thin for her roles? Except that she was no longer acting, so she ought to be able to eat. His mother never encouraged anyone to not eat. Love and food went hand in hand for her. And for him, he guessed; since he'd been raised in an atmosphere that included food with any and every event in a person's life.

"Would you like something to eat?" she asked.

"No, that's—"

"Sure you would. You're always hungry. You have a very high metabolism rate." She stood up. "I'll get something for you. How about some buffalo wings?"

Mike rose partway from his chair. "You're not my servant. I can get my own stuff."

"You already walked three blocks," she said. "Now sit down before I knock you down."

"Oh, boy. Aren't we tough?"

"You betcha."

Her grin ignited a spark within him, a hunger to know her in ways as old as time. She could give as good as she got. It would be fun to tussle with her, to tease her and be teased. One thing he'd learned in the past few days, though, was to never ever push with Angie. He just grinned back at her, letting her take the lead.

"I'm glad you're not into violence," he said.

"Sit down," she said, giving him a quick glare. "I'll be right back with those wings."

He did as ordered, then watched Angie glide across the floor toward the buffet tables. She was so small and graceful, like a hummingbird.

Her beauty was a delicate kind, one that drew out the best in a man, the desire to protect. Her smile signaled an open kind of trust, but her eyes... her eyes spoke of mystery.

Experience told him to move cautiously, but desire made him desperate to find the key. How was it that she was free and unattached?

When Angie returned, she was carrying two plates. "I didn't want you to eat alone."

"That's very kind of you."

The table was small and as she hitched her chair up closer, her leg bumped his. He could feel the firmness of her limb. The hell with the food. He wanted to pull her to him. He still wanted to protect her, but that desire was mixed with a more primeval urge to protect her for himself.

She picked up a barbecued rib and smiled at him. Her eyes were filled with innocence. Could a woman in her late twenties really be so innocent?

Mike turned his attention to the Buffalo wings on his plate. They were very spicy. But Angie might be even more so. Her eyes told so many stories; he didn't know which one was true.

The band switched to a slower tune, and he recognized his chance to hold her. "Hey, this is danceable."

"For some people, yes."

He knew what she meant, but his leg was getting better every day. Besides, he wasn't entering a dance contest—he was using the music as an excuse to hold a beautiful woman in his arms. He got to his feet and held out one hand.

"Would you like to dance?"

"With a crutch?"

"No, with me," he said.

Angie shook her head, but he was sure her eyes were laughing. "I don't think your doctor would—"

"Hey, we can't let other people rule our lives."

Sighing loudly, Angie stood up. "Just one," she insisted.

"Absolutely." He would have agreed to anything at this point, just to get her into his arms. Once their one dance was up, he'd worry about how to keep her there.

They walked to the dance floor, and Mike took Angie in his arms. Suddenly, his whole body sang for joy.

Angie was great at giving conflicting signals. She looked delicate, yet her attitude could be joking and tough. Other times she seemed to be soft and withdrawn. Those sea-green eyes of hers were like barometers of her soul, and they were constantly changing.

But once he took her in his arms, all of Mike's doubt vanished, like the fleeting flakes of a late spring snow. Beneath the delicate structure of her feminine frame, he could feel strength. A wiry kind of strength that came from a love of life.

He pulled Angie a little closer to him, smelled the soft freshness of her hair and let himself feel good. His hopes turned to anticipation and his dreams turned to needs.

He had grown up watching his grandparents, parents, and other relatives dance to the rich, sensual tunes that were part of his heritage. The man pushed a little, then the woman. Sometimes the woman would take an extra step, sometimes the man. And if their desires were real, they would arrive at a common destination.

Where would this dance with Angie lead? Every molecule of his body strained and listened. He inhaled the scent of her. He wanted her. Now all he needed was for her to want him.

They swayed to the gentle rhythm of the music. He could feel her move slightly closer. Her movements were soft, just as she was, but also like Angie, they were tentative. Was she really attracted to him or did he just feel what he so desperately wanted?

He held her even closer, a little harder, a little more demanding. She didn't resist. He was sure of it. They were blending into one. Mike bent forward to kiss the top of her head.

"How's it going, Lieutenant?"

His body tensed, jarred from dreams that he did not want to leave. Maybe if he ignored the voice, the world would go away.

But he was too late. He and Angie were already pulling apart, admitting outsiders into their special garden. Mike sighed. "Hi, Polanski."

One of the officers from his unit was standing nearby, his bulk encased in a dark pinstripe suite. His very pregnant young wife was standing next to him.

"Hello, Mary." Mike turned back to Angie. "Do you remember Polanski?"

"Sort of," she replied.

Her voice had gone distant again. He needed to get rid of the interlopers, but had no idea how. "This is his wife, Mary," Mike said. "Mary, this is Angie Hartman. She manages the building I live in."

The women exchanged greetings as Polanski turned to Mike. "A bunch of us are here for a little party," he said. "You and your lady want to join us, Lieutenant?"

Mary quickly eyed the two of them. Then she shook her head with a slight smile as she touched her husband's arm. "I don't think they really want to," his wife murmured. "I think they'd rather be alone."

The big police-officer's face wrinkled in bewilderment. "Why would they come here if they wanted to be alone?" he asked. "I mean, look around. There's gotta be close to two hundred people in this joint."

Mary gave Mike and Angie an apologetic grin before pointing off in another direction. "Oh, look," Mary said. "There's your mother. Let's go talk to her."

"She rode with us."

Mary gave them a conspiratorial smile and her husband a mighty yank so that he would follow her away. Polanski raised his shoulders in a helpless shrug as his wife pulled him along.

"Your friends are nice," Angie said once they were alone again.

"Some a bit smarter than others," he said, pulling her back into his arms. "You didn't really want to join their party, did you?"

"Not really."

She snuggled up close to him, quickly returning to the rhythm of the music and that special spot in his arms, like returning to a favorite book. The soft smile on her lips caressed his soul. There was no other elixir in the world like being desired by a beautiful woman.

He bent down and kissed her lips lightly. They tasted just as delicious as they had in his dreams and just as addictive. He leaned down to kiss her again, slower, deeper and a little more hungrily.

"Thank you for going out with me," he whispered.

Angie brushed his lips with hers. A light touch that teased the growing ache in his belly, churning it into fire.

"Thank you for asking me," she said.

He stared into her eyes and felt as if he were swimming in the cool waters of a woodland lake. He could drown in her gaze, willingly and happily. He could happily live forever in their green depths.

The nightmares had come again.

Angie huddled up against Fudge in the big, old love seat in the corner of her bedroom. Marshmallow was curled up in her lap, fast sleep. The bedside light was on as always, but it hadn't helped keep the darkness at bay.

When would the memories ever fade? She had thought that if she started seeing Mike, she would feel normal again. She had thought that if she affected a natural reaction to a nice man, her heart would let her forget until it was truly natural. She was only partly successful.

She was enjoying Mike's company. She wasn't having to pretend much, but the dreams weren't fading as they should have. He'd kissed her, held her in his arms, and she had found that with each touch her fears shrank—but the nightmares still came back.

Maybe it was a stupid plan. Maybe she would never totally lose herself in a man's arms again.

"We had a very nice time tonight," Angie told Fudge.

The dog waggled one ear. Was he approving or saying he didn't want to hear about it?

"We went to the play and then we went to this country-and-western nightclub."

Marshmallow stirred slightly, his one ear twitching as if the words tickled.

"And Mike was the perfect gentleman the whole time."

Fudge let out a low mixture of growl and groan.

"It's true," Angie insisted. "He didn't yell. He didn't get mad even once. He talked, told jokes and made fun of himself. He was so comfortable to be with."

Neither of the animals replied, so Angie sat there in the silence. She was healing. She had to be. Maybe she was just too impatient. Maybe she hadn't done enough to erase those memories.

She'd really had a good time that evening. Carrying on a normal relationship with Mike couldn't do anything but speed her healing process. She should go out with him, let him kiss her, touch her, let him do everything normal men and women do.

She got up and walked back to bed, carrying Marshmallow with her. Fudge climbed up on the other side. "You have to learn to be nice to Mike," she told the dog. "He's liable to be around more than other people."

Fudge just grunted.

"I don't mean anything permanent," she hastened to explain. "I'm not a permanent-relationship person."

Then Angie leaned over a did something she hadn't done in almost a year. She turned off the light before lying down. All she needed was a normal relationship to be totally normal, she told herself as she tried to hold back the panic of the darkness. A really normal relationship and she'd be fine.

Chapter Six

Mike leaned back against the tiled wall and gazed unseeing at the institutional beige of Northside Hall. Angie's class would be out in another couple of minutes. Some of the teachers had already released their classes.

He let his cop eyes roam the halls, checking out the students. Indiana University at South Bend was one of those new-age community-based colleges filled with a whole range of students. Everybody from the recent high-school grad to the recently retired, although a good percentage of the students were from the early twenties set. Angie probably felt right at home here.

Suddenly, students began pouring out of Room 107, but he didn't see her. He held his breath a moment; he hoped she wasn't skipping class today. Then he breathed a sigh of relief. She was at the end of the exodus, talking with a young Hispanic woman.

"Hey, Angie," Mike called.

She stopped and looked toward him, her eyes widening as much as Bambi's mother's. Though it looked almost like an instance of fear, he knew it was just surprise at seeing him here.

"I can really dance now," he said, forcing himself into an awkward soft-shoe, being very careful not to wince.

The doelike look quickly left her eyes as Angie briskly strode toward him. A frown grew on her face.

"Why are you jumping around on your bad leg like that?"

That wasn't the greeting he'd wanted. He'd hoped for the light in her green eyes to grow brighter and for the sweet smile on her lips to widen as she realized that he was healthy and whole now. A real man again.

"Hey, I'm glad to see you, too," he said, kissing her lightly.

That brought the start of a smile to her lips. Another kiss was waiting for her, one with more hunger in it that would light up her face even more. He put an arm on her back to draw her to him.

"Mike," Angie said, pushing lightly against his chest.

Sighing, he dropped his arm. It was funny that someone who'd been an actress would be shy in public.

"Now why are you jumping around on your bad leg like that?" she repeated.

"It's not bad," he told her. "It's a nice leg. It lets me march in the Memorial Day parades and stand for the flag."

"You know what I mean."

"No, I don't," Mike insisted. "It's a leg with strong moral convictions. It will not kick puppies, kids or old women."

"Mike," she said.

Angie's laughter was soft and teasing, sliding under his skin and bringing a warm glow to him that he hadn't felt in a long, long time. He reached for her hand, but she was turning toward her companion.

"Christina, this is Mike Minelli."

The other woman's smile grew broader, and her dark eyes flashed. "Oh, the crippled cop dude."

Crippled cop dude? Mike felt his own smile wither and die. Is that how Angie saw him? He was a few years older than she was, but he wasn't ready for the old rocking chair yet. His leg had been hurt in an accident, something that could have happened to a young high-school stud. It wasn't degenerating with age. There wasn't a single part of him that was. Obviously she'd needed that second kiss. It would have convinced her.

"This is Christina Cardenas," Angie said. "She's helping me make it through my business-finance course. I'd be in flunk city if it wasn't for her."

The young woman's brown eyes swept him from top to bottom. "Not bad, Angie," she said. "Not bad at all. Even the gray in the hair is okay. It's just enough for that distinguished look."

"Christina," Mike said. "I think I hear your mother calling."

Christina just laughed and turned to Angie. "See ya Tuesday," she said.

"I guess," Angie said.

"Aw, come on," Christina said. "None of that. You're gonna do just fine. You've been passing all your tests."

"Only because of your help."

"Wanna come in early and study before?"

"I'd appreciate it," Angie replied.

"You got it." Christina gave them a wave and a wink before hurrying off.

Angie and Mike stood in the hall, students swirling around them like the waters of a river, but he felt alone with Angie. It was a comfortable kind of aloneness, the kind that two people who want only each other feel. He reached out and took her hand.

"This math course is awful," Angie said. "It's out to get me."

"A real killer cucumber, eh?" he said as he took her books from her.

"Not quite. I'll get through this class with Christina's help. There's no escape from a killer cucumber."

They walked toward the outside doors in silence. Christina's remark still rankled; and he put a little more spring into his step.

"The doctor took off the soft cast?" Angie asked.

"Yep, I don't need it anymore. Everything is ship-shape."

"Shouldn't you be using a cane or something for now?"

"No," he said emphatically. "In spite of some nasty rumors that are floating about, I am not a cripple."

She gave his hand a squeeze and rubbed her shoulder up against his. "Hey, I didn't mean it that way." Her voice was teasing, flirtatious.

A smile filled his heart and overflowed onto his face. He felt like breaking into a dance again, but that was too tame. Backflips would be more in tune with his feelings.

A beautiful woman responding to his overtures cured anything that ever ailed a man. Although he certainly wasn't ailing. He felt like running a marathon. Mike dropped Angie's hand and put his arm around her waist.

"Be careful not to overdo things," she told him. "That leg is likely to be tender for a while."

"My grandmother always said pain is good," Mike replied. "It's a sign that you're alive."

He liked the feel of her body next to him, small but wound tight. He wished that he were a college freshman again; then he wouldn't worry about how things looked. He'd just squeeze Angie's body to his and thank the gods that he was alive.

They exited through the north door, coming out onto the newly landscaped plaza. It was a perfect spring day, warm and sunny with a scent of flowers in the air and Angie by his side. He felt alive, reborn.

"What are you doing here anyway?" she asked.

"I came to take you to lunch," Mike replied. "Celebrate my return to the fully able."

She smiled up at him, the brightness of her face shaming the sun. "Whatever happened to asking?" she said. "You know, like your father used to do whenever he wanted your mother to go someplace with him."

Mike kissed her lightly on the cheek. It was nice, but he would have preferred to kiss her long and hard on the lips and to hell with breathing. "Would you like to go to lunch with me?"

"I appreciate your asking," Angie replied. "But you should have asked earlier. I mean, what if you came out this whole way and I had a class this next period?"

"You don't."

She pulled away from his arm's embrace. Something danced in the shadows of her eyes. It wasn't springtime.

"How did you know I don't have a class now?" she asked. "And how did you know where I was?"

"Ve haf our vays," he said with a grin.

"You mean police ways, don't you?"

Her frown had grown; winter seemed to be coming back. Mike shrugged his shoulders as he fired up the energy behind his smile.

"I just dropped by the registrar's office. On Thursdays, you're free from 11:30 to 1:00."

"And they told you where I was?" Her voice was rising. "Without a warrant or anything?"

"They know me." Mike hurried to explain. "I've been a cop in this town for almost fifteen years. I used to moonlight as security here for a while. Hell, I even went to school here."

Angie resumed walking. "I still don't like it. What if you were someone stalking me? You could go to the registrar's office and find out where I was."

An uneasiness settled in the pit of his stomach. This wasn't just caution; this was fear. Something or someone in her past had scared the hell out of her. Well, she had to know that she had nothing to fear when he was around, either from him or anybody else.

Angie looked around the plaza, her agitation obvious in her eyes. She looked as if she were fighting to get control of herself. "Well," she finally said. "There are a lot of people here. If you tried anything funny, I could just yell for help. With all these people around, you'd be put under control real quick."

"Until I shot the first one."

Oh, hell. That was stupid. Her eyes reminded him of Bambi's mother again. He thought she needed reassurance that he would protect her, but obviously he'd chosen the wrong way to do that.

"You seem to have a horrible fascination with violence," she said. A quiver in her voice made the words high-pitched. "I told you I abhor violence."

"I'm sorry," Mike replied. "It was just a joke. A stupid, sick joke, but still a joke."

"I don't like jokes about violence and oppression. They're not joking matters."

"I'm sorry," Mike repeated. "But it's a cop thing. We see so much crap and so many horrible things that people do to each other that we'd go nuts if we didn't indulge in some black humor."

"Humor legitimizes the violence. It puts a gloss on it and makes it easier to accept."

The hell it did. Why did she think cops played garbage-men to society? Because they thought violence was a good idea? He knew this wasn't the time to argue with Angie. She looked too damned scared.

"I'm sorry," he said again. "I have a rough job and I have to understand that not everyone, especially people outside my profession, will understand my coping mechanisms."

Angie just shrugged.

Mike forced a smile back on his own face. "Now let's go to lunch. I'm starved."

She nodded. He took her hand, and they made their way to his car. Walking along like two porcupines going for a stroll, they said nothing. Mike was never sure what might set Angie off.

He opened the passenger door for her before going around to the driver's side. His knee was starting to twinge a bit, but he didn't want to give her a reason to be even more aggravated, so he threw himself into the front seat with abandon.

"Want to go to the Oaken Bucket?" Mike asked. "The food is good and the service is reasonable. I'll be able to get you back in time for your one o'clock class with no problem.''

"Okay," she replied, then tried to force a smile. "Sounds great."

Her attempt was fairly pitiful as attempts went, but he wasn't going to challenge it. He let the silence ride with them to the restaurant and on into the building itself. Mike asked for, and got, a booth on the riverside. The table and benches were varnished planks, about as comfortable for sitting as picnic tables, but they had high backs that provided a sense of privacy. It was just the two of them and the slow-moving river.

"How does Emily like school?" Angie asked after they placed their order and spent several long minutes riverwatching.

"Good," Mike answered. "She feels like the kids have accepted her and she's enjoying herself."

"She's at the perfect age," Angie said. She paused a moment to glance at the river, looking almost wistful. "I've never been a real confident person, but I don't think I'll ever have the confidence I had when I was nine or ten."

Her eyes quickly returned to the river, and Mike thought about his own past. He'd never really thought much about his childhood and would be hard-pressed to recall specific instances from it. All he had were vague recollections of playing baseball, fishing on the river with his father and a zillion picnics and dinners with friends and relatives. Angie, on the other hand, seemed to carry her childhood around like excess baggage.

"Yeah," Mike said. "Now she wants me to sign her up for soccer."

"Oh, a school team? That should be fun. She looks athletic."

"No, it's some kind of league thing, like Little League for baseball." His reluctance must have been written on his face because Angie frowned.

"Don't you want her to play?"

"She's not going to be here that long."

"You've talked to her mother?"

Mike made a face and looked back out on the river. He felt the need for a little slow-mo water movement himself. "No, not yet."

From the corner of his eye, he could see Angie take a sip of her water.

"You should just sign her up," Angie said. "No one knows what's going to happen tomorrow."

"You sound like my mother," Mike growled.

"Women are born wise."

He turned to stare at her, but the waitress was bringing their soup and Angie was concentrating on that. At least she was back to her wisecracking. Mike picked up his spoon and began eating.

"Will she be on a girls' team?" Angie asked.

"Nah." He shook his head, trying to suppress a smile of pride. "It's mostly a boys' team. She was playing with some guys during recess, and they recruited her."

"Mostly boys?" Angie shrugged. "I hope that doesn't cause her any problems."

"Not at her age." He tipped his bowl to get the last of the soup. "Besides, she's tough. Any kid gives her grief, she'll just kick his butt."

Angie laughed, and the last of the shadows seemed to disappear. She reached across the table to place her hand over his. "Thanks for asking me out," she said.

He covered her hand with his. The warmth of her, sandwiched between his two hands, spread throughout his body. "Thanks for putting up with my big, bad mouth."

She just smiled, a strange light flickering in her eyes as she pulled her hand away to gently trace over the edge of his lips. "Oh, it's not such a bad mouth. In fact, it has some very nice qualities."

Mike looked into her eyes and he could hear it, that same old tune that Adam heard when he first laid eyes on Eve. The music that drove men and women through their ritualistic dance of love. Swaying and bending. Moving in and touching, but only for the briefest of moments before spinning away again.

Despite the many pleasures for the body, Mike knew a man could never be truly satisfied until he fed body and soul equally. At the same time, he saw Angie's body, felt it, sensed it. Yet he wanted more. He wanted to find the hungers of her soul. Deep within her eyes, he searched. A light flickered there, his heart quickened, he leaned forward—

"Who gets the cheeseburger?"

Both of them started, drawn almost violently back to the present. They stared at the waitress. She wasn't the same one who'd taken their order.

"I got the cheeseburger, no fries," the woman said, looking at the baskets in her hands. "And a patty melt on dark rye with fries."

Mike took a deep breath and shook his head with a sigh. They had been approaching the heavens, and the return had been rather bumpy. "I have the patty melt," he said.

Mike carried a cup of coffee through his mother's living room, sidestepping two kids racing plastic Easter eggs across the floor, and sat down on the folding chair next to Angie. The family's annual Easter dinner was over. Everything had been cleaned up. The adults were talking, and the kids were climbing the walls, working off calories.

"Sure you don't want anything?" he asked Angie.

Angie was shaking her head as Bobby came by with a tray of glasses.

"How about some of my homemade grape juice?" he asked.

"Something that's gone through fermentation isn't juice," Mike pointed out.

Angie just laughed and waved it away. "I'm fine. Really."

The two kids racing eggs suddenly started pounding each other with stuffed rabbits and Clara moved in on them, hauling them both off to a corner while she scolded them. His sister was probably telling them that the Easter Bunny would give them coal if they didn't shape up. Not that the kids were taking her talk to heart. Probably figured the rabbit wasn't coming back until next year anyway. As soon as Clara turned her back, both kids ran off laughing out of the room. Most likely looking for some other mischief to get into.

Mike felt a smile tug at his lips as he turned to find Angie smiling also. "Wasn't there a 'Night of Horrors' show about Easter?"

"'The Rabbits' Revenge,'" she said. Her eyes were sparkling, dancing with a delight that drew him in. "Poisonous pellets got into my garden, and a bunny died. Naturally, all the rabbits for miles around blamed me."

"Naturally," Mike agreed.

It was obvious that Angie's soul was in a good mood. Joy overflowed onto her lips, danced in her eyes, glowed from her heart. Even her voice seemed to be a song.

"And banded together to get their revenge," she said.

He looked away, trying to escape from the distraction of her... just of her. But he'd have to flee to the center of the earth to get away from Angie's distracting influence. She was overflowing with life. That and maybe his antenna was exceptionally sensitive today.

"I seem to remember you being chased by rabbits through a forest."

"Until they had me at the edge of a cliff." She chuckled at the memory. "I always wondered why my TV family never considered moving. I mean, there I was, their lovely young daughter, attacked by rabbits, cucumbers, giant ants and mutant dust bunnies. Sane people would have left when they saw the first giant ant."

"Oh, I don't know. I think it would take a mutant dust bunny to convince me."

She just laughed, resting her hand on his for a moment, setting alive some of the wildest dreams he'd ever had, awake or asleep.

"Hey, Mike." Emily was yanking on his shirtsleeve. "Krista wants me to stay at her house tonight." Emily was pointing at a cousin, a skinny girl with freckles and two braids sticking out of the side of her head like an extra pair of ears. "Can I? Huh?"

"Let me double-check with her mom. If she agrees, it's fine with me," Mike said and got to his feet. "What about some pajamas and stuff? And where are you going to sleep?"

"We're going to sleep in our clothes," Emily answered. "And Cousin Louie said I could use his sleeping bag."

"Okay." Mike smiled an apology toward Angie and turned back to Emily. "Let's find Krista's mom."

Just as Krista had said, Diane was quite happy to have Emily stay overnight. "It'll give the kids somebody new to play with and keep them out of my hair for a little bit."

"If you're sure." He gave Emily a half-stern look. "You behave yourself, young lady."

"Absolutely."

She and Krista raced off squealing, trailed by Diane, who was telling them to gather their things together because they'd be leaving soon. Mike's gaze slid slowly across the room, back to Angie. Margaret had joined her, and the two were laughing together.

Laughter looked good on Angie's face. It lit those gorgeous eyes and brought a glow to her cheeks. Of course, there were other things that could bring a glow to her skin, other ways to light those eyes....

"She needs time."

Mike just about jumped out of his skin. "Darn it, Mom. Do you always have to sneak up on people?"

"Your young lady will be fine," his mother said. "She just needs time—time and much patience."

"She's not my young lady, Mom. I don't own her. Besides, she looks fine to me."

His mother did not reply right away, choosing instead to watch Angie. "She struggles with a great pain," his mother finally said.

"What's this, Mom?" Mike asked. "Psychology 101?"

"Don't mock your mother, or God will freeze your tongue."

Mike let his eyes follow his mother's and watched Angie also. Though he saw no sign of pain now, he wasn't discounting his mother's pronouncements. She might actually be onto something. Most of the time Angie was fine, fun to be with, but other times he felt something he couldn't really explain, a sense of some dark undercurrent.

"Why do you think Angie is troubled?" Mike asked. "Have you talked to her?"

"Not in words," his mother replied. "But our souls have touched."

Feelings, that's what his mother was talking about. Just her own feelings. But that didn't mean they were something to be ignored.

"Mikey." His mother placed her hand on his arm. "You will be patient with her. Promise me."

"Sure, Mom. I'm always patient."

"No," his mother said firmly. "This is not like always. I want you to be truly understanding. I want you to dig deep within your soul, very deep."

He just nodded his head. "Sure, Mom."

"You promise me. You promise on your father's memory."

Mike blinked for a moment. This was serious. His mother wasn't the type to drag his father's memory out whenever she felt like it.

"I promise, Mom."

"You are a good boy," she said, patting him on the cheek. "The saints will reward you."

He smiled as he watched his mother hurry away. He wouldn't hold his breath for this reward. Experience had taught him that the saints did things in their own sweet time. Even then it wasn't always easy to recognize when they were doing a person good. He went back across the room.

"Oh hello, Mike," Margaret exclaimed. "We were just talking about you."

"Something great, no doubt," he said.

"What else?" Angie said with a laugh as she reached for his hand.

He took her hand gladly, not at all averse to proclaiming a bond between them. But even as he did, he studied her eyes, searching for a hint of the pain his mother said Angie was carrying. As far as he could see, the little lady wasn't feeling any pain at the moment. She had a large glass in her hand, an almost-empty large glass. He looked toward his sister.

"She's had some of Bobby's grape juice," Margaret explained and got to her feet. "You done with your coffee cup? I'll take it into the kitchen."

Before he could protest, she was gone. He sat down as Angie drained the last of her juice.

"That stuff's pretty potent," Mike warned. Bobby's homemade wine was as smooth as a lamb and kicked like a mule. Had she believed Bobby when he said it was only grape juice?

Angie just smiled at him. "I'm a big girl," she said.

Her voice was low and husky, without a hint of its usual caution. And the way she gazed into his eyes made him feel suddenly young again. Like a college kid. He stared into those shadowy depths, reading all sorts of interesting messages scrawled there, like graffiti of the soul.

"So you're going to be all alone tonight," Angie cooed. She turned his hand in hers, weaving her fingers between his with exquisite care. "If you want, you can come down and spend some time with me."

The smoldering fire in the pit of his belly flared up in anticipation. His hands tightened on hers. But then a certain presence came to mind.

"I'd rather we went to my place," he said.

Angie burst into laughter. "You're afraid of Fudge, aren't you?"

"I am not," Mike insisted. "I just don't like upsetting him. My father taught me that it was wrong to tease animals."

She put her finger to her chin as if in deep thought. "Where can we put Fudge?"

"How about my apartment?" Mike suggested.

"I don't know if he'd like that," Angie replied. "What can he do there?"

"I'll turn on the TV," Mike said. "What does he like? I have cable. We can turn on wrestling or maybe there's an Australian football game on."

Angie just shook her head. "He'll be fine in my kitchen."

"What if he gets lonesome?"

"He won't," Angie replied. "He keeps telling me to have friends over. He'll be the perfect gentleman."

Mike looked into her smoldering eyes and decided the poets had spoken the truth. Only a brave man won the fair maiden.

With her shoes in one hand, Angie closed the kitchen door behind her and tiptoed into the living room. A queasiness ruffled her stomach as the pink cloud of Bobby's grape euphoria began to dissipate. She wondered if Mike had brought any with him from the dinner. Probably not.

Mike turned from the glass patio doors in the living room and smiled at her. It was a warm and gentle smile, a smile that said she was attractive, desirable.

She could do this; she could. It would be proof that she was whole again. A tremor raced through her stomach, but she ignored it. It had been a while since she'd been with a man, so it was natural for her to be a little nervous. Besides, Mike was a handsome man. The tremor was more excitement than nerves.

"Your baby all settled down?" Mike asked, nodding toward the kitchen.

"I gave him eight rawhide chew bars."

"Eight?" Mike laughed and came closer to her. "Think that'll keep him occupied long enough?"

She swallowed hard. "It should."

"It should?"

"We'll have two doors between us," Angie said and felt the euphoria dissolve even further. "You didn't happen to bring any of your brother's wine, did you?"

Mike frowned. "No, I didn't."

"It doesn't matter." They had to get to it. If she didn't do it now, she might never do it.

Angie walked up close and slid her arms around Mike's waist. He just stared at her, with what looked like a quizzical expression on his face.

"Aren't you going to kiss me?" she asked.

"Sure."

His voice was soft and gentle, his movements too slow. She put a hand on the back of his head and pulled him to her lips, holding him there for several counts. When she released him a moment later, she could see a difference in his eyes. Their gaze was harder, full of desire, full of need.

"Why don't be go into the bedroom?" she suggested.

Angie took him by the hand, leading the way. She was unbuttoning her blouse before she even reached the side of her bed. Mike's arms slid around her from behind. The was a moment's flash of panic, but she fought it back.

"I could do that," he whispered.

His breath was hot against her skin as his lips touched her neck. His arms tightened around her, pulling her up against the hard muscles of his chest.

Dark panic swallowed her for a moment. She couldn't breathe. She was trapped. She closed her eyes and forced one breath, then another. The panic subsided.

"I could do a lot of things for you," he murmured. "If you'd just slow down."

Her stomach quivered and the tremor fanned out like an earthquake, shaking her foundations. Angie turned in Mike's arms to face him.

"Next time we can take the slow road, but right now my tank is overflowing. I need to work off some energy." He was looking at her strangely, and her stomach twisted a bit. God, what if he said no? "That is, if you want to."

The questioning look wasn't totally gone from his eyes, but his lips were smiling. "Whatever turns you on, babe," he said.

She didn't wait for any more reassurance, sliding her blouse off, then her skirt. Mike was watching her, his gaze hard. His eyes were filled with passion, but it was a passion diluted with confusion. She grabbed him, pressing her lips to his, her body to his. Moving against him, she felt his confusion melt away as his passion took over once again.

She pushed off his shirt, then fumbled with his pants. He gently moved her hands away and unbuttoned the waistband, then slid the zipper down. Panic was starting to creep back in from the corners again. She had to hurry, get going before it had a chance to grab hold of her.

She unhooked her bra and slipped her panties off as Mike shed his pants. Even with his underwear still on, she could see his desire.

She took him once more in her arms even as he was trying to work off his underwear. As soon as it was gone, she tumbled back onto her bed, pulling Mike with her. Her hand went down below his waist and started rubbing.

"Easy," he murmured, supporting himself on his elbows. "It's more fun if you lie back and enjoy the scenery."

"Next time," she said.

He was quickly ready, and she pulled him down on top of her. With his weight on her, she was pinned against the bed.

Then it happened.

She couldn't move. She couldn't breathe. The panic surrounded and swallowed her. There was nothing but darkness and this raging fear screaming in her soul.

"Get off," she gasped. "Please, get off."

Mike rolled to the side. "What's wrong?"

Angie just jumped out of bed and raced for the bathroom. She barely made it to the bowl before she began to throw up violently. Dinner, Bobby's joy juice, her belief that she was healing, her life, every ounce of energy she possessed—she lost it all.

When she had nothing left to throw up, when she lay exhausted against the cold porcelain bowl in ignominious disgrace, the tears began. Hot, coursing tears that streamed in burning rivulets down her cheeks.

"Angie."

She shrank back from Mike's touch. She just wished he would go, that he would just leave her alone to die.

He was back by her side a moment later, before she had even been aware that he'd been gone, wrapping a blanket around her. Her body snuggled gratefully into the folds of the blanket, but the pain inside her wouldn't stop.

"Maybe you ought to go now," she whispered.

But he sat on the edge of the bathtub. She could just see the cuffs of his pants above his bare feet; he had gotten dressed when he'd gone for the blanket. Some of the panic subsided, leaving all of the pain.

"You've got to be careful with Bobby's stuff," he said. "It has a habit of sneaking up on you."

Angie just shook her head. She couldn't explain. She wouldn't humiliate herself even more.

"Hey." Mike's voice was still as gentle as a sleepy puppy's kiss. "You're not the first one who's been caught. Bobby's infamous. In the family, at least."

"No," she insisted. "I didn't drink too much."

"Why don't you come into the living room? I'll make some tea. That'll settle your stomach."

He offered her his hand to help her stand up, but she couldn't take it. She couldn't even look at him.

"It wasn't the drink," she repeated. *Make him go*, a voice inside her said. *Make him leave now without giving him anything, not your body, not your secrets.*

"It's okay," he said. "Come on now, everything's cool."

But it wasn't. Her life was a mess, and it would never be right again. "It wasn't the wine," she said. "It was the memories."

He just waited. Having gone this far, Angie had to finish. She couldn't think of any gentle way to ease into it.

"I was raped last year," she said. "I thought I was over it, but I guess I'm not." That sounded so weak, so crippled by life. "Not yet," she added, though her heart mocked her for her obvious lie.

Chapter Seven

Mike just sat there on the edge of the bathtub—anger, guilt, pity and pain all churned together into such a bitter mass that he was ready to throw up himself. Slowly anger came out on top, dominating the other emotions.

How could anyone misuse someone as gentle as Angie? The promise Mike made to his mother that evening rankled, too. Hadn't he misused Angie, as well? Hadn't his mother warned him to go slow? But he'd ignored all the signs and raced ahead. The torment he saw in Angie's eyes echoed in his heart.

She was sitting there in the corner of the bathroom, scrunched up in the folds of her blanket, looking as if her world had been destroyed. A helpless rage engulfed him, an anger at himself, at whoever attacked her, at the whole world, until all that was left was the desire to gather her up in his arms, make a shield that would protect her from all harm forever.

But he couldn't do that with a victim when he was out on the street, and he couldn't do it now. Instead he sat there, looking quietly at her, desperately fighting to keep his anger from his eyes. All his police training and experience told him to move cautiously. He didn't want to remind Angie of her attacker. He didn't want to scare her.

"Why don't I go heat some water?" he said. "We can both use some tea."

Angie shook her head. "No, just leave. I've done enough to mess up your life."

"You didn't mess anything up," he protested.

She laughed, a sharp, brittle sound. "Oh, right. I'm sure you often make love with women who throw up, break into tears, and then end the whole thing by turning into a basket case."

"My father told me not to judge another until I'd walked a mile in their shoes," Mike replied. Great time for wisdom to surface. Now, after the damage had been done.

Damn, he should have known Angie was carrying some kind of load; his mother had told him as much. Sure, a lot of times she had a smart mouth, but he should have seen that she wasn't the aggressive type, certainly not the hungry woman driven by a hot passion that she had been trying to play. Hell, if he couldn't read people better than he had Angie, he'd better turn in his badge.

But no, the first time she was an extra sheet to the wind, he just accepted that she was hot for his body. Dumb, absolutely stupid. As a cop, he should have known that alcohol never changes a person. It may strip away some layers of inhibition, but it never changes the real person.

A shiver went through Angie's body, and Mike held his breath. She looked as if she were about to break. Maybe if he just held her hand?

But again his years of police training stopped him. It was a man who had attacked her. A pat from his own large, hairy hand might be all that was needed to send her deeper into her land of terror. He'd seen it happen with other officers when they tried to comfort a victim.

"Angie," he said gently. "Would you like me to call someone?"

She shook her head mutely.

"We have a lot of people who work with us in the department," he said. "Ministers, social workers, nurses."

She shook her head again, strong lines of stubborn settling on her face. Mike sighed inwardly.

"We hit a wound that hadn't quite healed, Angie. That's all. Maybe it needs to be sutured and bandaged again."

"No," she snapped.

In a way, her stubbornness could be good. It could be a sign that her spirit hadn't been destroyed. But it could also mean that she was running away from reality, refusing to face up to her problems. He wished he could see inside her soul.

"Okay." He nodded his head for a short moment. "I'll get the tea started. Why don't you get dressed?"

Angie did not stir, but Mike knew that this wasn't the time to push. He went back to the bedroom and slipped on his shirt and shoes, stuffing his socks in his pocket. Then he took a deep breath and went to face Fudge.

The giant dog looked up as Mike entered the kitchen, giving out a low growl. But it wasn't clear whether the warning was just a general one or a specific one to stay away from the chew bars.

"I'm making tea," Mike said. "Angie needs it."

Fudge grunted and went back to chewing, but it kept watching Mike suspiciously as he filled the teakettle with water.

The dog suddenly took on new meaning. Big and mean-looking, it was Angie's protector. Why hadn't Mike seen that earlier? That explained why she brought Fudge up with her when she came to fix his shower, and why the dog was in the car when she brought Emily to the hospital that first night.

Damn. He'd been so blind, so stupid. "You should chew on my bones," he told Fudge.

The dog looked at him, a chew bar hanging from its mouth. At the moment Fudge looked more comical than fierce. Mike had no doubt that Angie had reformed the beast. Squashed whatever mean there was with an overwhelming load of gentle love.

Mike put the water on the burner and leaned against the counter, his arms crossed. After a moment, little rumbling sounds came from the pot, echoing the rumbling down deep inside him. The steam would explode out of the spout in another minute. Would that be before or after he exploded, splattering pieces of his psyche all over the kitchen?

Damn, damn, damn. Mike took a deep breath and glared at the green and white tile floor. He was acting like a civilian—and a wimpy civilian at that. He should know what to do. His training and experience told him to be professional, to be objective. It told him to be empathetic, not sympathetic. Like a good doctor, he should be concerned, but he should also keep his distance. He needed to maintain his professional objectivity or he would be totally useless to Angie when she needed him most.

But that was the crux of his problem. Intellectually, he understood what he should do, but he didn't want to remain distant. He wanted to scoop Angie up in his arms. Shelter her from the storm that was battering her soul. Hold her, kiss her and protect her. Keep her safe from all harm.

The teakettle began it's tuneless whistle and still no Angie. Mike turned off the heat and poured the hot water over the tea bags in the mugs. Would she come out? She was scared, hurt and embarrassed. The odds certainly didn't look good.

"Fudge, old buddy." The dog looked up at him, leaving the chew bar on the floor. "Angie's hurting real bad. She needs you. Go to her."

Much to Mike's surprise, the giant dog got up and padded out of the kitchen and toward the bedroom in back. It wasn't just the thought of the dog understanding him, but to actually obey him was unbelievable. If anybody could get Angie out, it would be that dog.

And when she did come, Mike would be professional. Well, reasonably professional. He'd be cool but gentle. He'd be caring. Most important of all, he'd be there. He would move carefully and let Angie take the lead. He'd let her reach out and take as much of him as she needed.

His eyes bounced worriedly toward the door. What was going on in there? Maybe Fudge and Angie were deciding that they didn't want Mike around. Maybe they were deciding that the dog should just pitch him out on his butt.

Mike wiped his hands on his pants. He didn't want to get in a fight with the giant beast, but he didn't want to desert Angie, either.

The sound of soft steps drew Mike's gaze back to the doorway. Angie stood there, her furry bodyguard by her side.

"Hi," he said.

"Hi."

Her voice sounded weary and beaten, but she was dressed and in the kitchen. She was doing well. They were making progress.

"Tea's all ready," he announced. "What do you want with it? Cream, sugar or lemon?"

She shrugged as she sat down at the dinette table. Fudge walked over to the chew-bar pile and lay down among them. The dog divided its attention between the rawhide bars and Angie and Mike.

"I'd say lemon," Mike said. It was tough, but he managed to keep his words flying high. "You're sweet enough already, so you don't need sugar or honey. And I hate cream in tea or coffee. So that leaves us with lemon."

He searched the refrigerator. "That is, if you have any." He found a bottle of lemon juice and put a few drops in their cups before taking a seat across from Angie.

She didn't say anything, but she did sip at her tea. His father had said that sometimes you had to measure progress in fractions of an inch; otherwise you'd think you weren't making any headway.

Mike's heart rose as Angie took that initial sip, but the feeling quickly faded. She seemed to shrink inside herself again. She just sat there, staring at the tabletop. She was clutching the mug as if she were trying to suck the warmth from it.

A bubble of emotion welled up in Mike's throat, making it hard for him to breathe. He could warm her with his arms and his kisses.

But that idea was quickly drowned in a rush of shame. How could he think this way about Angie after the way she'd reacted? Was he some kind of animal?

Mike clasped his own cup.

Seeing the misery on Angie's face was torture. Mike's desire to protect turned into rage—the basic, animallike rage to kill the man who had done this to her. Destroy the beast who had given her fear instead of love. Who had twisted and perverted a natural human instinct so badly that instead of giving her comfort, it gave her pain.

He had to get out of this apartment now. No question about it. His feelings danced at the edge of total loss of control. He really needed to channel his pain before it strangled him, but he didn't want to leave Angie alone.

"You sure you don't want me to call somebody?" he asked again.

"Quite sure."

"I hate to leave you alone," he said.

A trace of a smile flickered at the corners of her lips. "I won't be alone," she replied. "Fudge and Marshmallow are here with me."

Mike glanced down at the puppy from hell. The old cat was sleeping off in some hidey-hole, but Fudge would keep Angie safe. Trouble was, all the dog could do was listen. As big and warm as Fudge was, the dog came up short in the advice-giving department.

Mike dumped the dregs of his tea in the sink. Given his own emotional turmoil, the puppy was probably a better companion than he would be.

"Get some sleep," he said and cursed himself for the inanity of his remark. Ranked right up there with "Take two aspirin and call me in the morning." As if sleep or aspirin could heal her wounds. Still, sleep would help.

"I'll see you tomorrow," he said, and patted her hand gently.

She didn't pull away. Another small victory. He left before risking a defeat.

Angie slipped out of bed and padded into the living room, where she curled up into a ball in a corner of her sofa. The drapes were cracked open slightly, and a street lamp threw its pale rays on the rug. She felt rather than saw Fudge's dark hulk follow her into the room. The big dog groaned as he dropped his massive body on the floor near her.

"You didn't have to get up," she told him.

He grunted in reply.

"You could have stayed in bed with Marshmallow. You know he likes a big, warm body to cuddle up to."

This time his grunt was more expressive. Sort of, who cares about the darn cat?

"I'm sorry, Fudge," Angie said with a sigh.

She heard the tail thump on the floor, as if the dog were telling her not to worry about things. A chill skipped through her body, and she slipped her feet off the sofa, putting her toes under Fudge's warm, furry bulk.

"I really messed things up."

Fudge muttered a few unintelligible words of comfort.

"Oh, I did," Angie insisted. "I really did."

The dog sighed. Maybe he was tired of agreeing with her. Poor puppy probably just wanted to sleep. But she needed to talk, needed to tell someone.

"One minute I was all over him like some sex-starved vixen, and the next minute I was barfing and crying." Angie shook her head. "Mike didn't know what to do. He was really glad to leave."

There was no sound from the floor. The big guy was zonked out.

"I guess I'll just have to face up to the fact that I'm not normal," Angie murmured. "I'm some kind of a freak, and I'll probably be that way the rest of my life."

Her chin started to quiver, and Angie took a deep breath. She didn't want to shed any more tears. She wasn't sure that she had any left anyway. Crying and sniffling was about all

she'd been doing since Mike had left hours ago. Fudge ha
to be getting tired of it.

After several long moments, Angie let her breath out. Sh
was better now. She had things under control. Now all sh
had to do was accept the fact that she would always b
alone, and then she'd be fine.

Her chin wanted to quiver again, and Angie held he
breath while she stared at the crack between her drapes.

"I wouldn't mind going for a walk right now," she said

Normally the word *walk* would have sent Fudge dashin
to the broom closet for his leash, but he didn't stir. Not th
least tiny bit. Even her big giant Fudge dog thought it wa
stupid to go for a walk at three in the morning.

But so what if it could be dangerous? She was alread
messed up. What more could anyone do her?

Hot, quiet tears were flowing down her cheeks once more
following paths the previous rivers had left. She sat ther
praying that the morning sunshine would come soon. Sh
had to get out of here. She had to walk around and at leas
pretend she was free.

It was still dark outside when Mike abandoned his bed
but the birds' welcome-the-dawn chorus was starting to picl
up, inviting the world to plunge headfirst into the new day

Normally Mike loved these early morning hours of soli
tude, loved listening to the earth's awakening. His job pu
him in such close and constant touch with the perversities o
man that he really needed this time of solitude for his soul
A time for him to see that there was more to this world tha
human beings. A time to reflect, a time to prepare himsel
for his day.

Thinking on the evil man inflicted on other men brough
Angie to mind. Actually, she'd been dancing around in hi
thoughts all night, sometimes in the background, some
times stepping forward and screaming for attention.

He leaned on his elbows and put his head out the win
dow, taking in a deep breath of the moist river air.

"Hell," he muttered. "Life sure can be a bitch at times."

Of course nobody knew that better than a cop. There were times when you wished you were a god, sitting high up on Mount Olympus. Then you could get a big dustpan and sweep all the crud into the trash, leaving the world free for the good people.

Unfortunately, the real world wasn't all that simple. There were a few cases where things were clear-cut, though, when there were no varying shades of gray. Like Angie's case. A pure example of good and evil. Good was Angie, a soft, vulnerable woman. Evil was the man who'd violated her.

The picture of Angie cowering in her bathroom danced and swirled in the mist coming off the river. It gnawed at him until he could taste the fear she lived with. The rage began to build in him again, and he turned abruptly from the window.

Grabbing a sports bag from his closet, he tossed his swimsuit and towel into it and headed down the street to the YMCA for their Early Bird Swim. A few laps in the pool would do him good.

Apparently, he was one of the few people in town who needed the exercise. The pool area was deserted; there was just a sleepy-looking lifeguard reading the morning paper at one end of the pool.

Mike liked the solitude and spent close to an hour in the water, forcing himself to swim one lap after another until he was too exhausted to think anymore. Too exhausted to feel the rage.

It was after seven o'clock when he left the building, but he felt cleansed. The exercise had taken his rage and honed it into resolve. First, he would have a little talk with Angie. He needed to get some details from her. Was her attacker in the South Bend area? Could she identify him? Then Mike could put together a plan to protect her, to help her heal. Plus give out a little payback.

The gods were smiling on him. Angie and Fudge were just crossing the apartment-house parking lot as he pulled in. He quickly parked and hurried out of the car.

"Hey, Angie," he called.

The words were barely out of his mouth when he wanted to pull them back. His loud voice seemed to make her shrink within herself, and raised the ire of the mud-colored mountain at her side. Fudge moved in front of her and roared out an unwelcome, baring fangs that would make a lion happy.

"That's okay, Fudge," Angie said. "It's just Mike. He's our friend."

The words were fine, but the tone lacked conviction. The mutant puppy didn't appear to be buying the friend bit, either.

"Fudge, please," Angie said.

Mike stopped. She looked exhausted. Dark shadows circled her eyes. Obviously she hadn't slept any better than he had.

"I was just wondering how you were," Mike said.

Angie looked away with a weary shrug. "I'm okay," she mumbled.

Okay? People who were okay didn't look like something a cat would reject. She should be in bed.

He played along anyway. "Bobby's stuff has been known to knock big men out for a week or more."

"I'm fine," she said. "I was even able to keep some tea down this morning. I'll be back to normal in a few hours."

That beaten-down look just tore at him, ripping his heart apart. He wanted to take her in his arms and hug her long and hard. Hold her until she was whole again.

But they were standing out in the parking lot. Other tenants were getting into their cars to go to work. Fudge was standing guard, and it was still chilly.

And, worst of all, Mike didn't know how Angie would react if he tried to touch her. Would she welcome the contact with another human being and relax in the warmth of his embrace or would she stiffen in fear?

Mike would never know. Her beast companion did not look in the mood to permit any experimentation. What had happened to the moment's rapport they'd had last night? Mike took a step back.

"Well, I was just wondering," he said. "Give me a call if you need anything."

She barely nodded.

"You helped me when I needed it," he said.

She walked slowly toward her door. A touch of panic crept up on him, a fear that he would never see her again.

"And Emily, too," he said. "We both owe you."

Angie opened the door for the dog; then she followed him in. They quickly disappeared down the hallway.

"And Minellis always pay what they owe," he murmured to himself. And what Angie owed to the bastard who attacked her, Mike vowed to pay.

He stood there in the parking lot for several long moments, fighting the urge to run in after her. They needed to get things settled. She had to realize that he was there to help her. All she had to do was confide in him. Trust him.

Sighing, he looked at his watch. Time to get cleaned up. He had a court date this morning and if he wasn't there to testify, one more bit of scum would get back on the streets.

He walked into the building slowly. Angie wasn't going to get out of this thing alone; it didn't take a rocket scientist to see that she needed help. And frankly, so did he. He was a cop, but he needed to get deeper into this victim-psychology stuff.

Chapter Eight

"S.O.S. How may I help you?"

The woman's voice was soft and pleasant, as if she were answering the phone for a doctor's office rather than Sex Offense Services, but then maybe they were much the same thing. Over the years, Mike'd referred more people than he cared to count to the social-service agency for help in healing.

"Hi, Mike. Sorry to keep you waiting."

Mike stood up to greet Barb Vogler, one of the agency's counselors. "No problem."

"Why don't we go into my office?"

Barb led him into a cheery room filled with plants. Mike sat in front of the desk, while Barb went around and took her own seat across from him.

"So, how have things been going?" Mike asked. "Keeping busy?"

"Quite busy, I'm sorry to say."

"I know what you mean. It's the same at our place."

Barb was a pretty woman, not far past thirty. She hadn't grown up in South Bend, but her husband had. He was Mike's age and had been a star pitcher for Riley High School on the southeast side. He had struck Mike out twice in the big game for the city championship in their senior year.

"How can I help you, Mike?"

"It's not me," he hastened to explain. "I'm fine. I don't need any help, but I have this friend who does."

Barb nodded, the expression on her face easy and non-judgmental.

"She's been—" Mike cleared his throat. All of a sudden, the words were hard to say. Having this discussion with Barb was like getting an enema from a young, good-looking nurse who happened to be his sister's best friend. He forced the words out. "This friend's been assaulted."

"I see."

"So she needs help," he added.

Barb looked firmly at him. "Does your friend feel she needs help or do you think she does?"

"Let's not play word games," Mike said. "She needs help. That's the bottom line."

"Mike."

This might have gone better if he'd gone to someone he didn't know, although in a small town like South Bend that would be hard to find.

"She knows she needs help," Mike insisted. He was sure of it.

Barb fiddled for a moment with a pen on her desk. "This friend should really come in herself," Barb said. "I don't feel it's right to discuss such a sensitive situation when the person concerned isn't here."

"Oh, I agree, Barb. A hundred percent." He cleared his throat. "I just wanted to check out a few things for myself, so I don't screw something up. More than it's already screwed up. Not that Angie's screwed up, you understand. It's just that things could get screwed up."

"How close are you to Angie?"

The question came out of the blue, and Mike's mouth went dry. Damn it. How did her name slip out? "We live in the same apartment complex. She manages the place."

Barb looked quietly at him.

"She lives on the first floor, and I live on the third floor, so we're sort of close. Only one story in between."

Barb maintained her steady gaze.

"It's just a little joke," Mike said. "Actually, we're just casual friends. Neighbors. We say hi when we meet. That kind of thing."

He hadn't expected this to be so hard. Angie wasn't the first rape victim he'd come across, plus he'd been to a number of S.O.S. seminars for police officers. Why were the words so hard to find now? He silently returned Barb's gaze, determined not to run off at the mouth.

"What can I help you with, Mike?"

"I just don't know what to do."

"It's very difficult to give you any general guidelines to follow," Barb said. "The circumstances and an individual's reactions to those given circumstances are all very unique."

Mike nodded.

"How much do you know about the particulars of Angie's case?"

An uneasy feeling waffled through his stomach. "Not too much. Just that some piece of scum jumped her when she wasn't looking and sexually assaulted her."

"She was assaulted by a stranger?"

"Sure."

His reply had been swift and to the point, but Barb didn't say anything. She just looked at him steadily for a long moment. Mike felt a warmness around his collar.

"She's not a hothouse flower like those coeds you got calling in here," he said. "She's not dumb enough to let some so-called friend jump her bones in a back bedroom while a party's going on out front."

"The biggest thing that a friend can do in a case like this," Barb said, with a heavy emphasis on "friend," "is not be judgmental."

Mike looked away. He wasn't being judgmental; he was being accurate. Angie wasn't naive and blindingly trusting. She was a smart lady.

"So you're sure she was accosted by a stranger."

He met Barb's gaze and shrugged. "Pretty sure."

Barb frowned. "Who told you about the assault?"

"Angie did."

"So she's talking about it?"

Mike shrugged again. "Sometimes."

Barb waited.

He took a breath and launched into the story. "Sunday was Easter, so we were at my mother's house. I owed Angie. She took my kid in when Emily got dumped here and hauled me around when I hurt my leg. And...and it's a long story. Just take my word for it, I owe her. Besides, she hasn't got any family. My mother didn't want her to be alone on Easter Sunday."

"I see," Barb replied.

Mike paused. He didn't think Barb saw at all, but he wasn't going to get into that. "Anyway, we all had a nice time, but Angie had a little too much of my brother Bobby's homemade wine."

Barb continued looking steadily at him.

"Angie wasn't feeling very good." He looked away from her steady gaze. "Actually, she didn't appear to be feeling much of anything. Bobby's stuff hit her pretty hard."

The silence closed in on Mike, a painful presence in the room that he had to overcome. "My kid was staying overnight at my brother's."

Barb didn't move or speak. It was as if she weren't even breathing. Mike felt all alone in the office with only a shadow of the social worker's presence.

"I was going to boil water for tea, but we got hot before the water. And before anybody knew what was happening, we were in Angie's bedroom, letting nature run its course." He coughed into his hand. "And then things didn't quite work out."

"I see." Barb's voice was very quiet.

"I didn't force myself on her," he snapped. "I don't believe in that kind of crap."

Those light blues continued to look at him, hard and steady.

"Rape is the ultimate admission of failure of a man," Mike said. "What the rapist is saying is that he's so undesirable, he has to use force to get a woman to want him. What kind of a man needs to do that?"

"Rape isn't about sex," Barb corrected him. "It's about power and anger. About a man being able to overpower a woman in the most private and personal of ways. It's about a woman losing control over her body. And in nine cases out of ten, society'll make her feel it was her fault. She wore provocative clothes. She led him on. She trusted him."

Mike looked into Barb's eyes for a long, long moment, the memory of his own blundering about with Angie fresh in his mind.

"Mike, what happened Sunday night? It's important."

"She really came on strong," he said quietly. "I swear."

"And then?"

"Then? Then she got sick and started to cry a lot."

Silence descended on the office again. Barb looked up at him, and Mike looked away.

"There's a great deal that we don't know about Angie's situation," Barb said.

"Yeah," Mike murmured. "I have to check some things out."

"Are you her friend or her police officer?"

"Both."

"No," Barb said firmly. "You have to pick one or the other."

He looked out at the trees and the river framed by the window.

"You know more than I do about investigative procedures," Barb said, causing him to turn back toward her. "But that's different from being a friend. As a friend, you have to give her space and you have to give her time."

Mike nodded.

"She's been violated, Mike. Used in a way that few men can comprehend. She needs time to rebuild. Time to regain her trust and, most of all, time to regain her sense of control."

"Okay."

"She'll need a lot of support, but she has to be in control. Angie has to call the shots in this."

"Sure," Mike replied.

Barb eyes narrowed as she continued looking at him.

What was this? Didn't anybody trust him? "I understand," he assured her. "I understand completely."

Jeez. You'd think he was some kind of buttinsky. That wasn't the case at all. He was a man, and a man took care of his own.

Angie watched Emily, her brow wrinkled with concentration, as she worked on a math problem. The child checked the answer in the back of the book, then threw her arms up in victory.

"Yahoo!" Emily shouted. "Another one right."

Although Angie was in no mood for joy, she couldn't help smiling. The kid went for the gusto in everything she did.

"Boy," Emily said. "Are we a team or are we a team?"

"We're a team," Angie agreed.

"Wanna do another one?"

"You've been doing them all by yourself," Angie replied.

"You're helping by being here," Emily said. "Honest."

The girl's complexion was a little lighter and her features were softer than Mike's, but she sure had her father's eyes— dark, compelling and jumping almost instantaneously from one mood to another. Right now her eyes were pleading.

"I have to take Fudge downstairs and feed him and Marshmallow," Angie said.

"Aw, Angie. Please."

"Marshmallow's old," Angie insisted. "He doesn't like dinner to be late."

"Just one more problem," Emily pleaded. "And then I'll help you feed everybody."

Angie glanced up at the clock over the refrigerator. With judicious use of her answering machine, she'd managed to avoid Mike since yesterday morning when he'd met her out in the parking lot. But her efforts would be for nothing if she stayed here much longer.

"Your dad will be home soon," Angie reminded.

Emily's lips twisted in scorn. "He don't know nothin' about math."

"I'm not good at math, either," Angie insisted. "And you've been doing everything by yourself anyway."

"But we're a team. You said so."

"I didn't say so," Angie said firmly. "You did."

"You agreed and that's the same thing."

Angie tried frowning, but she couldn't hold it. She had another fifteen minutes or so before he'd be here. She was safe from having to face her shame in the pity in his eyes.

"Okay," she said with a sigh. "One more."

"Aw right!" Emily shouted as she jumped off her chair.

"Now what?" Angie demanded.

"I gotta do my lucky hug." Emily was down on her knees by Fudge, scratching him behind his ears, then hugging him around the neck. "Mike says good preparation is very important. He says if you don't do the first steps good, you won't be able to do the last."

Memories of Sunday night filled Angie's thoughts and a hot embarrassment flushed her cheeks. Preparation. A little seduction to ease into the scene and maybe things would have worked out. Maybe the disaster could have been averted.

But she had been so frightened. Angie was ready to admit that now. After Sunday night, she had to admit it. She was a freak, and she couldn't deny it anymore. She jumped when Fudge started to growl and raced to the front door.

"Go get him, Fudge." Emily jumped off her chair to follow the dog.

Oh, Lord, Angie thought. Mike was early. "Emily, hold—" But Fudge was already at the door, barking furiously, the noise making the kitchen cabinets rattle.

The door swung open just as Emily got to Fudge and grabbed his collar. Mike stood framed in the doorway, his normally dark face white with tension. Fudge had gone from barking to a more serious growling. His teeth were bared.

"Chill it, Mike," Emily snapped. "You're making Fudge all mad."

"What the hell is that dog doing here?"

"He's helping me with my homework," Emily replied.

A blink of confusion interrupted Mike's glare.

"Angie's helping, too," Emily added.

"Fine," Mike snapped as he strode into the apartment and hurried on back to the sleeping area.

"Boy, is he grumpy," Emily muttered.

That was putting it mildly. "I should be going," Angie said.

"Bite him when he comes out, Fudgey," Emily said, scratching the dog on the top of his head. "Right on the butt."

"Emily, he could get hurt."

"No, he can't," the child replied, shaking her head. "Mike won't have his gun when he comes back. He always locks it up right after he comes home."

Angie stared at the girl. "I meant your father."

Emily still shook her head. "Grandma says that when Mike gets grumpy, he needs a whack. You and I are too small to do it, so Fudge has to."

Mike didn't need a whack; he needed her out of here. Angie suddenly felt very tired. She wanted to run away and hide. It was a mistake coming here. She should have just had Emily wait downstairs when her aunt dropped her off after school. Yet it was fun being with the kid. Any gloom clouds that wanted to hang overhead were quickly dissipated by her smile.

And Angie used to enjoy being around Mike. She tried to put those memories aside. That was all gone now.

"Come on, Fudge," Angie said. "We have to go home."

"No, no," Emily said, grabbing her hand. "We gotta finish our problem."

"Emily, I—"

"But you promised."

Mike came back into the room. He taken off his coat and his gun and put on comfortable shoes and a knitted sport shirt. His face wasn't as tight anymore, either, but he still carried a load of anger in his eyes.

"Emily, don't be a pest," he snapped.

"I'm not," Emily protested. "Angie promised to help me with my homework."

"I'll help you."

"You're not any good at math."

"I'm good enough."

They stood glaring at each other. Father and daughter, as alike as two peas in a pod. Their anger generated an uncomfortable tension in the air and Fudge whined quietly.

"I did promise," Angie admitted. "So let's finish that problem, Emily."

"You don't have to stay," Mike said softly.

Angie looked into his dark, angry eyes and wished she could fall into a hole down to the center of the earth. A huge cloud of depression enveloped her, squeezing her so that she almost couldn't breathe. It was obvious that he didn't want her there, but she had promised Emily.

"It's just one problem," she murmured, guiding Emily back into the kitchen.

Mike stayed in the living room while Emily worked her problem. Fudge resumed his position on the floor, and Angie sat down with resignation.

It didn't matter what Mike was doing in the other room; what mattered was that he preferred to be in there rather than in the kitchen with them. It was obvious that he preferred being alone. It wasn't Emily he was averse to, though; Emily was his daughter. Emily wasn't a freak.

Tears pricked at her eyes, but Angie blinked and kept them at bay. She'd had enough practice at holding back tears this past year; no need giving up that skill now.

Mike came quietly into the kitchen, carrying the evening paper. He put water into the teakettle. He looked nice in his after-work clothes, more relaxed. His shoulders looked so broad, his arms seemed strong enough to carry the most burdensome of problems.

Angie almost laughed and cried at the same time. How could she think that way after the other night? There was no way he'd want to help her carry her problems. He'd just want to run from them and her, and she couldn't blame him.

"Care for any tea?" he asked. "Instant coffee?"

She shook her head. "I have to get back to my own place. It's dinnertime for my boys."

Fudge lolled his tongue at her and whacked his tail on the floor a couple of times. Poor guy. She knew he'd be hungry by now.

"Yahoo!"

She and Mike both looked at Emily, whose arms were raised in victory. "You got it right?" Angie asked.

"Yep."

Well, it was time for her to go. Time for her to get out of Mike's hair. It was obvious that he was tense with her around. And who could blame the poor man?

Angie stood up and waited as Emily closed her books and stuffed them into her schoolbag.

"I'm gonna feed the guys," Emily announced as she put her bag in a far corner on the kitchen counter.

"That's okay," Angie replied.

"Fair is fair," Emily insisted. "You helped me and now I gotta help you."

"All right," Angie said, standing up. "Let's go."

"I'll do it myself. You can stay up here and sit around and rest up."

"No, Emily. I'll—"

"Come on, Fudge," Emily shouted as she grabbed Angie's key from the counter and raced for the door. The big dog clomped along on her heels like a small draft horse.

"Hey," Mike called after her. "How about wearing some shoes?"

"I can't find them."

"They're under the table," he said.

Emily opened the door to let Fudge out; then she flashed an impish grin back. "Well, since you found 'em, you can wear 'em."

The door slammed, and Angie was left alone with Mike. She knew she should leave, knew that Mike wanted her to, but she wasn't brave enough to do anything. She just stood there, her feet rooted to the floor.

Mike stared across the room at Angie. She looked like a small waif from a war-torn land, captured in a newspaper photo—bewildered and scared, not knowing where to turn, who to trust.

Anger twisted his heart so that he almost had to strike out. He wanted to smash something, to vent his rage against the evil that had wounded Angie. Why should she be suffering like this? She would never hurt anybody. What kind of monster would try to destroy something so fine and gentle?

Mike swallowed hard, then swallowed again, trying to lock up his wrath, to tuck it safely away in the far recesses of his soul. The rage was his ally, his friend. His weapon. He would keep it festering and waiting, just in case. Right now, he had a more pressing task—Angie.

It took a moment for him to tamp the anger back down, to feel certain that it wouldn't rear up again, and all the while Angie's eyes seemed to grow darker and darker. He wanted to reach out to her, to hold her safe in his arms. Instead he did nothing, afraid that his touch would bring real fear back to her eyes.

"Boy, that kid is a pistol," he said, shaking his head.

Angie shrugged, and a smile played briefly on her lips. "She carries a lot of sunshine with her."

"Yeah." He looked at the floor a moment. "But she needs a woman in her life. I wish I could get a hold of her mother."

"She's comfortable with you," Angie said.

"She argues a lot with me."

As that riveting dialogue concluded, he watched her. She was looking around the room, avoiding his eyes. The teakettle whistled for his attention.

"Hey, the water's ready." He rushed to the stove, glad to have another excuse to hold her there. "Want some tea?"

"No. I should be getting downstairs. See how Emily is getting along."

"She said she'd take care of feeding your guys," Mike pointed out. "You go down, and she'll think you don't trust her."

That seemed to deflate Angie even further, and Mike cursed his big mouth. Trust wasn't an easy subject for Angie, though at the moment he wasn't sure what was.

"Come on," he said. "I have a lot of hot water. No use letting it go to waste."

"Okay," she said and sat down at the table.

He filled two mugs to the brim with hot water and plopped a tea bag into each. "Is lemon okay?" he asked. "I have honey, if you'd like."

She shook her head, and Mike cut a thick slice of fresh lemon for each of them. He swished the bags in the water a few times, then left them on the sink.

He set down Angie's mug near her, his hand brushing hers slightly. Fear of her fear made him jerk his hand back, spilling a few drops of tea.

"Sorry," he murmured.

Angie just nodded, snatching up her cup as if to hide behind it. She looked near to tears.

Damn it. Now he'd scared her again. Barb had warned him Angie'd need a lot of space and time. That didn't mean just a day or so away from him, he thought.

Mike stared into his cup, the rage flaring up for a brief moment. He'd like to have the bastard who hurt Angie all alone for just a few minutes—less than a minute even—and the bastard would never harm anyone ever again. Mike realized he was gripping his cup too hard, squeezing it as if it were somebody's throat.

He forced his hands to relax. "Tea tastes good on a day like today."

Angie nodded.

A small response, but a response nonetheless. He pressed on. "Weather's been rather cool for this time of the year, but then that's the great Midwest. They say if you don't like our weather, just wait a minute."

Again she nodded, not even attempting a smile. Mike's heart cracked. She was imprisoned by her fear, her pain, her agony. There had to be a way to conquer her fears. His hand went out to hers, but he halted midway. Not yet, he scolded himself; offer support, but don't push for touch. He slowly pulled his hand back to his mug.

If he'd thought Angie wouldn't see his actions, he was wrong. They brought a painful smile to her lips, so filled with misery that he would have preferred tears.

"That's okay," she said in almost a whisper. "I understand."

"Understand what?"

Now the tears started welling up in her eyes. "Understand that you don't want to touch me."

Mike just shook his head. "But I do want to touch you."

She stared at him, disbelief crowding the pain in her eyes.

"Angie, I come from a big, ethnic family. We're always laughing, talking, hollering and hugging each other. I'm just afraid to touch you. Afraid of how you'll take it."

When she looked up, tears were slowly sliding down her cheeks. "I thought you didn't want to touch me," she said softly. "I'm all messed up."

That rage was there again, eating at him, but he mastered it. He had to allow her control. "You're not messed up, Angie. The creep who attacked you just gave you a few more problems than average."

Apparently unconvinced, she looked back into her cup.

Mike gazed at her a long time. He was no counselor, but he knew she needed to let go, to spill out some of the pain and anger so she could heal.

"I guess as a woman you have to watch where you go," he said. "You know, be careful of what neighborhoods you're in, where you go after dark, that kind of thing."

A bitter-looking smile twisted her lips. "That makes us prisoners when we haven't done anything."

It hurt to admit to himself that she was right. A woman was the victim, yet she carried the life sentence. That was the world they lived in. As a cop, he didn't know what else to advise, except to be careful.

"But that would be the easy part," Angie continued. "Even little kids understand stranger danger. But how do you protect yourself from your friends?"

Something was coming, something he wasn't sure he wanted to hear.

"I had known the man who raped me for years," Angie said. "He was an old friend. I called him when my mother was really sick and we needed money. I thought he could help me get back into films or commercials."

She took a deep breath. "He was having some friends over one afternoon and invited me to come. We had a light meal and some wine. Then we went swimming. Afterwards, I was showering the chlorine out of my hair, when he came in and . . ."

Angie straightened herself up, but could not look at him. "And that's when it happened."

"And that's the real reason you dislike showers."

She nodded.

He couldn't breathe. The silence stretched into forever. The electric kitchen clock whirred. The refrigerator hummed and assorted creaks echoed from the far corners of the apartment. The anger was growing stronger.

He looked at Angie and saw all the victims of violent crimes sitting before him. He heard their weeping. He mopped up their blood and tears. And felt the rage burn deeper. Why did they all have that beaten, hopeless look in their eyes? Why did they all seem so surprised that evil existed? And why did they all expect him to prove the world was filled with good people when he knew otherwise? Why'd they all come to him for protection when it was too late?

"Good God, Angie, why'd you go swimming?" Mike asked.

She stared, stunned at his abrupt change of mood. "It was hot. Everybody was swimming."

"But that was just asking for trouble."

"How? I wasn't the only woman in a bathing suit, and even if I was, am I supposed to go through life wrapped in a blanket, not trusting anyone, especially if they're male? If that were true, then I shouldn't be here with you."

It didn't matter that her words made sense. Too many emotions were churning in him. Anger, pain, confusion, inadequacy. He couldn't think—only feel. "It was stupid to have gone there alone."

"I wasn't alone. There were six other people there, not counting his staff. And I had known him for years."

"So did those others come when you called for help?"

"The house was huge. If anybody heard me cry out, they ignored it."

"Were they willing to back up your story?"

Angie laughed, though there was no humor in it. "I didn't ask them to. I didn't report it."

"Why not?"

"Why not?" The look on her face wasn't pretty. "Because it wouldn't make a damn bit of difference."

The rage was winning, seeing something—anything—to strike out at. "It's attitudes like that that keeps bad guys on the street."

"Oh, come on, Mike. Grow up and look at the real world. Things are tough enough for a woman if she's attacked by a stranger. What do you think happens when she's raped by an acquaintance? The system rips her to shreds. Just like you're doing now."

Her words slapped him in the face, and the memory of Barb's words taunted him. He had blamed Angie, made the victim the guilty party. The rage still burned, the fury that naiveté and goodness were suicidal virtues.

He took a deep breath and forced his anger down again, though he wasn't quite ready to give up the fight. "You really should have turned the rat in. That's the only—"

"I should have stayed downstairs in my own apartment." Angie got to her feet and stomped out.

The slamming of the door echoed for a long time after Angie had left. He looked at his tea and his stomach soured. Lord, but he had screwed that up royally. He was a professional; he should know how to handle his anger. It was just that she'd thrown so much at him.

An acquaintance rape. Her attacker was on the loose.

The anger flickered deep in his belly, and a tight smile came to his lips. She knew who her attacker was, so that meant she could give him a name. And the bastard was free, so some civic-minded citizen could accidentally come upon him.

The door opened and slammed again. Emily stood there accusingly, hands on her hips.

"What did you do to Angie?" she demanded.

"I didn't do anything."

"She's all mad and crying."

"I'm sorry."

"Sorry don't pay the rent."

Both his hands went to his mug. He wrapped his fingers around the porcelain surface and squeezed hard. One of the great joys of parenthood was having your own words thrown back in your face. He sure didn't have a handle on this full-time father business at all.

"I'm going to try your mother again tonight," he said softly. "Things are just too—"

Oh, no. Now tears were flowing down his daughter's face.

"You don't want Angie around. You don't want me around. You don't want anybody around!"

She turned and ran to her room, presenting him with another slammed door. Damn.

Angie patted Fudge's giant head as it rested on her lap, but his massive warmth couldn't stop a shiver from dancing up and down her back. Mike was right; it was rather chilly for late April.

She sighed and looked off toward the window. Mike was right about a lot of things. She should have reported the rape. If not to the police, then to a counselor, a women's support group, somebody. It was too big a load to carry herself. He was right about her being stupid, too; she had trusted so blindly, so implicitly, so dumbly.

The telephone rang, and Fudge jumped off the sofa to run ahead of her into the kitchen. Angie followed along and answered.

"Angie, this is Mike. I'm sorry about everything."

She paused to listen to her heart pounding. Why did he bother? "That's okay," she assured him. "I shouldn't be so emotional about things."

"I shouldn't have blown up like I did," he said. "I guess I'm just so frustrated that the world keeps right on being an ugly place, no matter what I do."

"You were right about some things," she said. "I should have been more careful and—"

"No, Angie. It wasn't your fault, and I'm sorry most of all if I made it sound like I thought it was."

His words surprised her and somehow made the empty feeling inside her lessen. "Okay."

"Anyway," he said. "I had a reason for calling. How about going to lunch with me tomorrow?"

She looked down at Fudge, lying on the floor, his tongue hanging out the side of his mouth. She was going to have to step out into the normal world one of these days. The image of her disastrous scene danced through her mind. That wouldn't happen again, she vowed. She wasn't going to rush things anymore. It was going to be slow and easy from now on. Besides, she liked being with Mike. He made her feel alive.

"Angie?"

"I was just checking with Fudge. He said that he'd love for the three of us to go to lunch." There was a dead silence on the line, and Angie laughed. "That was a joke."

"I knew that."

His voice was brusque, and Angie smothered another, genuine laugh. "Anyway, I'd be glad to have lunch with you."

"Great. I have a meeting late in the morning, though," he said. "Can you meet me at Tippecanoe Place around twelve?"

"Sure," Angie replied.

She slowly hung her phone up. She didn't exactly feel like waltzing, but maybe she could manage a little two-step.

Chapter Nine

Barb Vogler was just stepping out of her car as Mike pulled into the parking lot. She waved as he sped by and into a parking space on the south side of the old Studebaker mansion. The enormous three-story building, made of huge chunks of Indiana limestone, looked like a castle, but it was the home of Tippecanoe Place restaurant. Maybe today it would be a castle again, a castle where a fair princess would be rescued.

"Hi, Mike," Barb said as he joined her. "Where's Angie? I thought she'd be with you."

"She'll be here in a few minutes," Mike replied. "She's coming right from school."

Mike led Barb up the steps and tugged open the heavy oaken door. He entered behind her, stopping at the hostess desk in the foyer.

"Hello, Lieutenant," the hostess greeted him.

"Hi, Jenny," Mike said. "You have any tables on the porch?"

"Sure thing."

They followed the hostess through the dining room and he library of the old mansion, both now filled with tables or eating, and onto the screened-in porch with wicker chairs and tables.

"Care for anything to drink?" the hostess asked once hey'd been seated.

"Barb?" Mike asked.

"I have a heavy schedule this afternoon," she said, shaking her head.

"How about iced tea?" Mike said. "It's perfect for such a sunny spring day." He turned to the hostess without waiting for an answer. "Bring us a pitcher of iced tea, please." Then he turned back to Barb. "That'll be plenty for each of us."

"Were you always like this?" Barb asked, as the hostess ped away.

"Like what?"

"So—" Barb grinned and put a finger to her chin. "How shall I say it? So commanding?"

Why did everyone act like decision-making was a dirty word? "Someone has to take charge," he said, glaring around the porch. "Otherwise the world sits on its keister, staring at its belly button."

Fortunately the server came with their iced tea before Barb had a chance to push the subject further. The man pulled out his order pad. "What'll you folks have today?"

"Let's wait a minute," Mike said. "There'll be a third person joining us." He checked his watch as the server departed, little fingers of nerves pinching at his stomach. He knew he was doing the right thing, but that didn't mean it wouldn't be tricky. "I'd better check up front. Angie probably doesn't know where we are."

"You're well-known," Barb said. "All she has to do is ask for you, and the hostess will bring her back."

"Yeah, but this is a busy time for them." Mike stood up. "I'll just run out and see if she's up front."

"Oh, Mike." Barb's eyes held no laughter. "You did tell Angie that I'd be having lunch with you, didn't you? I don't want to be sprung on her when she arrives."

"Of course," Mike snapped as he hurried off toward th entryway. What the hell did Barb think he was, anyway? Sh should know him well enough by now to know that h wasn't into game playing. He was going to tell Angie abou Barb and counseling the moment she walked in. Angie wa just stepping through the door as he entered the large foye

"Hi, Angie."

"Hi, Mike," she replied. "I hope you weren't waitin long."

"Nah." He bent down and kissed her lightly on the cheek She didn't pull back, and he felt about ten feet tall. Angi just needed somebody to help her find herself again. H took her hand in his and backtracked through the dinin room.

"Oh, by the way," he said as they stepped into the l brary. "There'll be three of us for lunch."

"Oh?"

"Yeah, a Mrs. Barb Vogler is joining us." They steppe out of the library onto the porch. "She's an S.O.S. coun selor with the Madison Center here in town."

"SOS?"

Angie's steps slowed down a bit, but Mike had her han and wouldn't let her stop, just as he wouldn't let her linge in her pain and fear anymore. He led her to the table.

"Barb," he said, keeping Angie's hand firmly in his "This is my friend Angie Hartman. Angie, this is Bar Vogler."

"Hello, Angie," Barb said, standing and offering he hand.

Angie tentatively grasped it. "Hello, Barb." Her voic was wary, suspicious.

Mike picked up the pitcher. "How about some iced tea ladies?"

"What does SOS stand for?" Angie demanded of Mike

Barb shot a glare Mike's way but answered before h could. "Sex Offense Services."

He could feel the words hit Angie like a blow. Her ex pression hardly changed, but there was a flash of pain in he eyes before she seemed to distance herself.

"You told her?" Angie said in the half whisper of shock. He could hear the accusation of betrayal between the words.

"Not much," he said. Her pain tore at him, but he didn't back down. Someone, sometime had to stop the bleeding. "Just that you were too nice to have your life ruined by fear."

Color tinged Angie's cheeks, and her gaze fell to the menu in front of her. He could tell by the stubborn set of her jaw that he was anything but forgiven. Her hands on the menu shook slightly. Couldn't she see how much she needed help?

"Ready to order, folks?"

The server was back. Mike quickly ordered a bowl of soup and a sandwich, then held his breath. Barb placed her order, then Angie did, too. At least Angie wasn't going to bolt. Good thing, because he hadn't prepared himself for that possibility and might have done something dumb.

"I'm sorry that Mike brought you here under false pretenses," Barb told Angie once the waiter had left.

"I did not," Mike argued. "I told her who you are."

"Oh, right," Angie jeered. "Just as we stepped out onto his porch."

"I told you in the library," Mike said.

Angie rolled her eyes heavenward.

"Would you have come if I'd told you about Barb yesterday?"

Angie just looked away toward the far end of the porch.

"Okay," Mike said. "So I didn't do everything by the book, but now that we're here, there's no use letting the opportunity go to waste."

Barb looked at him a long moment. Her eyes glowed, but he couldn't tell whether it was with pity or aggravation. She turned to Angie. "I would never have come if I had known you hadn't agreed to this meeting. That's not the way I operate."

That seemed a deliberate slam at Mike. He pretended to ignore it. "You aren't the first one I referred to S.O.S.," he said to Angie. "We refer all rape victims to Barb and her group. They have the necessary people and facilities to help."

The waiter brought their soup and, for a moment, they were just friends sharing a lunch. But no one seemed to eat all that vigorously once the server departed again.

Angie played with her soup, taking at most a spoonful or two before pushing it back slightly. "Look, I'm sorry Mike went to all this trouble," she told Barb slowly. "But I'm fine. He really shouldn't have bothered you."

"For God's sake, Angie—"

Barb just shot him a look. "A free lunch is never a bother," she said lightly.

Angie fiddled with her soup spoon, laying it on the plate one way, then another. Her eyes looked everywhere but at him or Barb. "I know I was a little upset the other night, but really I'm fine."

Barb's look told him to keep his mouth shut, and he did. She was the expert here, after all.

"I'm glad," Barb said. "Some of us have a harder road back."

Angie looked up at that.

Barb nodded slowly. "Twelve years ago I was raped by my boyfriend. The person I thought I loved."

"But you're married now," Angie said. "Aren't you?"

Mike didn't understand the connection, but Barb did. She smiled. "I learned to trust again," she said. "It takes time."

The waiter brought their sandwiches, and they all ate. Or pretended to eat. Mike wasn't fooled by the way Angie rearranged the food on her plate, nibbling from one side of her sandwich, then the other.

"Boy, those South Bend Sox are starting out pretty good, aren't they?" Barb asked.

What the— Mike just stared at her. "I guess."

"You a baseball fan?" Barb asked Angie.

She shook her head. "I don't follow much of any sport."

"Well, you have to here," Barb said. "If it's not the South Bend White Sox, then you've got be a rabid Notre Dame fan."

Angie's laugh was shaky. "I don't even know what sports they play."

Before Mike knew it, they were done eating. Even Angie had eaten most of her sandwich as Barb had kept her chatting about nothing in particular.

Barb laid her napkin on the table as she looked at her watch. "I'm afraid I've got to get going. I have a meeting at one-fifteen." She stood up, putting her card on the table next to Angie. "Think about us. If you don't need us, we might need you. Maybe you could help someone in one of our group sessions be healed faster."

Angie nodded silently. She stared for a long minute at the card, then slipped it into her purse.

Barb turned to Mike. "Goodbye, Mikey." She patted him on the cheek. "Try to stay out of trouble."

She left the two of them at the table. Mike was suddenly tongue-tied. A thin wall of ice separated him from Angie. How could he break it down without shattering the fragile relationship they were building?

Angie didn't seem to have such worries. She pinned him to the wall with her gaze. "You had no right to tell Barb about me," she said. Anger raced through her words, but so did sorrow, fear and bitterness.

"No," he admitted and caught her by surprise for a second. "But luckily I had the courage to anyway."

She recovered enough to glare at him. "It's not your problem. It was for a short time Sunday night, but not anymore."

"It is as long as you're hurting."

She got to her feet. "I'm not. I'm fine." She folded her napkin and started to put it back on the table. Playing the perfect little girl, even when she probably wanted to strangle him.

He grabbed it from her hand. "Why don't you just throw it at me? Show that you're mad if you want to."

"I abhor—"

"—violence. Yeah, I know." He got to his feet, too. "But if you abhor it so much, why are you letting the violence done to you win?"

Angie said nothing. She looked at him for an eternity, as if searching for the smile or wink that would say he was joking, that she didn't have to think about his words. But he just looked back, his eyes telling her to trust. She turned and walked away.

Mike watched her go, then sank back down into his chair and signaled the server for the check. His father said that progress always took the crooked road. He sure hoped the old man was right.

Mike frowned and rapped on the door extra hard. Where was his sister? Her baby was due in a couple of months. She should be home resting, not out gallivanting around.

He noticed a shadow behind the curtains in the door as he shifted his package to the other arm; then the back door opened. Margaret was dressed in an old shirt of her husband's and jeans. Her hair was wrapped with a bandanna.

"What are you doing?" he asked as he came into the kitchen.

"Painting the baby's bedroom."

"Why isn't Ted doing that?"

"Because I won't let him. He's a klutz, and I wouldn't let him paint a stick."

"You're supposed to be resting."

"You're supposed to be minding your own business. Why are you out bothering me, anyway?"

"I got a good deal on strawberries." Mike slid the package onto the table. "I left some at Mom's, and I've got more in the car."

Margaret grimaced as she looked in the bag. "That's a lot of berries to clean, big brother. If you really want me to rest, you should have cleaned them first."

"Get that bum of a husband to do that," Mike said cheerfully. "He ought to be willing to do something for free food. Besides, fresh fruit is good for pregnant women."

"You need a family of your own, Mike."

"I got Emily," he replied.

"Apparently she's not enough to keep you busy," Margaret said and made another face at the bag of strawberries.

Mike sat down at the table.

"Get a hold of Sue yet?" Margaret asked.

He shook his head. "I don't understand it. She's never done anything like this before. A girl needs her mother."

"A girl needs her father, too."

Why was it women didn't understand that little girls needed mothers more? He stood up abruptly. "Well, I gotta get going. Got a load of strawberries to deliver."

"You really ought to get married, Mike."

"Get outa here," he said. "I tried it once. Remember?"

"So if something doesn't work out the first time, you quit? Come on, Mikey."

It was his turn to grimace.

"I mean it, Mike. Find somebody or we will," Margaret said. "We're tired of you always trying to butt into our lives. Get your own tribe to boss around."

He ignored her. This wasn't the first time she'd given this particular speech. "Tell your husband to clean the berries," he said. "After he cleans up the mess you made in the nursery. He can handle that, can't he?"

"How about that apartment-house manager at your place?" Margaret asked. "You've been seeing a lot of her, haven't you?"

"She's a neighbor," Mike pointed out. "Not my doing that I see her often."

"So? There some law about fraternizing with a neighbor?"

"She's a friend. She's been real good to Emily."

"Ah, that explains it," Margaret mocked. "Can't get romantically involved with someone you like and who likes your kid."

"Jeez, you've really got a bee in your bonnet today," he snapped. "Angie's been having a rough time lately, and I've been giving her a hand. That's what cops do, give people some help when they need it. Once she's back on her feet, I'll probably hardly ever see her."

"I see, so all you were doing Sunday when you were hovering over her, granting her every little whim, was being a good cop."

He didn't like the smirk in Margaret's voice, but he was mature enough to overlook it. "I was making sure she was comfortable, seeing as how she was among strangers."

"A real gentleman. I'm impressed."

"You should be." He walked over to the door and turned back. "So you can stop planning the wedding. Cops don't make good husbands."

"Mom tell you that?"

"Dad was the exception. Cops these days don't make good husbands." He opened the door. "Can't make a silk purse out of a sow's ear."

"My, that's original."

"Original and true. Say hi to Ted for me."

He went out and hurried across the backyard to his car in the alley. Margaret was sure on a tear. Maybe he ought to drum up some decorating business for her. She obviously didn't have enough to do.

Him get married again, right. Just went to show that he had to watch his every move around his family. They didn't seem to understand anyone helping a friend get back on her feet.

Angie looked up at the clock on the wall of Mike's kitchen. It was almost six o'clock. He was normally home long before now.

An uneasiness settled in the pit of her stomach as she remembered the day Emily arrived. Could something have happened to him again? Police work was dangerous, and his leg was still healing.

No, they would have called Emily or his mother, and then she would have called Emily. Emily wouldn't be down in Angie's apartment happily feeding Fudge and Marshmallow if she'd gotten such a call.

Though why Angie should worry was beyond her. After all of Mike's interference, she should be hoping that something happened to him so he would leave her alone. But even that thought was worrisome. She got to her feet, wandering into his living room. That old movie magazine still lay on an end table, open to the article about her. Which of them had been rereading it? Emily or Mike?

She went to the window, staring out at the river lazily gliding along beneath the late April sunshine. This had been one hell of an afternoon. First learning that Mike had told Barb about the rape, then having to deal with the rush of anger that had caused. She guessed she hadn't exactly told him not to tell anyone, but she hadn't expected him to. Somehow learning that he had told someone else added to his betrayal, even if she intellectually knew he had just been trying to help.

She took a deep breath and exhaled, ridding herself of the traces of pain that wanted to creep back in. She'd dealt with the anger, the pain that had taken its place and the weariness that was finally all that remained.

The sound of a key in the door made her turn and for a panic-filled moment, she cursed herself for leaving Fudge downstairs. Then relief washed over her when she saw it was Mike.

She went into the foyer. "Hi."

He had a grocery bag in his arms and was obviously surprised to see her there. "Hi," he said, then looked quickly down the hallway.

"Fudge is downstairs," Angie said.

"Since I was allowed in, I figured he wasn't here."

"And Emily is with him."

"She is?" He went on into the kitchen. "She told me this morning she was going to Moira Conners' house, that they were going to do their science project and then Mrs. Conners was taking them out for a burger."

"I guess her plans changed," Angie said as she followed him.

"I guess." Mike put the bag on the countertop. "But she should have called me at the station and told me. I would have been home sooner."

"I think Emily likes her independence," Angie said.

"Yeah, I know, but she should let me know if things change." Grimacing, he sat down at the table. "Boy, I don't know how Sue handled this single-parent thing. I'm a basket case.''

"You'll get used to it."

"Oh, no," Mike insisted. "A girl belongs with her mother. Once I get a hold of Sue, this whole thing will be straightened out."

Poor guy. He seemed so confused. He wasn't the arrogant know-it-all he seemed this afternoon; he was just a man trying to do his best and fearing he wasn't. Her heart went out to him. She sat down across the table from him.

He looked at her and frowned. "You get some new clothes?" he asked. "Something about you looks different."

Her decision must have shown. She twisted her hands together for support. "That's actually why I'm here," she said.

His confusion deepened. "To show me your new clothes?"

"No." She waved dismissively at her jeans and sweatshirt. "These aren't new. I'm here because I was waiting for you."

A smile grew, tiny and barely there, just enough to make the lines at the corners of his eyes crinkle just a tad. "This is a good place for that," he said.

"I was waiting for you because I wanted to apologize," she went on.

Mike looked like a little boy hoping for ice cream but given brussel sprouts. "I was hoping it was because you missed me."

"I'm sorry I got mad at you at lunch," she insisted.

"Go ahead if you want," he replied. "But you could still say you missed me."

"Mike, this isn't easy."

"I'm sorry," he said. He reached across the table to take her two hands in his. "I'm sorry. You're sorry. We're all sorry. Now let's forget it. No harm done."

His hold on her made her feel safe, as if there were something she could cling to, someone she could count on. Life seemed easier, rosier.

"I made a call to Barb this afternoon," she told him. "I'm going to try counseling."

He just stared at her, his slow smile taking three centuries at least to curve his lips. "That is wonderful," he said, his hold tightening. "That is just super."

There was no way to misinterpret the real joy in his voice and in his eyes. It spread to her, and she smiled back at him. The worries that had been gathering since she made the call this afternoon seemed as substantial as cobwebs. Her uncertainties just couldn't stand up in the face of his certainties that this was the right thing.

"I'm attending my first support-group meeting tomorrow night."

"Good luck, kid."

She tightened her grip on him. "I'm a little nervous about it," she admitted.

"That's natural. A lot of victims I've worked with find they relive the crime a little bit when they retell it, but it gets easier each time."

"I hope so."

"Nothing to hope about. It's a given. Didn't I just tell you it would?"

His teasing brought laughter into her heart, a surprising and wonderful thing that had seemed impossible a while ago.

"I have you to thank," she said. "I wouldn't be going if you hadn't pushed me into it."

Mike just shook his head and slowly released her hands as he got to his feet. "Nah. You would have. Maybe not tomorrow, but you would have. You had the strength to do it, not me. Seeing as you're a little nervous, want me to drive you?"

"That would be nice."

"Great then. So do you like strawberries and ice cream?" Mike asked.

She was getting used to his abrupt changes of mood and subject. "Sure."

"I got two big boxes of fresh strawberries in there," he said, pointing at the bag he'd placed on the countertop.

"Why don't you get Emily on up here and the two of you can clean them?"

A good, solid frown took hold of her face. "Why do *we* have to clean them?"

"Because I have a number of other tasks to do."

"Right."

"Hey." He raised both hands up high. "Hear me out, will you?"

"Maybe I should put on some boots first." But she laughed, even as she recognized the strong odor of a con job.

"First, I have to go get the ice cream," Mike said. "Second, there's a container of my mother's spaghetti sauce in that bag, so I have to get some pasta. Third, we gotta have a salad. I was gonna put something together at the salad bar. Then, last but not least, I gotta get some wine. A meal without wine is like a day without sunshine."

"You really don't want to clean the strawberries, do you?"

"Angie." His face turned so full of sorrow and pleading that she could hardly keep from laughing. "I want to put together a celebration, and you want to bicker about one little task. Where is the sense of proportion here?"

What a con artist. He could talk her into almost anything. "I'll be glad to clean the berries," Angie said a touch magnanimously.

"Great." He burst into a wide smile that she just had to answer with her own.

Chapter Ten

Mike eyed the parking lot surrounding the Madison Center. The rambling brick structure was in a reasonably safe neighborhood with a hotel and some restaurants nearby. But the cop in him knew that no place in the world was absolutely safe. So while he waited for Angie, his eyes searched and his ears listened for any sound or sight out of the ordinary.

Female voices, laughing and talking, floated out onto the spring night air. He turned toward the front door of the counseling center as a group of women stepped out into the bright light. Angie was among them. Mike walked in their direction.

"Evening, ladies," he said when he was about ten feet away.

All eyes turned toward him. He couldn't really see the expressions on their faces in the streetlight, but the group's body language wasn't anywhere near friendly.

"Oh, it's just Mike," Angie said.

Just Mike?

The women relaxed and resumed their chatting as Angie turned away to meet him, calling out goodbyes to the others. Her step was so light that she seemed to glide across the lot.

"Just Mike?" he asked when she was close enough for him to touch, to feel her smile.

She just took his hand. "Oh, you know."

He did, so he let it go, pleased to feel the strength in her touch. He walked her to his car and opened the passenger's side door.

"How'd it go?"

"Fine."

Fine. It was like talking to Emily. He walked around to the driver's side and got in.

"You seem pretty chipper," he said.

"Yep."

Mike pulled out into the street and then took a right at the stop sign. It wasn't that he was nosy; he just wanted to know where she was emotionally. That way he wouldn't say the wrong thing.

"As scary as you feared?"

"Nope."

She was staring out the window. Not tense or avoiding him, just watching the world in the circles of light from the street lamps. Her profile was so delicate. The anger that rumbled whenever he thought of what she had been through teased at him, but he wouldn't let it surface. He didn't need it now, except as a reminder that there were still questions he wanted her to answer. Questions he couldn't even ask just yet.

"Going again next Thursday?"

She turned to face him then. "We're meeting on Wednesday next week. It's more convenient for most people."

"Oh." He frowned and plowed mentally through his schedule for next week. "I was supposed to speak to the Jackson Middle School PTA on Wednesday, but maybe I can get someone else to do it."

"Why?"

"So I can drive you."

"You really don't have to. I was just nervous about going the first time. I'm okay now."

"I know, but it's dark when you'll be coming home," Mike said. She of all people should understand the need for precautions.

"The parking lot's well-lit, and we all come out together."

"Hey, I still owe you. Emily stays with you almost every day after Lisa drops her off."

"That doesn't mean you need to drive me everyplace for the rest of my life."

His hands tightened on the steering wheel, but he tried to keep his voice calm. "Not everyplace, just to your group sessions when they're at night."

"I need to do it myself." Her voice was rising. Her words were clipped.

"That's crazy," he snapped.

His words, his impatient tone hung in the air for a lifetime and a half. Neither of them spoke as tension crackled in the air. She was mad, but he was right. She needed protection, and he would provide it.

"Mike, let's go someplace and have some coffee or something." Her voice was tired, tense and spoiling for a fight, he feared. She was no longer smiling.

"How about a sundae?"

"Okay."

He made a U-turn and headed east on LaSalle so he could pick up 31 North.

"Isn't that against the law even for a police officer?"

"Not if an emergency requires it." He would make her smile again.

"What kind of emergency do we have?"

"You look like you're in need of a heavy infusion of sweets," Mike said.

"What?"

Whoops. Her frown was definitely in charge. The light was green, and he made a slow, careful turn.

"You said you wanted a sundae," Mike explained.

"You asked me if I wanted a sundae. I said that was fine. How did you jump from that into deciding I had an attitude problem and needed some sweetening?"

"I didn't say you had an attitude problem," Mike insisted and stared at the road in front of him. He hadn't meant anything but a little joke, something to ease the tension from her voice. He was getting addicted to her smile, to that sparkle in her eyes. They rode the rest of the way in a heavy silence.

He pulled into a parking spot in front of Bonnie Doon's where he turned off the ignition. "You want to eat inside or in the car?" he asked.

"Let's sit at a table inside."

They both exited the car and Mike waited for Angie, tentatively holding his arm out to her as if he were testing for rain.

She took his arm, and he relaxed a bit. She probably wasn't really mad at him. She'd have some ice cream, they'd talk, and she'd see how much safer it was for him to drive her. She just wasn't used to having friends to lean on.

"They have great ice cream here," Mike said. "I should take a couple of cartons home for Emily."

They sat in a corner booth. In the bright light Angie looked even tenser than he expected. She needed to relax before they talked.

A waitress came, and Angie ordered a banana split. He asked for a hot-fudge sundae. She paused a moment to savor some of the silence surrounding them, and he was glad. Too much had been happening to her lately. She needed time to get things in order. She needed a friend to help carry the burdens until she did.

"I appreciate your coming to pick me up tonight," Angie said.

"No problem. Like I said, I owe you."

She looked at him a moment. Her eyes were saying something, but he couldn't read their message.

"The thing is, I don't need an armed police officer around me all the time," she said. "I'm not in any danger."

Angie spoke calmly and without any visible tension. That meant only one thing to Mike—that the man who assaulted her didn't live in the area. Most likely, he was back in L.A. It was a step in the right direction.

"It's rough world out there," Mike said.

"It is for everyone else," she replied. "And they get along."

Mike shrugged. "Luck has a lot to do with it."

"I don't want any special favors."

"Hey, you're special to us," Mike said and meant it. "I don't know what Emily would do without you."

"She'd do just fine."

Their orders came, and they ate in silence. Once he finished his, Mike sipped at his water and tried not to openly watch her. A lot of her toughness was just a veneer he knew now. Inside she was a fragile flower—something to cherish, not abuse. He felt the anger returning and looked away.

Finally, Angie finished, pushing her empty dish to one side. She looked at him. Only the faintest of smiles touching her eyes.

"You have to understand, Mike," she said. "For a long time, I hid from the world. Staying in my apartment. Hardly ever going out."

"That's not abnormal." He gently took her hands in his.

She let him hold her hands but carefully held something in her soul distant from him. He felt cheated, then ashamed at himself for the feeling.

"I don't see where hiding behind your back would be any better."

"You're not hiding behind me," he protested.

"I am if I don't do things on my own."

This was crazy, but he knew better now than to tell her that in so many words. "I can't give you rides or help you in any way?"

"You can if I ask you."

"Okay." He shrugged. "Go ahead and ask."

"Mike," she said. "It's my life. I have to be in charge of it. I'm not a little girl."

She wasn't all that big, either, but he didn't say that. She twisted her hands so that they were holding his now.

"I have to be in control," she said. "I won't be healed until I am."

Mike stared down at her little hands, fingers spread wide, trying to cover his big mitts. She was trying to be so strong, to prove that she could handle all the garbage life tossed at her. She just didn't realize yet that she didn't have to face it all alone. He was there to help her.

One thing was certain, though: she'd feel more in control if her attacker was locked up.

"Good job, Emily!" Angie shouted.

Mike watched as his daughter captured the soccer ball from an opposing player, moved it downfield and then passed to a teammate. Unfortunately, the boy didn't move fast enough, and the ball was lost out of bounds. Emily was the last one to touch it, so it would belong to the other team.

The coach shouted words of encouragement to the boy who'd lost the ball but said nothing to Emily. In fact, he quickly substituted a boy for her. Mike glared at the man's back as his daughter trudged off the playing field to the sideline.

"You're supposed to be cheering for your daughter and her team," Angie reminded him.

Mike just grunted, continuing to glare at the coach. The whistle sounded for halftime, and the kids all rushed off the field.

"Boy," Angie said. "You change moods quicker than the weather."

Mike just shrugged.

"Maybe you ought to broadcast a periodic Mike Minelli mood forecast," she said. "Give the rest of us fair warning if a storm's coming up." Her green eyes smiled but brimmed with concern as well.

"Sorry," he growled.

"I forgive you," Angie said. "But you're in deep trouble if you don't dump your grumpies and put your happy face back on."

"Anything to get you to quit your nagging."

But Angie was right. He had been in a good mood when the morning had begun. He'd convinced Angie to go into counseling, and her first meeting had done wonders for her, left her feeling better about herself than she had since he'd met her. He was even willing to let her drive herself to meetings, just so she could gain that sense of control Barb said was so important.

He glared at the soccer field. His good spirits had taken a definite nosedive as the game progressed and he saw how rarely Emily was on the field. Was there no place in the world free of injustice, not even a children's soccer team? That anger deep in his belly was getting to be more than a constant companion; it was more like an old friend, ready to flare up at the first hint of unfairness. He'd set things on course for Angie, and now it looked like he was going to have to do the same for his daughter.

The referee blew his whistle to start the second half. Emily remained on the sidelines.

"All the kids are supposed to play at least half a game," he grumbled.

"That's hard to keep track of. The coach keeps switching them in and out." Angie frowned a moment. "Well, he's switching some of them in and out. There's a nucleus that he keeps on the field."

And that nucleus was all boys. "I think you've broken the man's code," Mike said.

She turned toward him, frowning. "Do you see a plot behind everything a person does?"

"I've been a cop a long time," Mike said.

"Maybe too long?"

In truth, being a cop had nothing to do with it. He'd just been raised on a heavy dose of fair play.

There were about sixteen kids on the team and only three girls. Yet by the time over three quarters of the game had passed, none of the girls had played much. Certainly nowhere near their league-specified half game.

And it wasn't as if it were a close game. Emily's team was five or six goals down. The girls couldn't do any more harm than had already been done. Not even if they were one-legged, blind, and weighed three hundred pounds.

The ball went out of bounds and the referee called a halt in play for substitutions. Mike looked on sourly as Emily and another girl, a tall, strong-looking kid, were put in.

"About time," he growled to himself. But there was no way the girls could get in their half game.

Suddenly, Angie was screaming. "Go, Emily! Go!"

The tall girl was playing the back line and had given the ball a mighty wallop when it came near her. She'd sent it sailing toward the middle of the field where Emily sprinted after it, outrunning everyone on the field. Dancing and dodging like a rabbit through the woods, Emily raced toward the opponents' goal. She sent the ball soaring past the goalie's head and into the back of the net.

"Way to go, Emily!" Mike shouted as she was mobbed by her teammates.

The game was over a few minutes later, and the parents started to straggle across the field to gather their kids.

"I need to talk to Emily's coach," Mike said.

"Not now." Angie had a firm hold on his arm.

Mike looked over at the team. Someone had brought cans of soda pop and the kids were shaking them, spraying everyone within striking distance. The coach was trying to gather up the equipment and stay dry at the same time.

"Yeah," Mike agreed. "Probably a practice day would be better."

"Maybe," Angie replied.

Angie didn't understand. Confrontations were necessary sometimes. "No maybe about it. I'm going to straighten a few things out with that guy." Actually, it felt good to know that action on something was imminent.

"Why don't you wait?" Angie said. "See how things work out."

"You let things go, and they usually go to hell."

"She played well today," Angie said. "She scored her team's only goal. I'm sure she'll play more."

"That's assuming her coach is smart enough to recognize her talent."

"Mike, let her handle it."

He looked away from the intensity of Angie's eyes. She'd been raised in a different way, taught to be submissive and pleasing. Not to rock the boat, he'd bet. But that kind of thinking didn't do anything but invite people to walk all over you. She should see that by now.

People were milling around the field, the kids who had played were leaving and others were arriving for the next game. Emily was coming toward them with a group of friends.

"Emily needs my help. She's just a kid," Mike said.

"So give her help, in the form of advice. But let her do as much as she can herself."

"I can settle things in a few minutes," Mike insisted.

"Yes, you can," Angie agreed. "But what is she going to do when she runs into a problem and you're not there to take care of it?"

Mike just answered with a glare. The last thing he wanted to hear was that he would someday fail those he cared about, even if it was inevitable with kids who would outlive you. Right now, though, he wasn't going to sit back.

Emily threw herself into his arms. "Hi, Mike! Did you see my goal?"

"Sure did, kid!" Mike put his arm around her shoulders. "A hundred times."

"Huh?"

Emily looked quizzically at him while he watched her coach getting into his car. Angie was partly right; he should take care of things later.

"Let's go, kid."

He followed Angie and Emily, his two ladies, to the car. No matter what anyone said, he wasn't letting anyone hurt either of them again.

Angie stewed all afternoon over Mike's protective attitude toward Emily. In her session on Thursday, they'd talked about control, how all people need to be in control of their own lives. Did that extend to young girls with soccer coaches or did one only get the right to control one's life when one reached a certain age?

Emily was staying overnight at a friend's house, so Angie and Mike went down to Middlebury for dinner. They had an hour's drive down to the Amish town and another pleasant hour while they ate, but Angie still couldn't find the words to express her concerns to Mike. As he paid the check, she worried that she was going to be wimpish and afraid of confrontation. She vowed to fight for Emily's right of control. As they left the restaurant, she told herself it was now or never.

"Oh, my," she said. "I'm stuffed. I don't think I'll ever walk again."

Mike paused to hold the door open for an elderly couple just coming into the restaurant; then he stepped over to her side.

"What do you mean you'll never walk again?" he asked. "What are you doing now?"

Angie smiled. "I'm waddling. You know, like a fat little duck."

"I don't think you'll ever make it as a duck," Mike said.

"Oh, darn."

"Yeah, you'll never be able to play Donald."

He smiled down at her, a broad, male smile of appreciation. Rather than shrink from it, she felt a warm glow spread through her body, a pleasant, womanly kind of glow. It was the hint of a fire starting, the rekindling of ashes she'd thought long dead. She was starting to find trust. Healing was coming; she just had to be patient.

She slipped her arm through Mike's. "Donald's a guy duck," Angie said. "I was thinking I looked more like Daisy Duck."

"Donald. Daisy. What's the difference? One duck looks like another to me."

"Daisy has a ribbon on her head," Angie reminded him.

"Ah, that makes it all so clear."

They crossed the parking lot. A breeze wafted over the open fields around the restaurant, carrying the smells of newly turned earth and manure. There was something good here, something strong and real. She could fight all sorts of battles here and win.

They got to Mike's car, but he made no move to unlock the door. He faced her, looking deep into her eyes. Then, just as naturally as green followed the rain, she leaned into him. He kissed her lightly, and she kissed him in return.

There was strength in the touch of his lips, strength that gave her courage and healing. She could enjoy a man's touch and not feel afraid. Better yet, she could feel joy and life. They pulled back, acting as if they were one, and Angie basked in the warmth of Mike's gentle smile.

"Can we stay here a little longer?" she asked.

"Sure."

He took her hand, and they wandered toward the complex of shops. They went into the clothing store first. Though tourists were the obvious market, the store sold only traditional Amish clothing. Angie paused to look at a mannequin dressed like a little Amish girl with a long dress and bonnet.

"I wonder if Emily would like being an Amish girl?"

"She'd go for the barefoot summers and the farm animals," he replied. "But she'd draw the line at the long dresses and bonnets. I can't get her to wear any kind of dress."

"I guess most of us are like that," Angie said. "We'd like to pick and choose bits out of what life serves us."

"This is getting deep," he said.

"Don't you know how to swim?"

He just laughed and followed her down the main aisle. The women's dresses were all somber, solid colors and plain styles. The girls' dresses were exact miniatures of the women's. Serviceable clothing, but nothing to appeal to the needs of the soul. Just as the baggy, dull clothing Angie had been wearing for the past year didn't appeal to her soul. She needed colors and styles. She needed to feel like a woman again.

"I'd really like to get something for Emily," she said. The next rack displayed aprons, all white and in a variety of lengths. Definitely not Emily material.

"Get a hold of her mother," Mike growled.

"You'd better stop talking like that," Angie scolded. "Emily will start thinking that you don't want her."

His face assumed the grim set of the police officer. "Girls should grow up with mothers and boys with fathers," Mike said. "The Amish have real close families and that's how they do it. The mothers teach the girls and the fathers teach the boys."

"The Amish also have a very rigid society," Angie replied. "They're old-fashioned in what they allow girls to do. Would you like Emily to grow up in that kind of environment?"

He made a face without replying.

"Would you like to have grown up in that kind of society?"

"You really know how to fight dirty," he said.

She passed by the counter of shawls and the rack of men's black suits. "Actually, the kids in traditional Amish families grow up with a mother and a father in the home. That's not possible in your case, so I think what's happening to Emily now is the next best thing. A little time with her mother and a little time with her father."

"Boy," he said. "For a young kid, you certainly sound all wise."

"I grew up without a father," Angie pointed out. "So I think it's wonderful that Emily has a chance to stay with you, and I know that she agrees with me."

She stopped at a display of bonnets. Some had lace trim and others were plain. This was a life of rules and regulations, of strict do's and don'ts. Would she have been protected in such a society? Only if everyone obeyed the rules. But that held true for all societies.

Mike looked at her and sighed. "Remind me not to ever argue with you once you've made up your mind."

"Just don't argue with me when I'm right."

"And how will I know when that is?"

She just gave him a look.

"How about if I assume you're always right?" he asked.

She threw her arms around his waist. "Okay by me, pal."

"I thought so," he murmured as he leaned down to kiss her.

The kiss was a tad longer than the last one. Actually, a big tad, but she didn't care. She liked being in his arms. She liked the feel of his body next to hers. She felt alive and whole and ready to take on...some challenges.

They left the clothing store and wandered into the gift shop next door. The walls were covered with grapevine wreaths, embroidered sayings and painted wooden cutouts. The row of dolls near the back wall drew her attention. She picked one up that had Emily's dark hair and eyes.

"Emily doesn't play with dolls much, does she?" Angie asked.

"Nope. She's more into rough-and-tumble-type activities. A set of Amish boxing gloves might be more her style."

Angie put the doll back down and turned to face him. "If that's her style, then why won't you let her fight her own battles?"

Her question seemed to take him by surprise. "Who said I'm not?"

"I know you," she said. "You want to slay everyone's dragons for them."

His eyes darkened. "Maybe I'm good at that."

"Maybe you are, but the one thing I'm learning is that it's wrong to lean on someone because they're good at the things we're not."

His mouth was tight. A full-fledged storm was approaching. "For God's sake, I'm her father. I'm supposed to take care of her."

"You're supposed to teach her to take care of herself."

He sighed, long and hard. "Is this one of those impossible situations where I can't win?"

"You can win, and so can Emily, if you'd just give in a little."

Angie turned down a side aisle and found a display of handmade stuffed animals. One was a dog, big and brown and wonderful.

"Look, it's Fudge!" she cried. "I have to get this for Emily."

"Check to see if it's got teeth first. I want to know what I'm letting myself in for."

"Trouble probably," she said as she carried the dog to the counter.

"No doubt about that."

Darkness had fallen more thickly across the farmland when they got outside. There was a distinct chill in the air. Angie moved closer to Mike, taking not only his hand but warmth from his body.

"I didn't mean to make you mad," she said. "I just wanted you to understand."

He brought her hand up to his mouth, brushing her fingers lightly with his lips. She no longer felt any chill, just the sweet, wonderful warmth of being a woman.

"I understand that I'm with a very special lady," he said.

"That's a start, I guess."

He slipped his arm around her shoulders, and she snuggled into his embrace. The night seemed a blanket of protection, a cocoon of safety.

"A good start?" he asked, whispering the words into her lips.

"A very good start."

She let his mouth take hers, and the stars seemed to dance in the heavens.

Chapter Eleven

Mike sat outside the small office building, his left elbow leaning out the open car window as he tapped his fingers on the door. Mr. Soccer Coach worked in the building up ahead.

It wasn't that Mike was ignoring Angie's advice; she just didn't understand. Sometimes a man had to take charge. That anger demanded it; justice agreed. All he needed to do was decide on his approach.

As he sat there, pondering his course of action, the subject himself stepped out. He had his briefcase in hand as he hurried to his car.

"Nuts," Mike murmured. Now what?

The man fastened his seat belt, like a perfect citizen, then backed up his car before pulling forward into the street. A broad smile split Mike's face; the coach's left brake light was out.

Mike stuck his portable beacon on his roof and pulled out after him. The man slowed his car, pulled over to stop and turned on his flashing hazard lights. Mike got out of the car to approach him.

"Good morning, sir," Mike said to the man. "Your left brake light is out. Could I see your driver's license?"

Mike feigned surprise when he saw the man's name. "Barry Sommerset! I think you're my daughter's soccer coach." Mike stuck his hand out. "I'm Mike Minelli. Lieutenant Minelli."

"Minelli?" He carefully shook Mike's hand, his grip light and furtive like a bird ready to dart.

"Emily's father."

"Oh." His head bobbed, a hopeful smile flickering uncertainly on his lips. "Pleased to meet you."

Mike nodded, letting the silence hang in the air. The coach cleared his throat, obviously uncomfortable.

"You know, I'm glad to have this chance to meet you, Barry," Mike said. "'Cause I'm an old-fashioned kind of guy. And you know what an old-fashioned kind of guy wants most of all?" Mike paused. "Fairness, Barry. Fairness."

"Fairness?"

"Like in fair and equal. Equal opportunity. That kind of thing."

Barry swallowed hard. He wasn't slow about catching on.

"The game sort of got out of hand for me," Barry started to explain; then the words tumbled out. "I mean, I've played the game before. You know, high school, college, that kind of thing. But this is my first time coaching. And especially coaching nine- and ten-year-olds."

Barry wet his lips. "I know that all kids are supposed to play at least half a game, and they will. I promise."

Mike continued watching him.

"I mean, your daughter will play more than a half game next Saturday."

"Only if she's earned it," Mike said softly.

"Hey, she scored a goal!"

"Yeah."

"I mean, like, our only goal."

"Yeah."

"I mean, she'll definitely play more. From now on, she'll be right up there."

"None of the girls played their fair share," Mike pointed out.

Barry shrugged. "The nine- and ten-year-old teams are coed," he said. "Next year, those girls will be playing on all-girls teams. I was just concentrating on kids who'll be with me next year."

"If the word gets out that you're not a fair coach, none of them will be with you next year."

The coach nodded, looking like he'd tried to swallow a watermelon whole.

"You got any girls, Barry?"

He shook his head. "No. I just have the one boy."

"Treat them fair, Barry. No better, no worse than anyone else. Just fair." Mike stuck his hand out again. "Nice meeting you, Barry."

"Yeah, Lieutenant." Barry gripped Mike's hand and shook it vigorously. "Nice. Real nice."

Mike took a step back from the car and nodded toward the back end. "Better get that brake light replaced," he said. "Some other cop sees that, he might give you a ticket."

"Thanks, Lieutenant. I'll take care of it right away. I mean, like immediately."

He started his engine, then called to Mike. "See you Saturday, Lieutenant?"

"I'm not planning on missing a single game, Barry."

"Great," Barry said. His lips almost made it to a smile. "The kids appreciate that kind of support."

Mike went back to his own car and watched as Barry drove down to the end of the block and turned into the service station there. Mike congratulated himself. He'd straightened things out with Emily's coach. There'd be no repeats of the injustice; he'd gotten her a level playing field. The anger had subsided again.

Now it was time to get back to work on Angie's problem.

Mike pressed the bell, then stepped back as the roar of the devil puppy rattled the door. It quickly opened.

"Hi, Mike."

His smile stayed on with no effort, almost as if it had a life of its own. She was wearing jeans, as usual, but she had on a green blouse that seemed to cling to her lovely curves.

"Anything I can do for you?" she asked.

Any number of suggestions came to mind, but he brushed them aside. She was smiling. She looked happy. That was enough for him, for now.

"I wondered if you wanted to go play some tennis. I just dropped Emily off at soccer practice."

"Did you talk to her about talking to her coach?"

Mike shook his head. "Nah, I just thought we'd wait and see how the next few games go."

"I think that's a good idea. I'm sure the last thing the coach needs is another pushy parent complaining about their child's playing time."

"Yeah, I'm sure that's the case."

They stood in the doorway, as if frozen. She looked so great, so womanly. He wanted to feel her in his arms, to feel her softness pressed against his steel. It was a need as old as time, yet felt as fresh and strong as if it had never been felt before.

A movement made Mike's eyes drop. The dog was next to Angie and was either smiling or showing off its big teeth. It's okay, he silently told the dog. We're on the same side.

Mike smiled at Angie. "I got a present for Fudge."

"Oh?" Angie bent down and petted the beast. "Did you hear that, Fudge? Mike brought you a present. Isn't that nice of him?"

Fudge didn't verbalize, but Mike was sure that the dog's eyes said that all depended on what the present was.

"It's a mammoth chew bar." Mike pulled it out of his grocery bag. "Over a foot long. Something that would fit his giant mouth."

"Oh, wow." Angie ruffled the dog's ears. "Fudge says thank you."

Mike and the dog stared at each other; then he held out his offering and held his breath. The beast's jaws locked around the rawhide toy. It had been the largest chew toy in the store, and it looked small in Fudge's mouth.

"Why don't you come in?" Angie asked. "I have to run over to the next unit and replace a light bulb, but I'll be back in a minute and then we could go."

Mike and Fudge stared at each other. Man and beast. Mike was proud that he didn't break into a sweat. "Sure," he replied. "Glad to."

"It'll give you two a chance to get acquainted," Angie said before grabbing a light-bulb box and slipping out the door behind him.

Mike and the beast were together, locked in a small apartment entryway. He took a few deep breaths until he was sure he had the hang of it.

"You and me ought to be buddies," he told the dog.

Skeptical didn't being to describe the look on the beast's face.

"I mean it," Mike insisted. "We both take care of our women. You gotta admit that Angie's been feeling a lot more cheerful lately, and I'd bet my last dollar that Emily's going to play more."

The dog seemed to ponder Mike's words for a moment. Then the beast gave a grunt and went into the kitchen, where it flopped down and began to do serious harm to the chew bar. Mike followed it into the kitchen and sat down.

"Although we do have some unfinished business, pal."

Fudge paused and looked knowingly at Mike.

"Yeah, the bastard who hurt Angie is still walking free and easy."

A growl echoed in the huge throat and escaped out around the chew toy.

"I agree, big guy. That ain't right."

Fudge grunted agreement.

"We're going to fix that." Mike sat and listened to the dog's chewing. "But first I have to get a name."

"Hey, Al."

Angie hung back while Mike approached the man standing on the edge of the tennis courts. He was probably the manager of the Leeper Park courts. Mike seemed to know everybody in this town.

"Any chance of a court opening up?"

"Yeah," Al replied. "Another fifteen minutes and this high-school team will be off."

Mike's face seemed to fall as he nodded. Poor guy, Angie thought. He just wanted everything to be perfect for the people he thought he was responsible for. She certainly wasn't disappointed that they had to wait. Heck, they'd decided on this tennis date on the spur of the moment.

"I imagine you heard what Al said?" Mike asked as he came back to her.

She nodded. "A fifteen-minute wait is nothing. In L.A., you had to plan something like this days in advance."

He shrugged, obviously still not pleased with himself. Angie felt like mussing up his hair and giving him something real to worry about. Amazing how much more comfortable she was with touching him after only two sessions with her group. She wasn't whole by any means, but the fear that she never would be was gone.

"Do you want to wait in here or out in the park?" he asked.

"Isn't there a duck pond here?" Angie asked. "I thought you could see it when you drive by on Michigan Street."

"Yeah, there is." His face brightened a little. "I even have some old bread in the car. I keep planning to bring Emily over here but with school and soccer practice and sleepovers at friends and relatives, we haven't gotten around to it yet."

A flicker of guilt dashed across his face. Angie took his hand as they walked back to the car. He was going to tear himself apart trying to do everything for everybody.

He'd had suffered major trauma last night when she drove herself to her counseling session. There were four messages from him on her answering machine when she got home, all checking to see if she'd made it back safely. She was surprised he hadn't followed her to the Madison Center and then home again.

"I promise not to tell Emily that you took me to the duck pond first," Angie said.

"You're a real smarty-pants, aren't you?"

"The rest of me isn't too dumb, either," Angie replied. Then a frown settled on her forehead. "Except when it comes to math."

"Hey," Mike said. "Everyone has their strong points and their not so strong points."

"I'm not going to be much of a financial planner if I don't do better in my math courses."

"There are other professions out there," he replied.

She made a face. "I probably should be home studying right now," she said. "I'm in the middle of finals."

"I'll make you a deal," he said. "You help me feed the ducks, and I'll help you study tonight."

"Okay."

They left their rackets in the car and got a plastic bag full of bread crusts out of the backseat; then they followed the curving walkway to an enclosed duck pond down by the river's edge.

Her hand fit so easily and naturally into his. She felt almost a part of him. Actually, what she felt like around him was a woman, all woman. That warm, delicious tightness of desire seemed like magic to her. And it was all due to him— to his pushing her to start counseling and to those strong muscles that could hold her so wonderfully.

"You're awfully quiet today," he said, suddenly interrupting her thoughts.

"Am I? It's a good quiet, if I am," she said. "A relaxed quiet."

"So long as you're not quietly plotting against me."

"Not plotting, not brooding, not anything. Just vegging out a little." She slid her arm through his and leaned in close as they walked along, savoring the unseasonably warm day.

Actually, she didn't know where people got off calling the weather unseasonable. The Midwest tends to be conservative in many things, but anything goes when it comes to weather. It doesn't matter what the forecast is, you can't be sure what the weather will be like until it comes.

Angie looked up into Mike's face which, as usual, was wearing the stern mask of a police officer, his dark eyes scanning the landscape before them. He was a lot like his midwestern weather. You knew there was a solid foundation of old-fashioned values within him; you just never knew which emotions would bubble to the surface on any given day.

Even his mood swings were becoming less and less of a problem for her. She rather enjoyed the challenge of reading his tempers and responding to them. It added a certain spice to their relationship. Not quite full of the richness of a complete man-woman relationship, but it was getting there.

The ducks and geese rushed over to the fence as they neared the enclosure, demanding to be fed. Some days she felt just like them, rushing forward, demanding to be complete again. Up until recently, though, there was nobody who listened and knew what she was saying. Not until Mike.

He handed her the bag of bread crusts. "Want to feed these guys?"

She did, but first she stepped in front of him and stood on her tiptoes to kiss him. Her touch was anything but gentle. It reflected the hungers that had been buried for a year, the relief she felt as her fears ebbed and the joy she felt in being a woman.

When she pulled back, Mike looked puzzled. "What was that for?" he asked.

For tenderness. For understanding. For everything. "For nothing." She forced a fierce tone into her voice. "So don't try anything funny or else you'll be in real trouble."

"Is that a threat or a promise?"

She was still standing close, leaning into him. Her hand went up and smoothed the hair on the back of his head. Her memory of their previous disaster, her common sense, and the prevailing wisdom of her support group all cautioned her not to rush anything, but there were times when she felt she was getting closer.

"One of these days we may just find out," she murmured.

Mike's eyes burned with an answering fire, but he just sighed as the ducks raised an unholy din. "Let's feed these guys before we go deaf," Mike said, his voice definitely husky.

Angie reluctantly disengaged herself. "Yeah."

They leaned on the fence, tearing the bread and throwing the pieces in a wide range around them so that all the ducks had a fair chance at the food. Even though she wasn't looking at him, the air around them seemed to sizzle with unspoken desire.

"How are you adjusting to our little town on the banks of the old St. Joe?" Mike asked.

She threw a handful of bread over toward her right as far as she could. "There are times when I miss the unending sunshine, but otherwise, I have no complaints. It's a quiet little town. The people are nice. I'm glad I came."

"I'm glad you came, too."

"Oh, yeah?"

"Absolutely," he replied. "If it wasn't for you, I might never have met Fudge. And then I would never have known real fear."

"I thought you guys were getting to be friends!"

"Sort of."

"Just sort of?"

"I'm trying to do everything he tells me, but I don't always understand him. In fact, except for a few basic growls, I really don't understand anything he says."

Mike looked so serious that, if it wasn't for the subject, Angie would have thought that his communication problems with Fudge were uppermost in his mind.

"Maybe I should get you an English-Doggie dictionary," she said.

"I'd appreciate that."

The bread was all gone, and they stared out at the pond before them, standing close and holding hands. A few of the web-footed tenants were hollering for more, but most had given up and, grumbling, were moving away. The sun was warm on her face, and Angie felt safe and secure, wrapped in the coziness of her world.

"Although we do talk about some things."

Mike's words startled Angie out of her pleasant daydream. "What things? What are you talking about?"

"Me and Fudge," he replied. "I'm talking about the conversations we have."

"Oh?" Angie looked suspiciously at him. She wondered what sort humorous remark would fall from his lips this time, but he didn't say anything. Apparently he was waiting for some kind of lead into his punch line. "You want to tell me what kind of conversations you're having with my dog?"

He shrugged and pretended to watch the ducks, apparently gathering his thoughts. "Well, we both agreed that we're going to take care of you," he finally said.

"I'm not a little girl," Angie reminded him.

"I know, but everyone can use a little help. Our police procedures insist that an officer always call for backup, no matter how innocuous the situation he's investigating may look. And that's talking about armed and trained personnel. Not a plain-vanilla civilian."

"Well." She slid her arms around his waist. "First, let me, as a plain-vanilla civilian, express my appreciation to you and Fudge for your concern."

"Accepted."

Angie gave him a quick kiss and sighed to herself. He looked so serious. "But let me emphasize that I'm just fine."

"No more nightmares?"

"None." And there hadn't been any recently, even if her stomach did tighten at the mere thought. She was focusing on the positive future she was building and not the dark happenings of the past.

"I'm fine," she said. "Things are coming together just fine."

"Fudge told me that he'd really like to know who assaulted you."

The words took Angie by surprise. She looked up into Mike's face; there was a hardness there. His eyes were cold and staring off at some distant villain.

"Fudge said if he knew, he'd make sure you never had a reason for any bad dreams ever again." Mike finally met her eyes. He quickly went on to explain: "He said that he'd make sure that this guy didn't come near you."

The whole subject made Angie uneasy, like finding a spider in the back of a cabinet she'd reached into hundreds of times. "I can't imagine him ever coming to South Bend," she said slowly. "But if he does and if any problems come up, which I have a hard time visualizing, I'll take care of things."

Mike didn't blink, and his eyes held an icy hardness. It might not be enough that her own attitude was changing. He also had to understand that she was looking forward to a positive future. Focusing on problems in the past would just hinder her own development.

"Come on," Angie said, reaching up to muss his thick, dark hair. "Those high schoolers should be off the court by now. Let's go so I can get started on beating you. I mean, like totally destroying you."

"Boy," he said. "I used to think it was Fudge! Now I can see that you're the mean one of the family."

"You better believe it, buddy." Relieved that he'd dropped the subject, she stretched up to kiss him again. "Care to make any side bets?"

"My mother doesn't want me to gamble," he replied.

"'Fraidy cat!" she sang. "Mike Minelli is a great big fraidy cat!"

Mike sighed and shook his head. "This is a rough world. Nice guys not only finish last, they get stomped into the ground."

"Don't worry, Mikey," Angie said. "I'll take care of you."

It was a challenge, but she'd keep him focused on the positive track.

"Define iamb."

Angie groaned and sank lower into the sofa. "I don't wanna."

Mike couldn't help but smile. She sounded just like Emily had about two hours earlier when he'd told her to go to bed. Emily had been determined to stay up to help Angie study for her "Introduction to Poetry" test and had required a slightly raised voice on Mike's part to convince her to go to bed. There would be no raised voices for Angie, though.

"Come on—iamb," he repeated. "After that, we've only got three more definitions."

"I'm tired. It's past my bedtime."

It was hard—Herculean, in fact—but Mike ignored the opening she'd presented him. "Hey, I promised I'd help you study, and we're going to. You're not going to be able to blame a bad grade on the fact that we played tennis this afternoon."

She gave him a look that was no doubt intended to wither his soul, except that her eyes were laughing. "Iamb. A metrical foot in which a stressed syllable follows an unstressed one."

"Very good. Now how about trochee?"

Her sigh must have come from the very depths of her soul. She looked so delicious half lying there on his sofa. She was tired, quite obviously, and seemed to have let go of all her fears and tensions. The more she relaxed, though, the less relaxing he found the situation.

At times like this, it was hard to remember that she was still hurting deep inside. Her eyes held only wonder and laughter, no shadows. Her lips were moist and tempting. There was a very good reason for him to sit in the recliner on the other side of the room.

"Trochee," he repeated.

"Do you know how useless this information is?" she asked. "Has any arrest you ever made been dependent on knowing the definition of trochee? Not unless you're arresting people for bad poetry."

"I think you're stalling."

She lay back and closed her eyes with a groan. "Trochee. A two-syllable foot consisting of an accented syllable followed by an unaccented."

"Anapest."

"How about Mike's-a-pest?"

"Do your teachers know about your bad attitude?"

"Of course not. I use my acting ability to fool them."

"Use your acting ability now and pretend you know these definitions."

She made a face at him. "Anapest. A three-syllable foot consisting of two unaccented syllables followed by an accented one. And then dactyl, a reverse anapest. So there, meanie."

He allowed her a moment to gloat as he closed the notebook. "Anything else you need to review?"

"Are you kidding?" She got to her feet slowly. "I know everything there is to know after this evening."

There were things she didn't know about him, about the ways he could make her feel and the joys that he could bring her. But this wasn't the time to show her.

She was picking up her books and papers that were scattered across the sofa. In a few minutes she'd leave, and he'd be missing her.

"Want something to eat? I've got some cold ravioli."

She paused in her gathering to glance at him over her shoulder. "My, that's tempting."

"How about some coffee?"

"I want to sleep tonight. Soon tonight." She got down on her hands and knees. "Now where's my pen?"

He came over to help her, feeling between the sofa cushions. He found twenty-eight cents, one of Emily's barrettes and a TV-listings book from three weeks ago. No pen, though.

"Maybe it fell under the sofa."

He reached under the sofa at the same time she did, and their hands met. He sensed rather than saw a flash of hesitation on her part, but he didn't want to lose his chance to touch her.

"Look, a hand!" he cried suddenly, pulling hers out, then feigned surprise that it was attached to her. "Hey, is this yours?"

She started to laugh. "Yes, I think so."

"Jeez, and you didn't even notice it was lost?" He shook his head, all the while still holding her hand. "I don't know, lady. You'd probably lose your head if it wasn't attached."

"Sometimes I think I have," she said, but there was more sadness in her voice than laughter.

He didn't know what to do, what move he could make that would keep her at his side, but she did all the deciding. She took her hand from his and turned so that her back was against the sofa. Since she was resting slightly against him, he chose to gamble. He leaned against the sofa, too, sliding his arm around her shoulders. Rather than move away, she leaned against him with a sigh.

He closed his eyes and savored his moment in heaven. She smelled so good, like springtime. There was a warmth about her that made him think of the sun, and her gentle fragrance was like apple blossoms. He could almost hear the birds in her voice.

"I didn't know how I could face you again after acting so weird the other night," she said.

It would have belittled her suffering to pretend to misunderstand, but neither did he want her to dwell on it. "You're not the first person to do something embarrassing."

"'Embarrassing' is putting it mildly. My God, I pulled half your clothes off!"

"Hey, that was okay by me." He waved his free hand at his body. "In fact, you can do it every day for a month until it gets to be ho-hum. Not that I really want a beautiful woman to think my body is ho-hum."

She just laughed and laid her head on his shoulder. "And I took all my clothes off. I hardly know you and I stripped in front of you."

"I didn't look. Honest. I told you I was raised to be a gentleman. I had my eyes closed the whole time."

"Right."

She lay silent against him. The air turned thoughtful, and with that change came tension—but it wasn't a good kind. He tightened his hold on her slightly and reached down to brush the top of her head with his lips.

"When we're hurting, we all do things we'd rather not admit to later. I guess it's just part of being human. You have to accept yourself as you are and go on."

"I can't imagine you ever acting so dumb."

"Oh, no? How about trying to leap over that fence when I hurt my knee? Or for the next week when I acted like a super-macho stud to make up for the crutches I had to use?"

"Okay."

He laughed. "Hey, you were supposed to argue a little! Make some excuses for me."

"Well, you were chasing a would-be robber."

"That's better."

"And as for your super-macho-stud act, you are male."

"Whoa! That hurt."

She pulled away from him so that she was on her knees, facing him. "Aw, did I hurt your itty bitty wittle feelings?" she cooed, pinching his cheek exactly the way his grandmother used to when he was seven.

"As a matter of fact, you did."

But there was no way he could even pretend to be upset. The laughter in her eyes was so welcome. She looked alive and lively, all woman, with no more shadows than the next person.

Their laughter died at the same moment, and she moved slowly into his arms. He held her gently, as if he were afraid she would break. She slid her arms around his neck, and his heart felt glad. She was holding him just as he was embracing her.

As if by magic, his lips met hers and tasted all the sweetness in the world. She was honey and nectar. She was a drug he could become addicted to. She was the air he breathed and the sun that warmed his heart.

His hands slid over her back, pulling her into himself as if to prove they were truly one. The sweetness of her touch changed to fire. His hands felt burning, but he had to explore, had to feel her softness. She seemed to come alive in his arms, and something inside him grew until it wanted to explode.

Then he sensed something. Almost as quick as the blink of an eye, he felt it. A flicker of hesitation. He might have thought she was trying to catch her breath, but he knew better and slowly pulled himself back. His own breathing was raw and ragged.

She frowned at him. "What?"

"What what?" he repeated with a gentle smile that belied the pounding of his heart. He brushed the hair back from her face and found the strength to give her a light kiss on her forehead. A blessing that would keep the nightmares away.

"Don't you want to...."

"I want to very much," he said. "But we're not. Not tonight."

"Why not then?" She looked away, her cheeks flushed. "Was I coming on too—"

"You weren't anything but wonderful," he said, knowing just what she meant. "We're just going to go slow this time. If we both want it, it'll happen."

"But I want to now."

He smiled and got to his feet, then took her hand and pulled her to hers. "On a school night? What are you thinking of, young lady? You have exams tomorrow, and I expect you to get a good night's sleep."

"You could help me sleep better, you know."

"And this way, I probably won't sleep at all, so get out of here before I change my mind."

She grinned, and it almost broke his heart. She was such a rare person with her mixture of vulnerability and toughness. "Yes, sir." She grabbed up her books and headed for the door, peeking back at him. "'Night, Mikey."

"'Night, Angel."

But she had already gone. He closed his eyes and tried to let the tension, the desire flow from him. It would be a long night. Good thing the shower was fixed. He just hoped the city had enough cold water in its system.

Chapter Twelve

"We shoulda beat them bums."

Mike looked into the rearview mirror at his daughter slumped down in the backseat of his car. She'd played about three quarters of the game today and had played well, but her team had still lost by a goal. They needed more time to gell together as a unit.

"Don't call the other team bums," Mike told Emily. "Because then it doesn't matter how you do against them. You can beat them ten to nothing and it still doesn't mean anything because they're just bums."

"It's the coach's fault," Emily grumbled. "He let Larry Kingsley play too much."

"Everybody has to play at least half a game," Angie pointed out.

"I guess." Emily slumped over Fudge and gave up the discussion.

Mike looked over at Angie and smiled. She inched closer, taking his hand that rested on the seat between them and holding it. With each and every day, she seemed stronger. And as she grew stronger, so did his hunger for her.

"Whatcha guys doing?"

Both jerked their hands away from each other, and Angie bounced toward the passenger door. Emily fell back in her seat, shrieking with laughter.

"You do that again," Angie said, "and Fudge won't play ball with you."

"Yes, he will," Emily argued. "We're buddies."

"Not if I tell him you weren't behaving."

"He wouldn't believe you."

Mike took a deep breath and concentrated on the traffic. Angie was stronger and more confident and, best of all, more fun to be around. They made their way to the Knights of Columbus parking lot.

He parked the car and waited while Angie put Fudge on a leash. Then, with Emily bouncing ahead of them, they walked across Leeper Park toward the river.

The park was bursting into spring. The grass was a warm, moist green and beds of spring flowers scented the air. It made a person believe in new beginnings, in rebirths. Fudge was too busy investigating the smells around them to pay any attention to Mike, so Mike was free to concentrate on Angie, holding her hand and dreaming of being reborn in her arms.

"Neato!" Emily exclaimed. "Look at all those crazy boats."

They'd gotten near enough to the river to look down on its wild collection of crafts. There were decorated canoes and rowboats, but the rafts were the most fun. People had built castles on them, spaceships, and even a basketball court that dragged a Michael Jordan look-alike in a recliner on his own miniraft. Emily ran down to get a closer look.

"They have this race every year?" Angie asked.

"Yeah," Mike replied. "The River Run is an annual event held every May."

A large sign was strung across the park drive, listing all the events and starting times. Angie stopped to read it.

"They have a father-daughter canoe race," she said. "You and Emily should enter."

"I don't want to leave you here all by yourself," Mike said.

"Mike. I'll be all right. This park is filled with people."

Mike clenched his teeth. Emily had come running back to hear the end of the exchange.

"Fudge doesn't want to stay here, either," Emily said. "He wants to go for a ride."

"He doesn't paddle very well," Angie said.

"Can't he do the dog paddle?" Emily asked.

Angie laughed. "I don't know. I've never seen him in water."

Mike just frowned and stared off at the river. It would be fun to take Emily canoeing, but he didn't like leaving Angie alone. And it had nothing to do with safety or security. It had to do with those green eyes that could light a fire in him anytime she chose, the way her laughter could imprison him. He wished he'd made a raft. Then they could all go. Suddenly, his eyes lit on the last listing on the schedule.

"Hey! We can all go. We'll enter the four-person canoe race," he said.

"There's only three of us," Angie pointed out.

"No, we have four," Mike said. "You, me, Emily and Fudge."

"Yeah, Fudge is our fourth person," Emily agreed.

"He's not a person," Angie argued. "He's all covered with fur."

"Not any more than that guy," Mike said, pointing to a shirtless man well-covered in body hair.

"Fudge doesn't talk," Angie said.

"He talks," Emily insisted. "He just doesn't talk English."

"That's right," Mike said. "We can't discriminate against him for not speaking English. He could sue us."

Angie looked exasperated. "I don't want him in the river without a life jacket."

Mike made a face. Damn. She was right, something could happen. But now that he'd found a way for all of them to go, he wasn't going to give up. A wide smile split his face a he saw a police car parked over to one side of the park.

"What if I get him a life jacket?" he asked.

Angie rolled her eyes. "You get him a dog's life jacke and we'll go."

Mike took off at a trot toward Corporal Willie Snider an his canine partner Dieter. As it turned out, Corporal Snide had two doggie life jackets in his car and was happy to len one to Mike. All Mike had to do was promise dinner for tw at Tippecanoe Place.

Emily hopped up and down for joy when he returned wit his prize and Angie's eyes sparkled. The canine life jacke was worth the hundred-plus dollars it would cost him ju to see that look of laughter in her eyes.

Two reserve police officers were managing the fou person canoe race. They gave Fudge and his outfit a strang look when the four of them presented themselves for a ca noe, but neither objected to the dog. Angie, Mike and Em ily secured their own life jackets and shoved off into th river.

Mike had positioned himself in the stern of the canoe Angie in the bow, and Emily and Fudge in the middle.

"I don't know about this," Angie said as the cano rocked slightly.

"It's great," Mike called to her. "Fudge loves it."

As if in answer, the dog turned around to give him th eye. Mike just grinned at the beast.

"Look, Fudgey, there's ducks." Emily poked at the do as she pointed. Two ducks were swimming placidly near th shore. They disappeared in and out of the low-hangin shrubbery.

"I hope he's not part bird dog," Mike said, bracing him self for Fudge's expected outburst, but it never came. Th dog watched the ducks but sat as still as a statue.

"He's been taught manners," Angie pointed out.

"Wonderful things, manners," Mike said. "Maybe w should spend most of our time in a canoe."

They passed the ducks, and he relaxed. It was pleasant o the river, the current carrying them without much need fo paddling. Faint noises of the hustle and bustle of town wafted down to them, but they were easily ignored. There was no stress, no fears, nothing threatening. Just the cool river scents carried on the breeze.

They passed under the Angela Boulevard Bridge and then the old railroad trestle. Some kids were fishing from the concrete pilings and waved to them. Or waved to Fudge, more accurately, laughing at the sight of the big dog in his life jacket.

"I think Fudge looks cute in his life jacket," Emily said, her hackles up with her buddy under attack.

"I don't think they were laughing in a mean way," Angie said. "There just aren't too many dogs out here."

Even Angie's voice sounded slower, less intense. She was feeling it, too, feeling the river drain away worries and stress. Mike watched her. She paddled occasionally, but more often than not, she just sat there, soaking up the tranquillity.

Since it was a timed race, they had no competitors nearby, and Mike was just as glad. Who cared if they came in first or last? The peace out here was too precious to give up quickly. If this was what Angie needed to feel safe again, then they'd stay out here for days.

"Turtles, Fudge," Emily cried and pointed to two little turtles climbing the steep bank. "Aren't they cute? This is the neatest ride, isn't it, Angie?"

Fudge glanced at the turtles, then turned around and gave Mike a knowing, hard look.

Mike nodded his agreement. Certain business would have to be taken care of if he was to guarantee this kind of lighthearted happiness for all of them.

I need a name, big fella, Mike said silently.

Fudge blinked once. *Get it,* was the answer. Then the dog turned and faced forward again.

Angie was washing her car when Mike returned from taking Emily to soccer practice. Bent over a bucket, Angie was up to her elbows in soapy water. The trim shorts and sleeveless T-shirt she was wearing accented her slender figure.

Every little curve and dimple in that figure just naturally reached out and pushed all the right buttons in him. Mike hoped that someday, maybe soon, they'd be able to finish the little project they had almost started.

He parked the car and walked in the warm sunshine over to join her. Liberal amounts of the soapy water she was slopping over the car had landed on her, making her T-shirt-clad body even more appealing. The frown of concentration on her face told him to proceed with caution, though.

He slid his car keys into the pocket of his jeans. "Hi. Want some help?"

She shrugged as she stood up and scrubbed at some highly offensive spot. "Doesn't matter."

Fudge came around from the other side of the car. He greeted Mike with his usual snarl.

"My, my," Mike said. "Sounds like there's a whole lot of grumpy around here." He wondered whether he should go around the block and try again. But instead, he picked up the long-handled brush with the hose attached and began to wipe off the roof of the car. "So how was your day?"

"Great." Her tone said otherwise.

"Got your grades today, huh?"

"C+ in math."

"That's not bad," he said.

"Not good, either," she pointed out. "Not for a financial planner."

"So be something else. What were your other grades?"

"A- in Poetry, Bs in biology and history."

"So be a poet."

She just gave him a look before dumping her sponge back into the water. "Do you know how much financial planners make?" she asked.

"Didn't your mother tell you that you can't buy happiness?"

"I'd rather be unhappy with money than without it." She slopped some more soapy water onto the hood of the car.

Mike turned the switch to let water trickle through the brush and slowly wiped the roof. "You need the money to pay off debts?'' It was a touchy subject, but he was feeling brave. ''How much do you—''

''No, I'm not in debt,'' she said quickly. ''Health insurance covered most of my mother's bills, and her life insurance paid the rest after she died. There was even a little left over.''

''Then why so desperate for a high-paying job? You don't act like a big spender.''

''Money is power. You have enough and no one can own you.''

Her voice was matter-of-fact, not angry, not even eager, but Mike found the whole subject sad in some way. Had the rape done this to her or was it her lonely early life with her mother?

''I guess I never thought about it,'' he said. ''Being owned, I mean. In some ways I've never felt owned, and in others it seems like everybody I know owns a piece of me.''

''I couldn't stand that,'' she said, then stopped to eye the car critically. It must have passed muster, because she tossed the sponge into the bucket and left it there. ''I want to belong to me and nobody else.''

That would make for an awfully lonely life, he thought, but just turned the water on harder to rinse the car off. It gleamed as if it owned a piece of the sun.

He belonged to his family, to Emily in particular, to his friends and to the people he protected. His family, his community, his friends all belonged in some way to him. Owning and being owned. He couldn't imagine living any other way, but then he hadn't walked in Angie's shoes.

He wished he could open her up to life as he knew it, to the joys that filled each day. Sure, the look in Emily's eyes when she ran over to greet him after soccer practice made him feel he could never give her up, but there were smaller pleasures, too, ones that came with less baggage. Like having a job you loved, that gave you a sense of satisfaction. Or just enjoying the sunrise, looking forward to the day. Angie was like a bud, closed up tight. The rain had kissed her roots, the sun had caressed her leaves, but still she wouldn't open up.

"Hey, how'd we get so serious?" Angie asked suddenly "That's another thing that's not going to own me—moods I'm not going to be sad and serious all the time."

He was more than willing to change moods. He though they both could use a few laughs. "Ah, do I detect a party girl in the making?" he teased. "That's just what I'm look ing for. I was going to pick up a movie when I got Em from her soccer practice. Want to join us for an orgy of pop corn?"

"I don't know." Her eyes had a hint of laughter in them as she pretended pensiveness. "Is this homemade popcorn or the kind you buy already popped at the store?"

"Does it matter? Aren't our sparkling personalitie enough?"

Those eyes had definite mischief in them. "Speaking o sparkling, I think I detect some dirt."

She reached into the bucket even as she spoke and flicked soapy water at him. What came out of the bucket couldn' have been more than a few tablespoons at most, and what reached him wasn't more than a few drops. Nonetheless i demanded retaliation.

"That's what we law-enforcement experts call water vio lence, ma'am," he drawled. "And I'm afraid I can't over look it."

He didn't wait until he was done speaking, but turned the switch on his brush as he flicked it in her direction. Drops snaked through the air, landing mostly on the pavement, but a few were on her. And a few even landed on the monster dog, who immediately leapt to his feet and began barking ferociously.

"Oh, Fudgey," Angie crooned. "Mikey is so bad."

"What's the matter with that beast? Afraid his ugly wil wash off?"

"Don't listen to him, Fudge," Angie said, pressing her hands over dog's ears. "He's just a mean old man."

Then she looked up at Mike. "You're the one who can use a bath," she said. "Something to wash away your ugly at titude."

"Change that bath to a shower, jump in with me and you got yourself a deal, lady."

She disappeared behind the car briefly. Then the sponge, dripping water, came flying at him. He ducked, and it landed on the roof of the car, splashing water on his head and shoulders.

"This is your last chance to surrender," he called out. "A nice, pleasant buddy shower or a cold spray. Your choice."

"Don't hold your breath, fella!"

There was nothing Mike could do but spray her again. He turned the water on and stood up to peer over the top of the car as he flicked the hose in her direction. Or what used to be her direction. She wasn't there.

He heard a laugh behind him and spun around just in time to catch the contents of the bucket face-on. He was blinded for a moment as the water ran down him, plastering his shirt and jeans to his body before puddling in his shoes.

Slowly opening his eyes he found Angie in front of him, still clutching the bucket. Her lower lip was caught in her teeth, her eyes were as wide as the prairies. She looked totally astonished at what she had done. And more important to him, paralyzed by it.

He lifted the hose, which had been forming a lake around his feet, and fired the spray at her. Drops rained over her face, and her T-shirt took on a rare form before she recovered her wits enough to hold the bucket up in front of her as a shield.

"Hey!" she said. Laughter was back in her voice.

The bucket was deflecting as much back on him as was hitting her, but he didn't care. He'd gladly hold his head underwater to hear Angie laugh like that. He felt like a little kid on Christmas.

"Surrender?" he asked.

She peeked around the bucket. "Fudge abhors water violence."

Mike suddenly noticed that the beast, tongue hanging out and dripping water, had come around the car and was at Angie's side. His expression was that of a shopper checking the cuts in a butcher shop. Ever so slowly and carefully Mike turned off the water and lowered the hose.

"You don't play fair," he told her. "You know that, don' you?"

Angie just laughed and patted Fudge's head. The beast relaxed. "People my size can't afford fair," she said. "Besides, you didn't have to stop. It was your choice."

"Stop or die. Some choice."

Her laughter followed her, floating in the air like the fragrance of her perfume, as she went around the car. "Don' be so picky. It's still a choice."

Mike followed her, dragging the useless hose behind him. She had found a dry towel and handed it to him after wiping her own face.

"Sure Fudge doesn't want to use it first?" Mike asked as he watched the beast shake himself dry.

She just smiled and came into his embrace, slipping her arms around his waist and holding him close. Their wet clothes might have been made of cobwebs for all the protection they gave. He could feel every curve of her body pressed against him. Every breath that she took seemed to come through his lungs.

He slid his hands over her back, pressing her closer. Steam could have been rising off them by then, but his eyes, his mind, were too befuddled by her nearness to notice.

Their dance was changing. The sedate waltz had been replaced by a torrid tango. He felt it, felt the heat rising and the tension climbing to overload. She was staring into his eyes, telling him she felt it, too—and she wasn't afraid.

Mike slowly lowered his head and met her lips with his. It was like steel meeting flint. Like cold air meeting hot air. But what happened was hotter than a spark and louder than thunder. Their hearts were in tune, dancing to the same steps of an ageless rhythm as their mouths sang of their desires to each other's soul.

A woof dragged them back from the edges of paradise. Judging by the bewildered look in Angie's eyes, she was mentally staggering just as much as he was. They parted slowly, as if not certain they were two separate beings, afraid that they could not exist apart. A sound rumbled deep in Fudge's chest, a definite muttering under his breath.

"Well," Mike said and ran his fingers through his hair. "So are we on for tonight?"

"Sure. I've got a leak to fix in 4B, but that shouldn't take too long." Angie bent over to gather up her rags, tossing them into the bucket. "How about seven-thirty?"

"Great." His heart was still pounding in his ears.

Emily was back from answering the phone in about a half second. "It's Moira. Her mom's taking them out for ice cream and wants me to come along. Can I, please?"

Mike looked up from the VCR where he was about to insert the movie. "I thought you wanted to see this."

"I said it was good," Emily pointed out. "I already saw it ages ago."

"Then why..." He just shook his head and got to his feet. "They've taken you a number of times already. How about if I give you money and you treat them? Minellis always pay their debts."

"Okay." Emily waited as he got some money from his wallet. "Want me to bring you guys home anything?"

Angie just shook her head. "I've got all I want here." Mike's look was hopeful, and she just laughed and patted the popcorn bowl. "Here in the bowl, I mean."

"Rats." He pretended disappointment as he walked with Emily to the door. "Have a good time and don't let them talk you out of paying."

"I won't. 'Bye, Angie."

The door closed as Angie was calling out her goodbyes, and then Mike was walking back into the living room. She didn't know why, but she felt suddenly nervous here alone with him. No, she did know why. After that hot and heavy session washing the car, she was more than a little conscious of him and of her own womanliness.

"So you have all you need right there, do you?" Mike teased as he sat at the far end of the sofa.

"Well, maybe most of what I need." She patted the sofa next to her, surprised and a little anxious at her bravery. "Come on down and I'll share my popcorn with you."

He needed no second invitation, and he came down to sit next to her. He seemed close, but astonishingly, not close enough.

"So how are you feeling about your grades now?" he asked.

She shrugged. "About the same. I'm not quite ready to give up financial planning."

He took her hand in his, entwining his fingers with hers. "Want my instant diagnosis?"

"Sure."

"You're looking for a career that's nonthreatening. You want to be financially secure without having to deal much with people."

"That's crazy." She tried to pull her hand away, but he wouldn't let go.

"Is it? I don't think you trust very easily. In your situation, I wouldn't, either, so I'd look for something that would put the trust on someone else's shoulders. They would have to trust me, not me trust them."

"That makes me sound so...unhealed," she said.

"No, cautious."

She leaned her head on his shoulder. "I like the idea of the financial security," she said. "I like the idea of not having to beg someone for help."

She looked up at him and found a curious look in his eyes. Too curious. She didn't want him back on that old kick. He didn't need to know who had attacked her.

"It's not that I've discounted your advice altogether," she said quickly. "But I've decided to try another semester. If I have as much trouble with my second business-math course, I'll switch to something else."

"Poetry?"

"Roses are red, violets are blue, if I can't hack math, then poetry I'll do."

His laugh was so deep, so rich, it seemed to surround her. She could feel it inside him as she lay against his chest, a wonderful rumble that seemed to come from his very soul. She turned to look up into his eyes, and the laughter stopped. Something else took its place, something new and exciting and altogether wonderful. His lips came down to meet hers, and she gave herself up to the moment.

She sped away from the world of worries and fears, of shadows and uncertainties, and into a universe of sunshine and sweetness. Laughter was everywhere, mingling with the song of the birds and the scent of flowers wildly in bloom. Magic was in the air, dancing among the sunbeams and calling to her.

As his lips sang love songs to her heart, Mike's hands moved slowly over her back, pulling her closer with such a gentleness that she felt no panic, no fear. She liked the feel of him up against her, liked the solid, rock-hardness of his muscles. His lips left hers briefly and he looked down at her.

"You okay?" he asked.

"Lonely all of a sudden," she whispered into his lips. "Why'd you leave?"

"Maybe for a breath of air," he said, a gentle smile riding in his eyes. "You are one potent lady."

"Second helpings are available."

His smile deepened, his eyes took on a darker cast as his mouth met hers. It was a sweet dance of courtship. In and out, they touched and swayed as if they both moved to the same haunting melody. Man and woman they were, yet one in spirit in some way.

"Angie?" Mike's voice was a whisper, a prayer, a breath that spoke of springtime and new beginnings.

She got to her feet and took his hand. "Yes," she said and led him into his bedroom.

It was right, it was now. Her heart was soaring and her hunger waited to be satisfied. His room was shadowy, holding a mystery about it that teased her desires. She moved into his arms and let his lips dance on hers.

It was different from before, different from what it had ever been before. His hands lit a fire in her that would not be doused this time. She wanted his lips on hers with a certainty that amazed her. There was no fear, no panic, just a sweet joy at the coming of their love.

Mike pulled her gently down on his bed and with slow hands, unbuttoned her blouse. With every button he freed, he leaned in to kiss her neck, her chest, the curve and fullness of her breast. She felt the heat rise, a flush of desire that washed over her. when the blouse was gone, he lay alongside her.

"You all right?"

She smiled and reached over to push the hair back from his face. His eyes were always dark, but somehow they were darker now. Passion, hunger consumed them, and they burned with its intensity.

"I'm fine."

Her hands slipped under his shirt and traced the solidness of his muscles. His strength wasn't something to fear, it was something to marvel at, to delight in. She ran her fingers through the hair on his chest and knew that steel lay beneath it.

Suddenly, her lips were eager to taste more than just his mouth. She pushed his shirt out of the way and, even as he stripped it off, she was pressing feather-light kisses along that sculpted hollow in the center of his chest.

"Angie, oh, Angie," he sighed, and the words rippled over her.

A hunger seemed to race through the air, igniting everything it touched so that fear and memories had no room to exist. Mike pushed her back, leaning over her as his hands ever so gently skimmed over her skin. His touch was strong and sure, awakening such a longing in her.

She'd never thought she'd come this far, never expected to feel that rush of hunger again. It seemed such a miracle to be here with Mike, to lie in his arms and feel no shadows falling across her. She reached up to touch his cheek. He stopped to gaze into her eyes with a tenderness that seemed to rock her foundation to the core. What magic had led her to this man and how had he found the key to her heart?

"You okay?" he whispered.

"Oh, yes," she said. "More than okay. Great."

Her smile was barely formed before he was kissing it from her lips, searing it into his soul, and her heart tried to encompass the world. His kiss deepened, reaching into her core and rousing her whole being into life. Maybe the magic was Mike himself, with his ways that were both gentle and strong.

Mike's hand slipped below the waist of her shorts and down into the moist warmth of her womanhood. His touch was teasing and light, even though she was more than ready for solid and strong. He tickled and tantalized, kindling all sorts of fantasies in her soul. She moved under his delight, the world fading into nothingness.

In moments they had shed the rest of their clothes. Angie had never felt so alive, so hungry and yet so wondrously free. Mike's hands were bewitching. His every touch brought wonder into her heart and hunger to her lips, her soul.

"Are you certain?" Mike asked.

Unspoken words hung in the air around them, questions and answers, fears and assurances. She knew what was on his mind as he lay back and pulled her on top of him. He was a strong and solid base, a foundation to be sure of, a rock to place her trust in.

With him a firm ground beneath her, she came down on him and they were one. She felt the joy in his face echoed in her own as they danced to the age-old rhythm. She was free, a bird soaring in the heavens, a cloud floating on the breezes, free to reach ever higher and higher.

His hands reached up to touch her breasts, to adore with his hands her smooth skin. His touch was a fuel that set her heart beating even faster, that made her hungers even deeper. They rode up to the stars together, bound as one as the world exploded. Then ever so slowly and sweetly, they rolled to one side to lie in each other's arms as they glided slowly back to earth.

She felt a wetness in her eyes, but didn't try to blink it away. Pressed tightly up against Mike's chest, she let the silent tears cleanse her soul of the remaining shadows and memories so that she could rejoice in this peace he'd given her. Mike said not a word but gently kissed the tears away before folding her back into his embrace.

Magic indeed.

Mike and Angie were back on the sofa, dressed again, but holding hands like school kids. Angie stretched her head up and nibbled on his ear. He smiled and bent to kiss her.

"Do you want to have your way with me again?" he murmured.

"No, I just want to cuddle."

He held her a little closer and kissed the top of her head. Relaxing, he eased his breathing into sync with hers. It was so nice, so normal to just sit here, relaxed with a warm, loving woman. Unfortunately, the more he tried to savor their lovemaking, the less relaxed he became.

The anger that had been dormant for a while now refused to stay asleep. The pleasure that they shared only intensified his rage all the more. It wasn't right for Angie to have to go through pain as she was. The bastard should be suffering, too.

"How are you?" he asked.

"Fine," she replied. "And you?"

"Hunky-dory."

Angie pulled away from him and sat back on her bare feet. "What's wrong?"

"Nothing." He forced a smile to his face. "I just made love to a wonderful woman and I'm exhausted."

"You look tense and irritable."

"I'm not, but I probably could be persuaded in that direction."

"You were very relaxed," Angie insisted. "But now you seem to be getting tight. Something has to be bothering you."

He reached out and took her hand. "I'm over thirty-five," he said with a grin. "And I was just worried whether I'd be up to another round of lovemaking."

"Mike," she said softly.

He dropped her hand and looked away toward the TV set that had never been turned on. "I keep thinking that there's guy out there who really did you bad and he'd walking free as a bird.''

Angie turned around and sat up straight, crossing her arms over her chest and putting her feet flat on the floor. ''That can't be helped.''

Mike shrugged, his expression tightening further.

''It's over and done,'' Angie said. ''What I have to concentrate on is my future. That's something I can affect. I can't do anything about the past.''

''Why don't you give me his name?'' he said softly.

''What for? It's too late to do anything now. People have a hard time believing the woman when it happens. What do you think would happen if I came out of the blue a year later and accused this guy?''

''I didn't say make a public accusation—I just said give me the name.''

She looked at him and exhaled slowly. ''I just want to put it all behind me.'' She looked at him, trying to force a smile to her lips. ''Please.''

''Sure.'' It wasn't time to push. He moved over and put his arms around her shoulders. ''Whatever you say, kid.''

They sat and stared at the blank TV screen for a moment, and then Mike jumped up. ''Speaking of kids, I better put this movie on,'' he said. ''Otherwise a certain, rather ornery kid will be wondering what we've been doing.''

''Good idea,'' she said with a short laugh.

He inserted the cassette into the player, then walked back to the sofa. He was willing to let the subject drop now, but he wasn't forgetting it by any means. That bastard was going to pay, and Mike was going to be the bill collector. He had just settled himself back at Angie's side when the door opened.

''Hi, guys,'' Emily said. She paused to look at the TV. ''How was the movie?'' she asked.

''Great,'' Mike said.

''Fine,'' Angie replied.

Emily continued staring at the screen. ''This is still the first part.''

"Yeah," Mike said. "It was so great that we're watching it again."

Angie laughed, making Emily stare at them suspiciously.

"I think it's time for me to go," Angie said, standing up. "My babies will be missing me."

"Yeah, it's getting late," Mike said, rising also. "I'll walk you down."

"That's okay, Mike," Emily said. "I'll take Angie down. I have to give Fudge a good-night kiss anyway."

"Aren't you going to have to take that dog for a walk?" he asked Angie.

Angie started to nod, but Emily broke in before she could say anything. "We can take him for his walk," Emily said. "Fudge doesn't go real good when you're there."

"What?"

"You make him all nervous and tense because you're always so scared around him."

"I'm not scared of him," Mike insisted.

"Right," Emily said and turned to Angie. "Let's go."

"I am not afraid of that dog," he repeated.

"Chill back, Mike," Emily said as she opened the door. "And watch the movie."

He knew why he was irritable. It was time things were settled. He needed that name.

Chapter Thirteen

A football came flying through the air toward Angie. She ducked, but it fell a little short of her anyway, bouncing on the concrete walkway and wobbling to a stop.

"Hey," Mike called to the two preteen boys. "This is a shopping center, not a playground."

One of the kids grabbed up the ball and sheepishly hurried away. Mike looked like he was ready to explode, so Angie took his hand. He'd been a walking time bomb lately, snapping at the slightest thing.

Well, no, that wasn't exactly true. He'd been incredibly patient and cheerful with her and Emily. It was when others seemed to infringe on them that he blew up. Like now, with the kids playing football. Even if it had hit her, it was only a foam-rubber ball, not exactly concrete.

"It's okay," she told Mike. "The kids were only playing."

"It's not okay. What if you weren't watching? You could've gotten hit."

"Than I'd take care of it," she said. "I can, you know."

"I was raised to be a gentleman."

"That doesn't mean that I can't take care of myself."

"It means you shouldn't have to."

"Hey, Mike." Emily and a friend from her soccer team came racing over to them. "Can we have some money? Me and Gork want to get some ice-cream cones."

"Gork and I," Mike said as he reached in his pocket for his wallet.

Emily had been calling the girl that all during their drive here to the Lighthouse Place, the outlet shopping mall in Michigan City. Angie's curiosity had reached its peak. "What kind of a name is Gork?"

"That's what we call her," Emily explained. "On account of she gorks real good."

"Gorks?"

Angie looked at Mike, who was pulling some bills out of his wallet. He just shrugged. "You may not want to know," he warned her.

Angie turned her attention back to Emily.

"Go ahead," Emily said to her friend. "Show Angie how to gork."

The girl shrugged and took a deep breath. Then, after swallowing several times, she let loose with a tremendous burp. Angie stared at her while Emily squealed with laughter.

"I told you," Mike murmured to Angie.

Before anyone could say anything else, Emily snatched the money from Mike's hand and the two girls ran off between the shops toward the snack bar.

"Don't forget!" Mike shouted after them. "Meet us in an hour at the information center."

The girls waved, indicating they had heard.

"Life is sure different now than when I was a kid," Angie said as they resumed their stroll along the pseudo old-fashioned clapboard storefronts. She took his hand again, as if by sheer willpower she could keep his dark moods away. "My mother would have killed me if I had burped like that."

"She had definite ideas on how a lady behaved?"

"Quite definite, and the first rule was not to call inappropriate attention to yourself."

"Isn't that a contradiction for someone in the entertainment field?"

"My mother had very definite ideas about what was appropriate and what wasn't."

"Burping was inappropriate?"

"Along with any number of bodily noises and functions. Strong emotions of any kind and impolite behavior, regardless of the situation. I was to say 'please' and 'thank you' to producers, directors, fellow actors, fans, and probably bank robbers and kidnappers."

"And rapists?"

His question, a natural extension of her statement, nonetheless startled her. The sudden knot in her stomach told her she wasn't sure just what he meant. And that it mattered deeply.

"You think I asked for it?"

"Of course not," he snapped, as if impatient with her for even asking. "But your background could have made it harder for you to kick the guy where it hurts and run."

She relaxed and gave his hand a squeeze. A week or so ago she might have taken this as criticism, but no more. "Actually, we discussed this very thing at my last session, how women are too often raised to be perfect victims. Our parents thought they were teaching us to be acceptable, but what they were actually teaching was to be accepting."

"The rules have changed for everybody," he said. "I'm not allowed to be a gentleman, and you aren't allowed to follow your mother's definition of what makes a lady."

"Things used to be easier."

"My parents knew exactly what was expected of them."

"Do you think we ought to go back to those times?" she asked.

Mike shrugged. "I don't know," he replied. "My mother seems to have made out just fine."

"Would you like Emily to have the same opportunities your mother had?"

He made a face. "Boy," he said. "You sure know how t zap a person!"

"Nonsense," Angie said with a laugh. "Zapping woul be inappropriate behavior. I merely asked a question."

He stopped walking, his hand on her back. "Then it's m turn to ask one. Am I allowed to open the door for you? O would that be being too gentlemanly?"

Angie turned and discovered they'd reached the stor they'd been walking toward. She'd been more conscious o Mike's hand on her back than their progress, and just shoo her head.

"How about if I hold the door open this time and yo take care of it on the way out?" he suggested.

"Very democratic," Angie said and made her wa through the door before curtsying to him. "Thank you, kin sir."

"My pleasure," he replied. "Although we've had bet ter."

Angie felt her cheeks glow with a hidden warmth. I seemed best to postpone this conversation until a more ap propriate time and place. "I'm going to look at skirts," sh said. "Why don't you look at the jackets here?"

"Too bad Emily isn't here," Mike said. "Then you' have help bossing me around."

"I don't need any help."

"That's for sure," he murmured as he walked over to th men's section.

Angie wandered through the women's section, a soft smil on her lips. There were men for all seasons and then ther was Mike, a man for all moods. He could be funny. H could be exasperating. He could be bossy and domineer ing. He could be gentle, and he could be a little boy. An those were just a few of his many faces.

Her smile flickered slightly. There was also a dark side t Mike. She had seen it in his eyes when he'd asked for th name of the man who'd assaulted her. It would be better fo everyone if he never knew.

* * *

Mike looked up to see Bobby ambling toward him and Angie. Bobby and his wife had purchased a big rambling home on the shores of Big Sister Lake in Michigan and were going to turn it into a bed-and-breakfast inn, with the family's help. It was renovation day, and Mike and Angie had taken on the porch railing, giving it new life with fresh white paint. Bobby apparently had taken on the job of distributing his homemade wine among the workers.

"Hey, little lady," he said to Angie, his deep voice booming out past the porch railing and probably across the lake to the other shore. "How about a little to top off your glass?"

Angie hesitated, her paintbrush in midair as she glanced at the half-empty glass at her side. Mike could see that she didn't want any more wine, probably remembering the last time, but seemed to be afraid she would hurt Bobby's feelings.

"That's okay, Bobby," Mike said. "She's fine."

His brother scowled as he looked from Angie to Mike and back again. "What did you do?" he asked her. "Hire him for your conscience?"

Angie shook her head and went back to painting the baluster. "Not that I know of."

"That's the trouble with Mikey," Bobby said. "He hires in even if you don't want him. Just ask anybody."

"Hey, I resent that. Can I help it if you guys need some advice now and then?"

Angie laughed. "He's right this time, though," she said. "I'm just fine, thank you."

"How about a little more spaghetti then?" his brother asked. "Or salad? Hey, we got a lot of salad."

"Thank you very much," Angie said. "But I'm full."

"How about another piece of pie? Ice cream? We got three different kinds."

"Hey, Bobby," Mike said. "She's a small lady."

"And she ain't gonna get no bigger the way you feed her."

"I ain't feeding her," Mike said.

"I can see that," Bobby replied, looking down at An
gie's trim frame and shaking his head.

"She feeds herself," Mike said. "She's a big girl and can
take care of herself."

"First, she's a small woman," his brother said. "And
then suddenly, she's a little girl."

Mike considered dumping the can of paint on his brother
Good old Bobby. He really loved what he called discus
sions. Good thing it wasn't Christmas or Easter. Bobby
loved to argue religion at those times, and he wasn't sure
how Angie would react to the loud and raucous "discus
sions" that developed.

"Hey, Mike." Emily dashed up the porch stairs.

"Watch it! This is all wet here." He waited until Emily
had screeched to a halt at a safe distance from the railing
"So what can I do for you?"

"Can I bicycle around the lake with some of the guys?"

He looked at his watch. "Yeah, but we need to leave in
about an hour."

"Okay," Emily replied before she dashed off.

"Don't the kid know you're her father?" Bobby asked
once Emily was gone.

"She thinks Mike is easier to spell." Actually, he wished
Emily would call him Dad, but she didn't, and he wasn't
going to push her into it.

Bobby went off to minister to his other guest laborers, and
Mike dipped his brush back into the paint to start on the last
baluster. Down the lawn, ahead of them, the placid water
of the lake rippled from the kiss of the breeze.

It had been a perfect day, in this peaceful setting. One
could almost forget that the world and all its troubles ex
isted. What would it be like to retreat to such a haven and
never see the darker side of humanity again? Mike doubted
it would that easy. The knowledge that the dragons were still
out there would haunt him, just as thoughts of Angie's at
tacker danced a heavy-footed polka in his mind.

"What should we do now?" Angie asked as the last of the
baluster was finished.

"Clean the brushes," he said, and standing himself pulled her to her feet. "No use starting anything new. We'd just get in the way of the second shift."

Angie looked down toward the street where another group of in-laws were getting out of their cars. "Big families are nice," she said.

"Sometimes."

"Don't be such a big cynic."

"Realist."

"Cynic," Angie insisted. "You can feel the love and caring in this group. How they're all willing to help each other."

Mike turned his eyes from Angie and looked inside the door at the milling groups of relatives filling the hallway right through to the kitchen in the back of the house. From brothers and sisters to shirttail cousins. Catholics and Protestants. Republicans and Democrats. Ph.D.s to high-school graduates. His family covered the whole spectrum.

"I don't know about the love bit," Mike said. "But if you need help, all you have to do is holler. We'll all come running."

"Family is where people want you," she said. "No matter what."

Mike grinned and shook his head. It was obvious that Angie knew nothing about large families. "Family is where people accept you even if they don't want you."

"You are a super cynic," she said.

"The family doesn't have to like you," Mike said. "But it's a place where they always have to take you back."

She looked a moment at the milling, laughing groups and smiled. Mike was sure that Angie would have a hard time visualizing this same group in a real knock-down, drag-out fight.

"Come on. Let's clean our brushes and then go for a walk along the shore," he suggested.

It took only a few minutes to clean the paint from the brushes; then they strolled down the path to the lake. It was a beautiful spring day coming on to evening. Earlier it had been warm, but the air now had a hint of a chill in it. Just as his relationship with Angie had a chill running through it. No matter how happy they made each other, there was unfinished business awaiting him.

"The family also takes care of its friends," Mike said.

Angie started, as if lost in the evening scents. "I'll remember that," she replied.

"Yeah," Mike said. "You help one of us, and we all remember."

She frowned at him. "I just baby-sit Emily some afternoons. No big deal."

He ignored the bantering tone in her words. "You do us a favor, and we remember. Your problems are our problems, and your enemies are our enemies."

For a moment she stiffened, but then relaxed and pointed off to their right. A male and a female duck were coming in for a landing. "Oh, look at the ducks. I wonder if they have a nest nearby."

"Maybe." *You can't keep shutting me out,* he silently told her.

Chapter Fourteen

"Mike!"

Emily was screaming for him. Something was wrong. He rushed out of his bedroom, in the middle of changing from his work clothes and still pulling his knit shirt over his head.

"Mike!" Emily hollered just as he charged into the hallway.

"What's the matter?" he asked.

"It's Angie," Emily said, her words tumbling out over her lips like water falling over rocks. "Something's wrong."

"What?"

"I don't know." Emily voice was becoming a wail. "She's been crying a lot, but she doesn't want to tell me anything. You have to talk to her. You gotta."

Mike's stomach tightened. Had Angie had a relapse? Barb said something like that could happen. An assault victim could be getting better and better and then, bam, she takes a step back.

"I'll look in on her," he told Emily. "Lock the door after me."

He hurried down the stairs, his heart racing more from concern than the exertion. Maybe her attacker had called her? Or worse yet, maybe he was here in South Bend.

Mike's lips stretched across his teeth, making a tight grin. Actually, that would be great. He'd like nothing better than to get his hands on the creep. A few minutes with the guy and the bastard wouldn't be able to attack a bug.

Mike range Angie's doorbell, then began knocking when she didn't answer immediately. A deep barking greeted his efforts.

"Shoot," Mike muttered. What if something was really wrong and he had to force his way in? Once he got inside he'd have to fight past the monster dog.

"Yes?" Angie called out.

He sighed in relief. Whatever was wrong, she could still come to the door. "Angie? It's Mike. Let me in."

Several long moments passed. Was Angie putting the dog in a back bedroom? Couldn't she open the door? Maybe she didn't want to.

Finally, the door opened, framing Angie with her fuzzy bodyguard just to the left and behind her. "What can I do for you, Mike?"

Relief that she was all right made his legs wobbly and weak. He put a hand on the door frame to steady himself. "What's wrong?"

"What do you mean, what's wrong?" Angie asked. "Nothing's wrong."

Nothing? Then why the red-rimmed eyes? Why the lines of pain crisscrossing her forehead? Why was all this tension radiating out into the hall? Was there someone else in her apartment?

"Can I come in?" he asked.

Angie hesitated and Mike stepped in, pausing only a moment to glance at her bodyguard. Fudge stayed put, not making a sound. Although Mike wouldn't swear to it, he thought the dog had almost wagged his tail.

There couldn't be anyone in here, not with the giant dog this calm, but Mike's cop eyes scanned the living room and kitchen as he stepped further into the apartment.

The television was on, a talk-show host spouting some philosophy or other, but it certainly didn't appear that anyone was there. The dog came by, and Mike's absently patted him on the head. There must have been a telephone call. The beast would never have let anyone in that Angie feared. Mike was sure Fudge would have died first.

"What made you think anything was wrong?" Angie asked, her voice snappish and demanding.

Mike looked into her eyes. He couldn't tell whether she was mad or upset or both. "Emily was worried about you."

Angie dropped her eyes, and the fight went out of her. "I'm sorry."

"Hey, what's there to be sorry for? She cares about you."

Mike stepped forward, taking Angie in his arms. He could feel her tension slipping away, flowing into his own body. It felt good to feel the tightness grow within himself. That's what a man did; he took the load off the shoulders of those he cared about.

"It's silly," Angie said. "I shouldn't have worried her."

"What happened?"

"Nothing."

"Angie." Mike's hand automatically moved to rub her back. She relaxed even more.

"It's nothing really." She shook her head and tried to push him away. "It's just silly."

But Mike wouldn't let her go. "Nothing's silly if it upsets you."

Angie pushed harder against him, and he let her go. She stomped determinedly into the living room and threw herself into an overstuffed chair by the window.

Fudge tentatively followed, and Mike came close behind them. The dog flopped down by the side of Angie's chair while Mike took a seat on the sofa. He wanted to yank the information out of her, then go chasing after her tormentor, but he knew that wouldn't work. He just waited. The television blared on. Now some vaguely familiar actor was cracking jokes.

Suddenly, Angie's shoe came flying at the screen. "The bastard," she cried.

Fudge flew to his feet, hair on end, growls emanating from all parts of his body as he raced after the shoe. He sniffed around it in confusion.

"Who's he?" Mike asked.

"Randall Sheridan. He always played the hero in 'Night of Horror.'"

Mike leaned forward, trying not to breathe as he stared at the screen. He sort of recognized the guy now. "He looks older."

"Stopped dyeing his hair," Angie said. "I guess since he's producing now, not acting, he figures he can look his age."

Mike knew what an actor did and was vaguely aware of what a producer did, but so what? What did this have to do with Angie's anger?

The answer lingered in the back of his mind, just out of reach. He could feel its presence. He could almost smell it, but he couldn't make out its substance or form.

"Why's he on?"

Angie glared in disgust at the screen, then turned to stare out the window. From where she sat, she couldn't see more than the treetops, but she still stared at them as if mesmerized.

"Apparently, a couple of weeks ago they had a young actress on the show. I didn't see it. I guess she was just damn sick and tired of the system and talked very frankly about the casting couch."

He leaned forward, elbows on his knees, hands folded.

"Today's show was supposed to be a rebuttal," Angie said.

"They denied her allegations?"

"Deny them?" Angie looked at him and laughed, a bitter sound with a solid foundation of rage and tears. "Not at all. Not one tiny bit. These aren't exactly decent men."

She took a moment to compose herself, those beautiful little hands fiercely punishing her shirttail. "Randall admitted it and laughed, calling it one of the perks available to any producer and director."

The tears were flowing now. No sobs, just silent tears streaming down the soft smoothness of her cheeks.

"He said that there was always a ready supply of young women desperate to break into the business, eager for any kind of part, walk-on, extra, commercials, whatever. Hungry young women willing to do anything and everything to get themselves in front of a camera."

Mike still didn't know quite what to do with the information Angie was giving him. It wasn't a nice story, but freedom of choice allowed consenting adults to do some very stupid and cruddy things to themselves. That had always been the way of the world.

"Randall Sheridan made it sound like there were women in every nook and cranny throwing themselves at men like him. Men who have the power to shape a young performer's career."

Mike took a deep breath and slowly let it out. From the stories he'd heard, that might not be too far from the truth.

"Although, dear Randall went on to say that some women needed more persuasion than others. That doesn't make sense, does it?" Angie was looking at him now, her eyes as hard and fierce as if he'd had something to do with the sorry state of the world. "If there are thousands of bimbos throwing themselves at his feet, why does Randall Sheridan have to pressure anybody?"

A sadness usually settled over Mike when confronted with injustice in the abstract, but that didn't happen this time. Instead, he felt himself growing cold. There was nothing abstract here.

"The answer is that he doesn't have to," Angie replied to her own question. "He doesn't have to rape. The bastard does it because he enjoys it. He enjoys the power trip."

Bingo. The monster jumped out of its box, all ugly and twisted. "He's the one who raped you," Mike said.

It should have been a question, an attempt to confirm his suspicions, but it wasn't. It was an absolute statement that Mike didn't doubt for a moment. He had his bastard. The anger in his soul grew into a cold, freezing rage.

She nodded, her face mirroring the strain of trying to control her agony.

The pain and anger in him twisted and stretched him to almost breaking. He'd dealt with victims for all his many years as a cop, but he'd always had the protective armor of the professional police officer wrapped around him. Why had he cast it aside?

"You said that if he wasn't stopped, he would just go on doing it," Angie said. "That's what you told me, and that is exactly what he's doing." She sprang up from her seat and walked to the window. "And you know what the worst of it is?"

The worst of it was seeing such pain in someone you cared about and being unable to prevent it.

"The worst is that he's laughing. The bastard rapes and then he laughs like it's all one big joke."

Mike could see one side of her face. This time it wasn't twisted up with pain but with a primitive kind of anger.

"Well, he's not going to get away with it."

"He'll stumble one of these days," Mike said.

"I have no intention of waiting. I've waited too long already. I'm going to put a stop to him."

Mike stood up himself, concern flooding in and pushing out all his other emotions.

"I'm going to tell the police what he did to me."

Oh, no. No, Angie. No. Mike wanted to scream at her. He wanted to sweep her in his arms. Tell her to put it all behind her. Tell her to look toward her future, just like she'd told him. But everything was rooted and frozen in place—his feet to the floor, his tongue to the roof of his mouth.

"And I'm going to tell the reporters." She spun away from the window. Her fists were clenched. Her eyes were blazing a white-hot heat. "I'm going to expose him to the whole damned world."

"You can't."

Angie could not believe her ears. For a moment, shock at Mike's words paralyzed every single muscle in her body. She couldn't blink, she couldn't breathe, and she certainly couldn't talk. The room swam before her eyes.

"Isn't that what you told me to do?" The words came out all hoarse. If she hadn't felt her lips and tongue move, Angie would have sworn it was someone else speaking.

"I thought that you should have reported it," Mike replied. "But that moment has passed. You report things like this immediately so that you can go to the hospital and have the appropriate tests done."

"Appropriate tests?" Angie snorted. "So that doctors and police officers can poke and probe me to see if I'm lying?"

Mike shook his head. "Doctors do the examination," he said. "Police officers interview you. We try to see who's telling the truth."

Angie felt the anger bubbling up, bringing the bile up to her tongue and spreading it throughout her mouth. The whole thing wasn't Mike's fault, but he was there and she felt her daggers of anger all turn toward him. Rationality be damned.

"Do you believe I'm telling the truth?" she asked.

"Of course I do."

"Then why do you see a problem with me telling my side of the story?"

"It happened over a year ago."

"It still happened!" she shouted.

He rubbed the bridge of his nose with his thumb and forefinger, a typical Mike Minelli gesture when he was trying to calm himself. But if she didn't want to be calm, why should he be?

"Angie," he said softly as he moved toward her.

She immediately stepped away. "Don't touch me," she snapped.

He stopped, his face stone hard as if she'd slapped him. "Let's both calm down."

"I've been calm too long," she replied. "It's time for me to kick ass."

"No, it isn't." His voice was growing louder. "The assault happened a year ago. Everyone is going to ask you why you waited this long."

Angie turned away and went to the window. She knew hi
words were true, but she didn't want to think about them
All she could think of was hurting Randall Sheridan, hurt
ing him bad.

"Talk about poking and probing, that's what they'll a
do now until they come up with a reason. They'll say you'r
a woman scorned. Or that you're mad because he wouldn'
agree to the sequel. Or that you hate all men." He took
deep breath, running his fingers through his hair. "Angie
please. You gotta play this smart."

Smart? If she'd been smart, she would have known wha
a rat old Randall really was, but it was too late for that now

"You know how people look at this kind of thing," Mik
said.

"Yes, every woman does." Angie was shocked at the bit
terness in her voice, but she put that concern aside. "It's th
only crime where the victim has to prove her innocence."

"I'm not saying it's right," Mike said. "But the medi
will rip you to shreds."

Her stomach twisted in pain, and Angie didn't reply. Sh
tried focusing on the dogwood blooming outside her win
dow, but it just turned into a blurry mass of white.

"You waited too long," Mike said. "You have no proof
And with both of you being in the entertainment business
the media will be all over you like vultures on a carcass."

A shiver went through her body. Was it fear or anger?
Angie didn't know. She just folded her arms across her ches
and held herself tight.

"Your picture will appear on the front page of every su
permarket tabloid in the world. You won't have a shred o
privacy left. And after they've chewed you up, they'll toss
you aside like a gnawed-over chicken bone, for the crazie
of the world to pursue."

She shivered again, but this time she spun around to fac
Mike. "I've been afraid too long," she said. "It's time fo
me to step out and take care of business."

"Let me do it," he said.

Angie shook her head. "It's my fight."

"You don't have to do it alone," he insisted.

"I was alone when he attacked me. I'll be alone when I rike back."

"Angie, please."

"It's my fight!" she shouted.

"This is dumb!" he shouted back.

Tears were about to flow again, but that single word opped them both cold. Dumb? Hiding from the bastard ll these months was dumb.

"Thank you," she said coldly. "I'm glad to know what ou think of me."

"Aw, come one," Mike snapped. "Don't be a Lone angerette."

His angry, frustrated words whipped up a matching an- r in herself. Maybe this wasn't the way to do things, but e just didn't give a damn anymore.

"What can you do?" Angie knew that her tone of voice ordered on contemptuous, but she didn't care about that, ither. "You just told me that I had no proof, no witnesses. fact, from your police point of view, I have no case at all. ight?"

"Just leave it to me," he said, his voice low and quiet.

"What are you doing to do? Hire a hit man?"

"Just let me take care of it." His face was growing red, nd the words barely slipped out between his clenched teeth. I'll figure something out. Just don't go making public ac- usations. That won't do any good at all."

"I don't need your protection," she said.

"Angie."

"I'm a big girl," she said. "It's my fight, and I'll take it the bitter end."

"I'm not telling you to quit." He was shouting again. I'm just saying there are better ways to fight."

"Like what?" she snapped. "Hide behind the big po- ceman?"

"What's wrong with that? That's what we do—we pro- ect people."

"Then why is the crime rate climbing?"

"Why are you attacking cops?"

For a moment he looked bewildered, standing there with his arms spread wide. She turned toward the window again, shutting that image out of her mind.

"We can't be everyplace all the time."

"Right," she replied. "And now you have a perp in your sights, so you're going to go get him."

"Yeah, I said I'd take care of him."

"Always the cop, aren't you? Except this is my fight," she said.

"It's my fight, too," he snapped. "You made it my fight when you confided in me, when you leaned on me and let me make love to you."

She spun at that. "I didn't sign my life over to you when we became friends."

"No, but you gave me the right to help. And that's what I intend to do."

"Whether I want your help or not."

He sighed and looked around him as if searching for any straws to grasp. "Angie, listen to reason. I just want to take care of you, not let you be hurt again. You're too precious to risk with this crazy crusade. You're too soft and gentle to fight those kinds of bastards. I'll take care of it."

"Just turn your life over to me. Trust me to do what's best for you, to make the right decisions," she mocked. "Well, thanks but no thanks."

She suddenly saw what she was to Mike, what their relationship was, and she felt as if her heart were being ripped out. She was just a possession, a notch on his belt. Not a living person with a life and mind of her own—just something to own. She could scarcely breathe, the pain was so bad. The hurt was so unexpected.

He wanted to run her life as he ran Emily's, making her decisions and fighting her battles, all to feed his male ego. Women and children, lumped together by the macho studs of old and necessary to support their selfish philosophy of life.

"Why are you pushing me out?" Mike asked.

"Because you're no better than Randall Sheridan." His eyes went wide, but she ignored the hurt in them. "He saw me as an apple in the tree. Something to pick because he wanted me. You see me as a delicate flower. Something to protect in your own little greenhouse. Both of you see me as a possession. Something to do with as you want. A piece of property that makes no decisions.''

"Well," he said quietly. "I'm glad we had this little chat. It gave us a chance to really get to know each other."

"Wonderful, wasn't it?"

Without another word, Mike turned on his heel and left. The slamming of her door would rattle well into the night, but Angie didn't care. She knew she wouldn't sleep anyway.

Mike took the stairs back to his third-floor apartment two at a time. He needed physical activity, a lot of it. He needed to burn off the anger within him before it ate out his entire stomach.

He was breathing hard by the time he approached his door and reached into his pants pockets for his keys. Damn. There was nothing there.

Another wave of anger washed over him. He'd been changing his clothes when Emily had run in, saying he had to talk to Angie. He'd rushed off before getting his keys or his wallet.

Mike tried the door. The knob wouldn't turn. Emily had locked it, just as he'd told her to. For once, the kid had listened to him.

"Emily," he called, knocking. "Emily, open the door."

"Who's there?" his daughter called.

"Emily quit fooling around—it's me," he replied.

"Me who?"

"Mi—" The hell with this nonsense. It was about time the kid recognized him for what he was. "It's your father. You remember him, don't you?"

"Do you have any ID?"

Little men ran up to the top of his head and began to beat on the inside of his skull with their tiny little sledgehammers. "If you don't open this door right now!" he said, "I'm going to kick the damn thing down!"

He heard the lock swiftly turn, and the door was opened. Emily stood there staring at him, concern alternating with anger on her small face. Her dark eyes flashed like his mother's always did when she was agitated.

"What's wrong with Angie?" she demanded.

Mike stomped past his daughter into his apartment. "I don't know," he snapped. "She wants to be dumb."

"She's not dumb," Emily snapped back as she shut the door.

"I didn't say she was. I said she wants to be."

"Were you hollering at her? How come you always have to holler at people?"

"I wasn't hollering at her."

"Did you holler around Fudge?" he daughter demanded. "I bet you did."

Those little men were beating an anvil symphony in his head. "Emily, please."

"You know he doesn't like you to holler at Angie."

An image of Fudge suddenly jumped into Mike's mind and he was surprised. He and Angie had gone at each other hot and heavy, yet throughout it all the giant beast had done nothing.

"I didn't holler at Angie. We just had a discussion, and that dog didn't do anything but sit there."

"I bet you made her cry," Emily persisted. "You're always making people cry."

"If I'm so bad, why are you staying with me?" Mike snapped.

The sudden silence fell on Mike like a truckload of elephants. He wanted to grab Emily up in his arms and rain apologies on her little head. Instead he just stood there, hands at his sides, rooted to his spot. His daughter's lower lip quivered and tears streamed down her cheeks, but the anger that burned out of her dark eyes would have put the fires of hell to shame. He wanted to hold her, but was scared she'd run away if he tried.

"You don't want me around!" she screamed. "You don't want Angie around! You just don't want any girls around!"

hate you!'' The tears were coming like a waterfall as she an wailing to her room.

Mike stared at the empty living room, sagging under the eight that was now his heart. He wanted to cry himself, but e felt all dry inside, unable to feel anything but pain. He ent to the window to stare out at the river.

Emily was right. He didn't know anything about caring or women. He'd been the first child and a boy, so he'd pent a lot of time with his father. Then he'd gone into po-ce work. Even with more women entering the force, it was till primarily a man's world.

He'd flopped as a husband, he'd flopped as a father, and e couldn't even hack it as a boyfriend. Hell, he ought to ist go away and join the Foreign Legion. Live in a world hat was totally male.

The river flowed slowly on down under the Twykingham ridge. Past the bridge, the river would turn north and flow n into the state of Michigan where it would eventually mpty into Lake Michigan. He wished he could go with it.

It would be nice to run, if he could. But he really didn't hink it would do him any good to run to a company of men ke the legionnaires. It wouldn't do any good because he idn't belong there. He belonged here, doing the things that ad to be done.

He'd given Angie the big talk about how he'd take care of hings, pressured her for a name so that he could person-lly deal with the problem. Well, he had the name. The man as alive and easy to find. It was payback time.

What he had told Angie was true. She had no real proof hat the man had assaulted her, nothing but her word. And, rithout corroborating evidence, that wouldn't hold up at all a a court of law. So staying within the law provided no av-nue for revenge.

It was time to do what was right, not what was allowed. man took care of his own.

''The man's name is Randall Sheridan,'' Mike said.

The man at the other end of the phone let go with a soft histle. ''You're after some pretty big fish.''

"The man's a rapist."

"Could be, but he's still a big fish."

"I really don't give a damn, Pete."

The man laughed. "Always liked going after big game eh?"

Mixed metaphors aside, Mike didn't feel like having deep conversation. This was business. "Look, I just war you to check this guy out. Find out his habits, his friends his weaknesses. Dig up all the dirt you can."

"Then?"

"Then nothing. Call with what you have. I'll take care o things from there."

"Sounds like fun."

Mike wondered why he'd called Pete. The guy was a goo private investigator, but also a jerk. "Just call when you ge the info," Mike said.

"Will do."

"I'm gonna go over and sit by my friends," Emily said getting up from her chair.

Mike only briefly considered telling her that she shoul stay with the people who came with her to this athletic ban quet before he just nodded instead. Forcing the kid to sta with such a jolly group would be cruel and unusual punish ment.

He and Angie were studiously avoiding each other. Hi mother was behaving very well about the whole thing avoiding even the appearance of prying as she concentrate on talking to an older woman sitting on her right. His siste Margaret and her husband had gone off to talk with an other young couple.

Besides, it looked like most of the kids from Emily's clas were sitting off in a group by themselves, throwing we napkins at each other. Maybe being a ten-year-old mean never having to sit with your family.

"Okay?" Emily was still standing there, waiting for hi permission to join her friends.

"Yeah, sure," Mike said. "Fine with me, kid. Just don' get too rowdy."

He wondered what was with the kid; she didn't usually ait for permission. She just told him what she wanted to do nd went ahead with it, leaving it to Mike to stop her if he ould.

Mike shook his head. He sure didn't understand females. It didn't matter whether they were one day old or a undred years. He just flat out didn't understand them at l. Now the kid wasn't calling him Mike anymore. Not that e'd started calling him Dad; she just didn't call him anying.

Mike let his eyes roam about the grade-school gym. The thletic-awards banquet was a standard grade-school function that hadn't changed all that much from when he had one to school here. Long tables covered with white paper blecloths, surrounded by metal folding chairs. Basketball ackboards pulled up to the ceiling. Paper plates and plasc spoons, food in warming trays at one end of the gym. A icrophone and a speaker's stand up on a stage at the other d.

Although, some things had changed from his day. When e went to school here, a majority of the kids were Italian. ow there were kids of all European extractions as well as rientals, blacks and mixtures of them all.

Maybe things would have been easier for him now if he'd own up in the same multicultural environment. Mike stole quick glance at Angie. She was sitting very stiffly, arms lded across her chest, staring off into some far space.

Hell, his problems weren't with different ethnic groups, en when he had to arrest somebody. Sure, there were lanuage problems, and sometimes he just didn't understand here they were coming from, but he always tried to show basic respect for people as individuals, and that attitude ad carried him through.

Truth be known, all his real problems were with the omen in his life. He'd always gone to coed schools, so hat the hell was his excuse? Maybe a serious case of terinal gender stupidity.

He looked at Angie again. She shouldn't have come. mily had invited her, and Angie was just living up to her

promise, but the cost was much too high. It was obvious sh
was suffering. She looked so damned miserable.

He would love to take Angie to a quiet, secluded spot, fa
from anyone's prying eyes, and sweep her into his arms. Pul
her down in his lap and nuzzle her hair, kiss the pain from
her eyes. But he didn't dare try it. He was afraid that Angi
would just spit in his face. Figuratively, of course, since sh
was too reserved and polite to really do it.

Maybe that was the trouble. Angie had been raised to b
too damned nice and polite. Now she was breaking thos
restraints and was trying for all-out tough. Trying to mak
up for a lifetime of submissiveness in a few days. Well, onc
Pete called him back, he'd see that Angie's problem wa
taken care of. She'd be angry with him for interfering—h
accepted that. But he was not about to let her handle thi
whole thing. He also knew she had about as much chance o
bringing Sheridan down as a butter knife cutting down a
sequoia.

Someone tapping on the microphone drew Mike's atten
tion to the stage. A smiling woman with short, graying hai
stood there. Mrs. Ketchum was Emily's track coach. Hi
daughter's group would get their awards first.

Angie turned her attention from the far wall to the stage
Mike's mother whispered to her companion that this was he
granddaughter's team, and the woman flashed her a smil
of sharing. His sister stayed with her friends. At least for a
few minutes Mike would have something else to concen
trate on besides his misery.

The coach spent a few minutes extolling the virtues of he
team. The girls hadn't won any championships, but they'
learned a lot and had had fun. The woman went on to spou
several more clichés about hard work, teamwork and al
ways doing your best. When did a basic truth turn into a
cliché? His father probably would have said when it's mixe
with cynicism. Mike felt worse about himself with eacl
passing minute.

Emily received a participation ribbon, plus the sports
manship award. She wasn't the fastest kid on the team, bu
she was something more important—the first one to chee

teammate. Emily's face glowed as she stepped forward to accept her award, and Mike felt ready to burst with overwhelming pride himself. He clapped until his hands hurt.

He wasn't the only one excited, either, for Angie's face shone with happiness for Emily. He wished he could keep that glow there forever, but he knew he couldn't. Angie wouldn't let him. Mike felt a tiredness settle on his shoulders.

"Like I was saying," the coach said, her words drifting into the haze surrounding all his senses. "We didn't win any championships, but we were close. And I do promise that we'll make a strong run for the intercity girls' soccer championship next fall."

The coach paused for some applause, then went on. "We have a very experienced group returning and Emily Micelli, who has recently moved here from California, will be here in the fall to give us that scoring punch that we've been missing so far."

The girls on the stage began jumping up and down, squealing as they took turns hugging Emily. His daughter stood in the center of all that attention, beaming with happiness.

Mike wanted to stand up on his chair and holler, "No!" He looked at Angie, but her face was impassive. Mike turned to his mother, but she was talking with her friend, telling the woman how Emily had left for California when she was just a little thing and now she was living in South End with them.

Damn it! Mike thought. She's not staying here! She's going back to live with her mother. She had to—that was where a little girl belonged. A girl needed to grow up with a woman so that she'd know how to act when she became a woman.

Mike wanted to scream. He wanted to stand up and wave, to anything to get Emily's attention, but she was surrounded by her friends. Mike sank back in his chair, feeling dull and all alone.

The girls went bouncing off the stage and another coac stepped up to the microphone. Mike felt himself sag an grow into a lump of clay.

Emily dashed over to show her awards. Mike stared at th ribbon and plaque, aware of the items without really seein them. Angie congratulated Emily, and his mother hugge her.

"Hold these for me, Grandma," Emily said, handing a the items to his mother.

Angie stood up and hugged Emily. "I'm really proud you," she said. "I wish I could stay longer, but I really hav to go."

"Already?" Emily asked.

"Fudge needs his walk," Angie replied.

Emily nodded, a wise expression on her face. "Tell hir I'll come by later and give him a good-night kiss."

"He'll like that," Angie said and exchanged hugs wit Mike's mother. They murmured goodbyes to each other.

She said something to him, but Mike didn't really hear He forced a smile to his lips and gave her a small wave, the watched until her trim body disappeared out the big doubl doors at the far end of the gym. Why did every time she lef hurt more than the time before?

He turned slowly back to his daughter. "Emily."

She turned to face him, her dark little eyes glittering har like two black aggies.

"We really need to talk," Mike said.

"Don't worry," Emily replied. "I've taken care of ev erything."

Mike didn't want to ask.

"I know you don't want me around," Emily said. "S I'm going to live with Mary Margaret."

Mike wanted to put his head down and cry, but he wasn' a little boy anymore. He was a man, and he needed to han dle things rationally and logically.

"Have you talked to Mrs. Sheehan about this?"

"No," Emily replied. "But it's okay. Her mother alway says that she can bring anything home as long as it's not at or a dog because her little brother Matthew has aller-ies."

With that, Emily dashed off to join her friends, leaving er words hanging in the air like the foul exhaust of a diesel ngine. He shook his head, trying to dispel the cobwebs. verything he did was wrong.

"I am so glad to see you've finally found someone to care bout."

Mike lifted his head, but could only stare at his mother. must have been several lifetimes later before his voice ould work. "Angie hates me, Mom."

"She is not a person who hates," his mother replied. "She just annoyed with you."

Annoyed? He would have laughed if he weren't afraid e'd break into tears if he did.

"And one can easily get annoyed with you. You are just ke your father. Everything has to be your way."

"Mom, I'm not like that. And neither was Dad."

"You have to learn to back off," his mother said. "You on't have to run everything."

He closed his eyes. He wasn't trying to run everything; he as just trying to take care of her.

"And I'm so happy that you and Emily have worked hings out," his mother went on. "It will be nice to have her round after all those years so far away in California."

He wanted to say something, but his tongue was stuck to he roof of his mouth.

"In a few short years, she will be a woman," his mother aid. "So enjoy your time with her while she is with you."

Mike wanted to scream, but he just murmured quietly, "She calls me Mike, Mom. She won't even admit that I'm er father."

"She is still not sure of things. Give her time. Once she is ure of you, everything will be fine." His mother got to her eet. "Ah, there's Margaret. We have to go now. Mrs. Ken-all is having her operation tomorrow, and I told her I vould drop in on her tonight."

"Good night, Mom," he said, barely able to summon nough energy to get the words out.

"We should have a party for Emily," his mother said. "To welcome her to Indiana. How about this Sunday?"

Mike shrugged.

"Good," his mother said. "And you can bring that nice little Angie."

He didn't reply.

His mother looked at him, then came over to his side. She gave him a hug and kissed him on the cheek.

"Mikey, Mikey," she said. "You have such a good heart. Relax and things will turn out well."

His mother hurried off to get Margaret. Mike sat there and stared at the table, only half-aware of the voices around him.

Right now he wanted to strangle Sue and whack old Randall Sheridan; then he wanted to break and smash all the furniture in this gym. After which, he wanted to toss all these happy-ass people out into the street.

He was glad his heart was good. No telling what he'd do if it were evil.

Chapter Fifteen

The ball was passed right to Emily's feet but, as she had all through the game, she fumbled around with it until an opposing player kicked it away from her. What was even worse, though, was that she didn't chase after it, trying to get it back. When Emily had an awful game, she had a spectacularly awful game.

It was a warm spring day, but the beautiful sunshine seemed a torture. Why couldn't a thunderstorm come up, complete with lightning to stop the game? It was a blessing when the final whistle sounded and she trudged across the field over toward Mike. He watched with a puzzled frown as the rest of the team joined the coach on the sidelines.

"Don't you have to see your coach after the game?" he asked her.

She just shrugged and walked on past him toward the car.

"Emily," he called, hurrying his steps to catch up with her just short of the parking lot. "Hey, we all have off days now and then. By next game, you'll be back to your usual form."

It was a definite glare that she sent his way. "Larr Kingsley said that the only reason I get to play so much because you said you'd throw Mr. Sommerset in jail if didn't."

"I would not. Where'd he get an idea like that?"

"You yelled at him. Bret told us. He heard his dad tell h mom."

Mike sighed. He ran his fingers through his hair, but didn't free any answers from imprisonment. "I talked t him. Talked, not yelled. And I never mentioned jail. I onl reminded him that everybody was supposed to play half game."

"Then why am I playing more?" she demanded.

"Because you're good."

Her look was skeptical, to say the least. "I was terribl today, and he didn't take me out."

"He probably thought you'd play through it."

"He probably thought you'd shoot him." She turned an trudged the rest of the way to the car. "I'm gonna have t tell Mrs. Ketchum that I'm not so good. And after she tol everybody at the banquet how great we'd be next year."

Mike unlocked the car door for her. "For God's sake Em, you're the team's top scorer. How can you think you'r lousy?"

She didn't answer him, of course, and lay slouched dow on the seat the whole way home. Another well-meant at tempt to help gone awry. So what else was new? He shoul be getting used to these silent drives home.

Angie was waiting for them when they came into th apartment lobby. His heart smiled at the sight of her, but hi lips took a cue from the frown in her eyes. She wasn't com ing to greet them because she'd missed him.

"A registered letter came for you," she said and handec him the brown envelope.

"How are you?" he asked.

"Fine." Her eyes softened when she smiled down at Em ily. "How was your game?"

"Terrible," Emily said. "Can I came in and talk to Fudgey?"

"Sure." Angie held open the door and let the girl go in, then, after flicking a quick questioning look at Mike, went in herself. The door shut, and he was left alone in the hall.

He could not move, afraid to breathe, as a wave of horror washed over him.

It couldn't be true. That tremor he had felt while looking into Angie's eyes must have been an earthquake. That stillness that settled over the world when she closed the door was the silence that came just before a storm.

It was not love.

He, Mike Minelli, super cop and loner extraordinaire, could not have fallen in love. He was too busy. He'd just been helping Angie out. He'd just been having a little fun. He couldn't be in love.

Then why had his world sprung into life when he saw her?

Why had it felt like a death sentence when she'd shut the door just now?

Mike turned and trudged up the stairs. He couldn't believe it. This wasn't what he had planned at all. He was too smart to fall in love. But then, if he was so smart, why was half the world mad at him?

Well, he'd found the real killer cucumber Angie had warned him about—love. It had sneaked up, twisting and slithering around him unnoticed until it was ready to move in for the kill. Then it gradually tightened around his heart until he couldn't breathe, couldn't think, couldn't do anything but ache with love. There was no escape, no machete sharp enough to cut it away. It choked and strangled him, until he agreed to its demands, which in turn would kill him anyway.

Love demanded that he give up Angie, no matter that he wanted to protect and safeguard her. In order for her to heal from the rape, she had to have control of her life, and that meant no interference from him. More than anything else, his love meant that he wanted her to be happy and whole. And she could only accomplish that without him and his interference.

He idly glanced down at the envelope. It was from Sue. No doubt, more great news. He unlocked his door and went in, opening the envelope as he did. There was a letter and an airplane ticket.

Dear Mike,
Well, you've had Emily for more than a month now. Knowing you, you're probably ready to kill me, but hopefully things have settled down and you're getting along fine. If not, here's an open-ended ticket to send her back.

Before you rush her to the airport, though, hear me out. I didn't send her to you lightly or on a whim. She needs you, needs to learn the toughness you can teach her. I don't want my daughter to feel like she's a failure if she's not married by age twenty-two and rush into a mistake like I did with you. Or to date a "fish face" (as she calls Ron) because she doesn't have enough self-esteem to date nobody while she's waiting for somebody good to come along. She's so strong now, I'm afraid she'll lose that going through her teen years with me.

I've caught myself several times in the last few months telling her she wasn't being "ladylike" when she was actually just fighting for her rights. Then early in April my office was getting restructured, and I was given the choice of a new position or quitting. The new job would have involved bringing complaints against negligent suppliers—constant arguing, in other words. The idea of it terrified me. I couldn't eat and I couldn't sleep and finally it boiled down to a choice between making myself sick or quitting. I quit, but then all I could see was Emily in the same boat twenty years from now.

Even though I'm going to be miserable every minute without her, I love her too much to risk having her turn out as weak as I am. She's the best of both of us, so I'm giving her to you with the hope that you'll teach her to be strong, to be proud of who she is and to never settle for less than the best.

Sue

Mike just sighed, closing his eyes as he leaned up against the wall. Not only did he have to give up Angie, but he had to let Emily go, too. Sue's letter must have been written in the middle of a bout of amnesia if she thought he could raise Emily to be strong and independent. Sue's main complaint about him when they'd been married was his domineering ways, that he never let her do things for herself. He hadn't learned anything, as Emily's misery this morning demonstrated.

The phone rang, and he trudged over to answer it. He hoped it was the station. Maybe somebody had called in sick and they needed him to work. He could do that. He could track down the bad guys and get them off the streets. Good people's lives he just messed up, but bad guys he could handle. Come to think of it, he messed up their lives, too, by sending them to jail, but that was all right.

"Minelli," he barked into the phone.

"Pete here. Got the lowdown on Sheridan. Man's got some peculiar habits. Send out the trucks—there's too much dirt to mail."

Mike sighed, his heart torn between the need to listen and plan, to strike out for Angie's revenge, and the need to let Angie strike back on her own. He saw the pain and doubt in Emily's eyes as she dragged herself to the car after the game. No, he'd interfered too much. He might be a slow learner, but he wasn't stupid.

"Forget it," he told Pete. "Send me a bill for your work."

"Say what?"

"I don't need what you've collected. It's over. Send a bill."

"Man, you been eating too much of that Indiana corn or something? I thought you said this guy was a rapist. Figured he'd hit on your sister at least. You letting him get away?"

Mike felt so weary. "No, I'm letting someone else handle it."

"Okay." There was a long silence. "You change your mind, give me a call."

"I won't, but thanks." Mike hung up.

The apartment seemed so dead and empty. Just as his life would be soon.

"He just shouldn't have said anything," Emily wailed for about the eight-hundredth time. "Now everybody on the team hates me."

"I doubt that," Angie said. She waited a moment while Emily took a slobbery tennis ball from Fudge's mouth and threw it across the yard. "Everybody wants things to be fair. Right now, some of your team probably thinks things haven't been fair because of what Bret told them, but that'll change."

Fudge bounded back, and Emily threw the ball again. It was a beautiful day—sunny and warm. You couldn't ask for more perfect spring weather. But the only one who seemed to be appreciating it was Fudge. Angie thought she was probably putting on a better act than Emily, but it was still just an act.

Angie turned back to the problem at hand. "You aren't playing more than everybody else, are you?"

"No."

"Are there others who play more than you?"

"Some."

"Then if the coach was really unfair, he'd play you the most, wouldn't he?"

Fudge had come back, but rather than take the ball from him, Emily had decided he needed a hug. Angie let the girl share her misery with the big dog for a few minutes. Lord knows, Angie had done the same thing enough over the past few days.

She'd been so angry at Mike for his blithe assumption that she'd just step aside and let him deal with Sheridan. How could he not understand that she needed to do that herself? How could he not see that she needed to face up to her fears as well as to Randall, in order to be strong again? She'd been so bitterly disappointed in him.

But why? He was an acquaintance, a friend, a cop. An A-number-one meddler. She was better off without him. Then why had the past few days been so lonely? Then why had othing seemed as much fun when she could no longer share with him?

"You know," Angie finally said. "Your father really does now the law. I can't imagine him threatening to arrest your oach if he doesn't play you enough. It might be unfair for coach not to play you much, but it isn't against the law."

"I guess not." Emily looked up over Fudge's back. "I ish he hadn't butted in, though. Now I'll never know if I'm y good."

"Sure, you will," Angie assured her. "If you can pass the all where it should go, you know you're good. If you can ove the ball around other players, you know you're good. here are lots of ways."

Emily frowned. "I was pretty bad today."

"Was that because you aren't a good player or because ou were being mopey?"

A grin peeked out of Emily's eyes before she buried her ce in a big furry back. "Mopey, I guess."

Angie smiled in return and got to her feet. "Come on, t's see if there's any ice cream left in the freezer."

Emily went back into the apartment much happier than hen she'd come out, which was more than Angie could say oout herself. In spite of all her anger with Mike, she missed im. He'd made her feel special, alive. Even when she was ost ready to strangle him, there was a bond there that An- e couldn't deny. Unfortunately, none of that mattered. He eeded a hothouse flower; she needed someone who valued er independence as much as she did.

Angie got the ice cream out of the freezer while Emily got ut three bowls—for herself, Angie and Fudge.

"Your dad only does those things because he loves you," ngie said.

"I know." Emily sat down to watch Angie dish up the ice eam. "My mom says that the more he loves you, the more e strangles you."

Angie grinned. "Sounds like a killer cucumber."

That sent Emily off into peals of laughter, and whatever aces of anger remained vanished. "That's great!"

"I'm not sure we should tell him, though."

"Aw, why not?" But Emily didn't press for an answe Instead, she took Fudge's bowl of ice cream and put it the floor. "Here you are, Fudgey. Ice cream of your ve own."

Once the girl was satisfied that Fudge found the concc tion edible, Emily came back to the table. She ate a fe spoonfuls of ice cream, then looked up at Angie.

"Do you think you could talk to Mike? You know, t him not to butt in all the time?"

This was the request Angie'd been fearing since Emily h. poured out her troubles a half hour or so earlier. Talk Mike, the very person she'd been avoiding so studiously f the past few days? Her anger with him had subsided, but deep disappointment remained. She'd thought he car about her, valued her as a person; yet he'd been unable allow her the very thing she needed to become who again—control.

It was so tempting in a way to just hand everything ov to Mike, to say, "Go ahead, take care of the bum for me But how would that help her? She'd just be in debt agai Maybe for a more positive reason, but still beholden to man. She needed to finish this on her own, as a player, n a cheerleader.

"Couldya, please?" Emily asked again.

"Wouldn't I be guilty of doing the very thing I was as ing him not to do?"

Emily looked confused.

"Wouldn't I be butting in by telling him not to butt in? Angie explained.

"I don't think so."

Emily looked so uncertain, so dejected, that Angie had relent. "I guess I can try," she said.

What difference did another conversation with Mil make? She was going to be seeing him around, anywa since he lived in the building. Might as well set the tone f the next seventy-five years.

"Now?" Emily asked.

Jeez, this kid was as pushy as her father. "All right." Angie got to her feet. No real reason to delay things. "You going to stay here with Fudge?"

Emily nodded, then eyed Angie's barely touched ice cream. "You gonna finish that?"

Angie pushed the dish across the table, then headed for the door. Her heart was riding somewhere around her ankles. Why did this feel like another attack of the killer cucumbers?

Mike's inclination was to ignore the knock at the door. Maybe the world would go away if he pretended he wasn't home. But then he realized it might be Emily, so he trudged over. He opened the door to find Angie there.

The first thing he noticed about her was the shadows in her eyes. Worry, uncertainty, concern all swam in those green depths. Was she worried about seeing him? Hadn't they progressed at all in their relationship or had they regressed in the past few days? Then he realized he was keeping her standing in the hall and stepped aside.

"Uh, sorry. Come on in."

She entered with all the bravado of a doe stepping into the middle of a pack of wolves. Her gaze skittered around the small foyer, as if avoiding eye contact with him. She went into the living room; he followed. She stopped and turned to face him.

"I'm glad—"

"Em asked—"

They both spoke at the same time, then both stopped. Angie tried to smile, but there was something about the way her hands kept wiping at her jeans that said the smile was a lie. Was this what his love for her had done—made her afraid of him? Maybe he should reconsider the Foreign Legion.

He motioned her to a chair, then waved for her to speak. "Ladies first."

She went over to sit on the edge of the sofa, ready to jump and run, he guessed. He sat all the way back on the re-

cliner, to reassure her she'd have a head start. Love was th
pits.

"Emily asked me to talk to you," Angie began. "I gue
you know she was pretty upset about your talking to h
coach."

Mike nodded. It was awful to sit here and watch her. H
face was pale, without that glow that she'd begun to hav
Her eyes were cloudy, a restless sea. He looked away to sav
his sanity.

"I did not yell at him," Mike said. "Or threaten to a
rest him." He sneaked a look back to find her smile w
slight.

"I told her that unequal playing time wasn't against th
law," Angie said. "So I doubted you would have threa
ened arrest."

"Did she believe you?" His voice came out sounding to
grim, if Angie's sudden start were any indication. He trie
for a lighter tone. "She wasn't too receptive to my expl
nations earlier."

"She's afraid the kids all hate her now. I think I co
vinced her all anybody wants is to be treated fairly. Th
other kids don't want her to get breaks, just as she doesn
want any. She just needs to prove she deserves her playin
time by playing well."

Hadn't he tried to tell her that? Obviously, he had bee
speaking the wrong language. "All I wanted was an eve
playing field for her," Mike tried to explain. "What sh
does with it is up to her. I just wanted her to have the sam
chances as everybody else. As the boys on the team have."

Angie nodded. "I understand and so does she, but yo
just went about it wrong. Next time, let her try to work
out before you take over."

Next time. He sighed and leaned forward, resting his arm
on her knees as he stared at the floor. "I doubt there'll be
next time."

"You're sending her back?"

It was more than a question; it was an accusation th
stabbed at the heart of him. He flinched; he couldn't he
it.

"Not until after the school year is over," he said and got wearily to his feet. He felt ancient, like something that had exhausted its usefulness long ago and was ready to be washed out to sea. He walked to the window, taking strength from the steady flow of the river. "She needs to live with me."

There was more to say, of course, about a zillion things his heart wanted to spill out, but there really was no point. Pain was not best when shared, no matter what some stupid poet said.

"I can't believe you'd do that to her," Angie said. "She loves you so much."

A ten-year-old didn't know what love was. He hadn't known until just recently, when it was about to kill him. He turned to face her. "I have seen the enemy and it is I."

Angie frowned.

"Look," he said. "I may be a slow learner, but even I eventually get the message. I screwed up every way imaginable. I have hurt people that I only wanted to help. I'm just not going to let that happen anymore. I quit. It's over."

Angie's frown deepened, and she got to her feet. "Just like that?"

"Just like what?" he snapped. "You think I haven't tried to do things right? I just frankly haven't got a clue. I think 'protect'—everybody else wants to fight for themselves. I think 'shelter'—everybody else wants freedom. I think 'help'—everybody else says butt out. Well, that's what I'm doing, I'm butting out."

He took a deep breath and tried to make the anger go away, but he knew better than to really make it leave. Once it went, all that would be left would be the pain.

"Don't you know how this will hurt her?"

Angie saw only Emily in all this. Had there been no real relationship between him and her? Had he imagined it or had it been so shallow that it was easily forgotten?

"She'll get over it," he said. He might not.

"Will she?"

Mike just turned back to the window. Why couldn't Angie just accept the fact that he was the flame to their moths?

He was poison. Whatever he did would be the wrong thing at the wrong time and would ultimately hurt them.

"I wanted to talk to you about something else, and I guess this is as good a time as any," he said slowly. "I know I made a lot of statements about getting the guy who attacked you, but I wanted you to know that I'm not going to do anything."

"I told you not to do anything." Her voice reflected her surprise.

He turned around, though his heart advised against it. Too many emotions were written on her face, ones he didn't dare to read.

He shrugged. "When did that ever stop me?" he said with a laugh. When she didn't join him, he sighed. "I called a private investigator I know in California and had him do some digging into Sheridan's life. He called back a little while ago and said he's found a ton of dirt."

Mike walked over to the end table and picked up Pete's telephone number. He gave it to her. "I don't know what your plans are, but you might want to call him and see what he has. It might be something you can use."

She stared at the number as if it were written in a foreign alphabet. "Why are you giving this to me?"

Hadn't she been listening? How many times did he have to rip his heart out? "I'm butting out, just like you told me to," he said. "I put together a little ammo that I'm not going to use now. Figured you might want it, that's all."

"I see."

What she saw, he had no idea. Nor did he want to. It was time for the curtain to come down. He'd set her free to become healthy and whole, to be in control of her life. He would do the same with Emily in a few weeks, send her back to Sue. Em would grow up strong there because she'd have no one fighting her battles for her. Angie would become strong because there'd be no more nightmares. As for him, he'd pay more attention to catching the bad guys. It had been enough before and would be again. Right.

"Well, I'll send Emily up," Angie was saying as she walked slowly toward the door. She seemed almost to be

aiting for something else to be said, but neither of them
poke. She stopped at the doorway and waved Pete's num-
er slightly. "Thanks."

He nodded and let her leave without saying another word.
He couldn't have spoken to save his life. The only thing that
ood between him and tears was his silence.

"I don't know, Fudge," Angie said. "It was the strang-
st thing I'd ever seen. Mike Minelli butting out."

Fudge didn't look all that impressed. He probably fig-
red they'd had enough midnight conversations about the
uy. He got up and found a new spot on the sofa to stretch
ut, his head facing away from Angie.

"I just don't understand it," she went on. "The guy has
terminal case of the meddling disease. He was meddling
he first time I met him, trying to tell me how to fix his
hower. If he's willing to interfere in the lives of total
trangers, why is he suddenly going cold turkey with people
e knows?"

Fudge yawned, showing his deep interest in the subject.
Angie just slid her feet under his body with a frown.

"The more he loves you, the more he strangles you." That
as what Emily's mother said. "So does that mean he
oesn't love Emily anymore?"

Fudge grunted.

"No, I don't believe that for a minute, either," she
greed. "So what does it mean?"

Fudge just sighed, a deep, meaningful sigh from the re-
esses of his soul.

"Emily was upset and wanted him to butt out, so he is.
Could it be because he loves her so much that he has to do
vhat she wants, even if it goes against his basic nature?"

It made sense. The slight wag of Fudge's tail said he
hought so, too.

"Could Sue be wrong? Maybe he used to be that way in
he past, but changed. What could make him change so
nuch, though?"

Fudge was asleep. His breath was rhythmic and slow, a gentle snore rumbling in the air. She must be on the right track or he wouldn't have left her to figure it all out.

"What changes a person so drastically?" She stopped, her words hanging in the air. One thing and one thing only. "Love."

Mike gave up Emily because he loved her so much. But he also gave up Angie, handed his ammunition on Sheridan to her. He could have kept it, used it even, and she probably would never have known. So why did the leopard change its spots and agree to become a nonparticipant?

She pulled her knees to her chest, wrapping her arms around them. Lord, what did this all mean? She was afraid to even make a guess and afraid not to.

Chapter Sixteen

'Mary's just about had it with these late-night shifts,'' olanski said. ''She says if I'm so good at staying up to all ours, I can get up with the baby at night.''

''It's hard on the families,'' Mike agreed and took another drag of coffee as he stared out at the rain-slicked treet. Nobody in his right mind was out on a night like this. he crooks sure weren't. He and Polanski been staking out his liquor store for three nights now, certain it would be the ext one in a string of five to be hit, but so far nothing.

''It must be even harder on you,'' Polanski said. ''At least 've got Mary around to take care of the baby no matter vhat hours I work. What do you do, hire a sitter?''

Mike drained the last of his coffee. ''My brother's oldest id is sitting with Emily tonight. Weekdays are a pain, hough.''

Not for much longer, though, a little voice reminded him. Ie didn't want to dwell on the thought so he shifted his stiff gs. The lighted sign above the store went off. The place was inally closing. He was beginning to think it never would.

It took another fifteen minutes of waiting around, but the store was finally locked up, and Mike and Polanski could leave. Trouble was, now that he could go home, Mike wasn't sure he wanted to.

He still hadn't told Emily she was going back. He knew he had to do it soon, but every time he tried, the words stuck in his throat. He had to tell her this weekend. No more delaying.

It was almost a week now since he'd told Angie. For the first few days, every time they met accidentally in the hall, she would treat him to a reproachful glare. The last few days, though, her attitude had been more thoughtful. And sight of her seemed to haunt him. Maybe he should move once Emily was gone.

Mike dropped off Polanski at the station to pick up his car, then drove home. The lights were on in his apartment. he hoped Emily was in bed. He couldn't bear to face her knowing he was sending her back to her mother. At the same time, he hated to miss any of the little remaining moments with her. Hell, there was no way he could win.

Mike opened the apartment door and was greeted by the low growl of the monster beast. What was that dog doing here?

"Hi, Mike," Emily called out as she came to retrieve Fudge. "Come on, Fudgey. Mike doesn't have any popcorn."

"What's the beast doing here?" he asked as he followed them into the living room. He got his answer when he saw Angie sitting on the floor in front of the television.

"Hi," she said.

"Hello." His tone was surly, but that was preferable to admitting the giddiness his heart wanted to feel at seeing her there. "Where's Dana?"

"The high-school boys' soccer championship was tonight." Angie said.

"So?"

"So she wanted to go." Angie voice rose just a trifle with irritation. "I wasn't doing anything, so I came up."

If he had wanted Angie here, he would have asked her. He is beholden to her enough. "Louie said Dana was available."

"Well, Louie was wrong." Angie turned back to the TV. He recognized the show as "Night of Horrors." "Em, this the good part."

Emily stopped stuffing her face with popcorn long ough to throw herself on the floor. They both seemed pnotized by the show, acting like he wasn't even there. ell, that was just fine with him because in a moment he uldn't be.

"I'm going to bed," he announced.

"Good night," they both called out. Neither turned to ok at him.

Not that it bothered him in the slightest. He'd had a long y, a long week, and he was going to get a good night's ep.

That wasn't quite as easy to achieve as it should have en, though. Angie and Emily obviously were staying up er, but it wasn't the lights or their occasional laughter that pt him awake. Maybe it was the knowledge that they dn't seem to miss him. Or the fact that they could still ugh. Finally, he buried his head under the pillows and went sleep.

Mike woke up groggy and fuzzy-headed. It was morning the blinding sunlight seeping through the crack in the apes indicated. It was also as quiet as a mausoleum in the artment. Emily must not be up yet. He rolled over to look the clock.

Damn—it was ten-thirty! Emily had a game at eleven. He apt out of bed.

"Em!" he cried. "We've got to get going."

He raced out of the bedroom, a million different things at needed doing speeding through his mind, and ran ack-dab into...plastic vines?

They stopped him, if for no other reason than the fact at they were taped from ceiling to floor to wall to ceiling. e looked around. The stupid things were everywhere. With me work, he found a path to Emily's room. It was empty.

"Emily?"

No answer.

What was going on? He turned to go back toward t
living room, but he didn't have the same luck. His fo
caught on a vine and pulled it from the wall so that the vi
and tape wrapped around his ankle. He tried to shake hin
self free, but it only made it worse, so he pressed on, dra
ging the vine behind him. It was soon joined by others.

"Emily?" he called again.

He stopped in the living-room doorway. That room w
clear of vines and Angie was there, sitting on the sofa, tl
newspaper in her hand. She looked so right there that h
heart wanted to cry out. He wanted to preserve the mome
forever and hold off her anger.

Angie looked up at him. "Emily's at her game," she sai
"Louie took her."

"Louie?" He tried to step into the room, but a vi
caught at his neck. He yanked at it in irritation, only to hav
a whole mess of them come tumbling down around hin
"What the hell is going on?"

Angie came over, not to remove the vines, but to lift
section still attached to the wall so that he could get into tl
living room. She led him by the hand over to the recliner. F
felt like an absolute fool, wearing nothing but his pajam
bottoms and plastic vines.

"These are killer cucumbers," she said. "Well, preten
killer cucumbers. You'll have to use your imagination a li
tle."

"Why do I have to use my imagination at all?" he askec
His first fresh joy at seeing her here had faded, replaced b
the irritated knowledge that she'd be going soon. "Have yo
draped them all here so you can watch me get strangled b
them?"

"You really don't know the first thing about killer cu
cumbers, do you?" she asked.

"I did my master's thesis on them," he grumbled. He
smile was too soft, too sweet. He was looking like a foo
and she was smiling. His irritation level rose a notch. "
know you can't beat them."

"You can't beat them alone," she corrected.

"Well, I admit defeat." He pulled a string off his shoulders and tossed it onto the living-room floor.

"You aren't listening, are you?"

Why was she so damned chipper? Didn't she know how much it hurt to see her there? "I'm listening," he said. "I always listen. That's how I know you can't beat them."

She pulled the vine from around his leg. The tape stuck for a moment to the hair on his leg, but that didn't hurt half as much as having her so close.

"Didn't you ever see 'Attack of the Killer Cucumbers'?" he asked.

"You were in the shower and they attacked you."

"Yeah, but if they'd finished me off, that would have been the end of the show. It ran for another four years."

"So?"

"So I survived the attack because I know the secret."

God help him, but he wanted to be pulled in by the sparkle in her eyes, by the laughter in her voice. He wanted to know the secret, as if it would make a difference. "And what is that?"

"You can only beat them if you have help."

"That's it?" He felt ridiculously disappointed. He'd wanted magic, if not a miracle. He wanted all their problems to disappear. He would become easygoing and noninterfering; she would become less independent, more willing to be sheltered by his love. "So you're my help?"

"Maybe." She sat back on her heels, smiling like the cat who ate the canary. "Why did you give me Pete's telephone number?"

It was a change of topic he wasn't prepared for, and he stared at her for a long moment. "Why? So you could use the stuff he'd found if you wanted."

"Why didn't you use it?"

What was all this, a test of some sort? "You didn't want me to."

"I didn't want you to tell Barb about the rape, but you did."

He shrugged. "So I'm not always a jerk."

"According to Emily, according to Sue, the more y
love someone, the more you strangle them."

Not a test, but a recounting of his faults. Just what
wanted at the end of a long, miserable week. "That ce
tainly makes me sound like a charmer. Emily will be glad
learn she's leaving, then."

"I don't think it's true."

He just stared at her, a certain cold fear creeping into h
heart. "What isn't true?"

"I think you'd do whatever you had to for someone yo
loved. Even if it meant butting out of their lives."

Her eyes seemed so piercing, so knowing. Could she r
ally see into his soul? Could she read his loves and desir
and his terrible fear that his love would cause more pa
than happiness? It suddenly because all-important to pr
tect those secrets, to keep those green eyes from seeing in
the core of him. He stood up abruptly.

"I think you've been watching too many soap operas,
he said. Fear made his voice snappish and he was gla
"There's no melodrama here, no hidden agendas. I want
simpler life, the way it was before all these entanglemen
came along."

He could feel her pull back. Though his heart proteste
he made himself look at her, made himself see the pain
her eyes. It was better to hurt now than to stay hurting an
unwhole for the rest of her life.

"Emily's an entanglement?"

"Emily, you, Fudge even. Marshmallow's the only on
I'd keep around. He doesn't want anything but food and
warm place to sleep. No killer cucumber vines to strang
me."

"Then you know," she said slowly.

"Know what?"

"That love's the real killer cucumber. That there's no es
cape from it."

"But there is," he said. They were talking about them
selves now, no more pretense of this whole thing being abou
him and Emily. "You simply see it for what it is and ru
before it catches you."

"And that's what you've done?"

"You'd better believe it."

The pain in her voice made him want to cry out. The deep as of her eyes looked awash with tears, but he made himself hold steady and strong. She was better off without him. e knew it, even if she didn't.

"Well, I guess I'd better go," she said.

He didn't try to stop her—that would have defeated all the gony he was going through. He put a barricade around his art and said nothing as she walked across the room and eaved in among the silly plastic vines. His life was growg colorless and dim. Her departure was taking all the joy om it.

She had never explained why she'd hung the vines, but king her would mean making her stay longer. And even other minute might be too much for his faltering resolve.

She stopped over one vine and slipped around another en as her steps faltered. "Oh!" she cried suddenly and umbled, grabbing her ankle.

"Angie?"

She tried to get up, but could only limp another step or vo before her ankle gave out completely and she sank to the oor.

"Angie." He sped after her, not taking time to move round the stupid vines, tearing them off the ceiling and the alls as he went. "Are you okay?"

He reached her with his hands filled with vines, the way ehind him clear and free. Her face was in the shadows as e tossed the foolish things aside and swept her up into his rms.

"I don't know what the purpose of these stupid things ere, but it was an idiotic stunt," he snapped as he carried er into the living room and put her on the sofa. "I thought nly kids did dumb things like this. You should have known etter."

It was only when she was settled and he knelt down beore her that he saw the smile in her eyes.

He refused to smile back. His heart was too confused, too opeful.

"You see?" she asked.

"See what?"

"The secret of the vines. You can only beat them if y
have help—if someone loves you enough not to fear the
for himself."

"That's stupid."

"No, it's the truth."

He got to his feet to put some distance between them. H
footing seemed rocky. "You mean your fall was all an act'

"'Jealousy of the Giant Ants,' act two, scene four," s
said. "Only there I was tripped by a giant ant and carri
away by them rather than a hero."

"I'm not a hero."

"You braved the killer cucumbers, risking your life f
me."

She was plainly crazy. "They're plastic vines," he to
her, exasperated.

"You could have been killed."

Her eyes were so bright, the sparkle wanted to touch hi
call him into their laughter. "They were taped to the wa
with cellophane tape."

"You gave me Pete's number because you loved me a
wanted to let me beat Sheridan, not you."

He sighed and turned away. The sunlight coming throug
the front window seemed blinding. "It doesn't matter," l
said. "I am what I am, and it's not what you need."

"Says who?"

Says who? What was this? He spun to face her. "Sa
you, if I remember correctly. I wanted to help. You told n
to butt out."

"I told you I needed to face Sheridan, that you couldn
do it for me." She got to her feet and moved closer to hin
His heart told him to run, but his silly feet wouldn't mov
"I never said you should go away completely. Emily doesn
want you not to be a part of her life."

She didn't understand. "I'm no good for you guys."

"Who made me see I needed counseling? Who made n
see that loving means owning and being owned? Who p

nily on a boy-girl team because she could handle any-
ody who gave her trouble?''

Angie came even closer. He could feel her breath on his
est, feel the way its tickling slid all the way into his heart.
e kept telling himself that she didn't understand, but there
as a little flicker of hope that maybe she did.

''I thought you were a brave man, Mike Minelli,'' she
id. ''I never thought you'd run from a difference of opin-
n.''

''It's more than that,'' he said. He had to make sure she
ally understood things. ''I tell everyone what to do. I boss
ople around. I take over without giving them a chance.
m always butting into everyone's life.''

''Yeah, so what's your point?'' She slid her arms around
s waist.

It was hard to think with her so close, with those eyes
ailing up at him and those lips so tempting and near. ''You
n't want that.''

''No, and every time you take over, which will probably
 often, we'll have a big fight. Then maybe the next time
u'll think a little before doing it again. I figure in forty—
fty years max—I'll have you thinking before you act.''

He was starting to believe, starting to hope. ''You must
gure I'm a fast learner.''

''Naw, but with me and Emily working on you every day,
u won't stand a chance.''

His lips needed hers, but he was still afraid. ''Are you
re?'' he asked. ''This can't be a short-term thing. If I
me back, it's for good. It's forever.''

''Well, I should hope so,'' she said with a sigh. ''It was the
ts hanging all these stupid vines. I don't intend to do it
ain.''

That was all the convincing he needed. He pulled her into
s arms and let his hands welcome her home. His lips spoke
—

He stopped and pulled away. ''You know I love you,
n't you?'' he said.

"Yes, I know. But it's lucky that you said it. I was beg
ning to think I was going to have to beat it out of you a
I—"

"—abhor violence."

His joy could no longer be contained. He swept her up
his arms, swinging her around the room until she laugh
with dizziness. This was magic he'd never thought possib
a lightness in his heart that he never thought he'd feel.

"Whoa, fella," she said with a laugh. "We haven't go
lot of time."

He stopped to frown at her. "I thought you said—"

"I mean, this morning. I told Emily we'd be at her ga
by halftime. That leaves us just enough time."

"For?"

"A shower."

He really stopped then, stopped breathing, stopped sm
ing. "You mean—"

She nodded, taking his hand. "Yes, the two of us. W
you at my side, I don't think there's any fear I can't cc
quer."

"Oh, Angie." He just held her tightly as if he would ne
let her go. Her belief in him was terrifying. He only hop
he could live up to it. "You are going to marry me, are
you?"

"Of course." She paused. "And we are going to ke
Emily, aren't we?"

He just laughed. If he ever started to falter, she'd poin
out to him. "You bet. We need someone to protect me fr
Fudge."

Press Release: December 5

LOS ANGELES—Morrison Productions, Inc. announced today that a sequel to their popular horror
television series, "Night of Horrors," will be produced sometime next year and is tentatively named
"Day of Terrors." Angela Hartman Minelli, better
known as Angel Heart, has agreed to come out of re-
tirement to star in the show and has pledged a part of
her earnings to the National Coalition Against Sexual

Assault. Hartman attracted a great deal of attention this past summer when she led the successful boycott of the movie *Time Will Tell,* produced by her former co-star, Randall Sheridan, who has been accused recently of several incidents of sexual harassment and assault.

The actual filming of the sequel is expected to take place late in the year, as Hartman is expecting her first child in April. Most of the former cast has been reassembled, with the exception of Sheridan who will not reprise his role in the sequel.

* * * * *

Silhouette

SPECIAL EDITION™

It takes a very
special man to win

That
SPECIAL
Woman!

She's friend, wife, mother—she's you! And beside each Special Woma[n]
stands a wonderfully *special* man. It's a celebration of our heroines—
and the men who become part of their lives.

Look for these exciting titles from Silhouette Special Edition:

April   FALLING FOR RACHEL by Nora Roberts
Heroine: Rachel Stanislaski—a woman dedicated to her career
discovers romance adds spice to life.

May   THE FOREVER NIGHT by Myrna Temte
Heroine: Ginny Bradford—a woman who thought she'd never love
again finds the man of her dreams.

June   A WINTER'S ROSE by Erica Spindler
Heroine: Bently Cunningham—a woman with a blue-blooded
background falls for one red-hot man.

July   KATE'S VOW by Sherryl Woods
Heroine: Kate Newton—a woman who viewed love as a mere fairy ta[le]
meets her own Prince Charming.

Don't miss THAT SPECIAL WOMAN! each month—from some of you[r]
special authors! Only from Silhouette Special Edition! And for the mo[st]
special woman of all—you, our loyal reader—we have a wonderful gi[ft:]
a beautiful journal to record all of your special moments. Look for
details in this month's THAT SPECIAL WOMAN! title, available at you[r]
favorite retail outlet.

TSW[

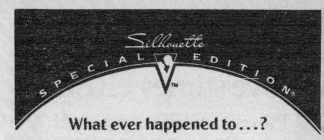

Silhouette
SPECIAL EDITION

What ever happened to...?

Have you been wondering when a much-loved character will finally get their own story? Well, have we got a lineup for you! Silhouette Special Edition is proud to present a *Spin-off Spectacular!* Be sure to catch these exciting titles from some of your favorite authors.

TRUE BLUE HEARTS (SE #805 April) *Curtiss Ann Matlock* will have you falling in love with another Breen man. Watch out for Rory!

FALLING FOR RACHEL (SE #810 April) *Those Wild Ukrainians* are back as *Nora Roberts* continues the story of the Stanislaski siblings.

LIVE, LAUGH, LOVE (SE #808 April) *Ada Steward* brings you the lovely story of Jessica, Rebecca's twin from *Hot Wind in Eden* (SE #759).

GRADY'S WEDDING (SE #813 May) In this spin-off to her *Wedding Duet, Patricia McLinn* has bachelor Grady Roberts waiting at the altar.

THE FOREVER NIGHT (SE #816 May) *Myrna Temte*'s popular *Cowboy Country* series is back, and Sheriff Andy Johnson has his own romance!

WHEN SOMEBODY WANTS YOU (SE #822 June) *Trisha Alexander* returns to Louisiana with another tale of love set in the bayou.

KATE'S VOW (SE #823 July) Kate Newton finds her own man to love, honor and cherish in this spin-off of *Sherryl Woods*'s Vows series.

WORTH WAITING FOR (SE #825 July) *Bay Matthews* is back and so are some wonderful characters from *Laughter on the Wind* (SE #613).

Don't miss these wonderful titles, only for our readers—only from Silhouette Special Edition!

SPIN